CAROLINE ROSE

CAROLINE ROSE

MARY TRIOLA

Quiet Storm Publishing • Martinsburg, WV

All Rights Reserved. Copyright © 2002 Mary Triola

No part of this book may be reproduced or transmitted in any form or by any means, graphic, electronic, or mechanical, including photocopying, recording, taping or by any information storage or retrieval system, without the permission in writing from the publisher.

This is a work of fiction. Any resemblance to actual events or persons, living or dead, is entirely coincidental.

Published by Quiet Storm Publishing

For information, please contact:
Quiet Storm Publishing
PO BOX 1666
Martinsburg, WV 25402

www.quietstormpublishing.com

Cover design by Sara Lindley

ISBN: 0-9714296-4-2

LCCN: 2002109418

Printed in the United States of America

DEDICATION

To my parents, Cathleen and Hugh Treacy, for teaching me that all things are possible. To my husband, Larry, who has always believed in my ability as a writer. His constant encouragement and support means more than I can say in words. And to Shannon, Chris and Lauren, my terrific kids, who cheered me on and put up with the process of writing *Caroline Rose*.

ACKNOWLEDGEMENTS

My publishers, Darla and Clint of Quiet Storm Books, have worked literally night and day to grow a company that not only produces quality books, but also educates and encourages its authors toward greater heights of success. Thank you both for your infectious enthusiasm and tireless dedication!

Sara Lindley, a long-time friend and gifted artist, created the beautiful cover art for *Caroline Rose*. Her ability to express the essence of a story in visual art never fails to astound me. Sara also assisted me in preparing my original manuscript to send to Quiet Storm. Sara, you have my heartfelt gratitude.

Sean Miers is a talented editor. His corrections and suggestions demonstrated his keen sensitivity not only to the story, but also to the style in which it was written.

Another thank you goes to authors William Saffell and C.E. Wells, who kindly took the time to write the quotes that appear on the back of this book.

My family and friends encouraged me during the long process of producing this novel, and continue to support me in my journey along the writer's path. I thank them heartily for all of their help and good wishes. I particularly want to mention my gratitude to Zach Bailey for his last-minute tech support during the late stage of the editing process.

I also wish to thank The Creative Writers Forum at Borders Books of Fredericksburg. They listened carefully to my first draft in weekly installments, offering thoughtful criticism, helpful suggestions and much encouragement. Without them I might never have finished writing the story of Caroline Rose.

CHAPTER ONE

My father was murdered.
He went out to pick up a few things at a nearby convenience store when two guys in ski masks came in to rob the place. One of them shot him even though he had his hands raised. The killer had no idea my dad was a passionate husband, that he was a kind and funny father who had a new story for his little girl every night. What was that to him? He shot him and got away with it. I could never understand why someone would want to kill my dad. He was a good man. I couldn't figure it out at seven; twenty years later I still can't figure it out.

I survived. Mom and I continued living. My mother was strong. She learned to go on without her husband. She learned to cook for just the two of us. She learned to sleep by herself in that big bed. Well, sometimes when I was little, I would crawl in with her. Mom never found another man that she could love like she loved my father. I never found another man who could be my father. I've been looking all my life, but he doesn't exist.

I miss my dad. I always will.

One of my earliest memories of my father was riding on his shoulders as he and my mother hiked in the Catskill Mountains. I remembered his laughter as he trotted along, pointing out the different flowers and trees; he knew them all by their Latin names. I had even learned a few from him, though I was only five at the time.

I held his forehead and played in his hair, pulling the long, black strands through my tiny fingers. Suddenly he stopped and held up a hand. Mom hung at his side and looked along the creek, following Daddy's gaze.

"What is it?" I tried to whisper in my child's soprano.

"Shh, honey. It's a bear."

"Oh," I added in a reverent tone. I peered through the leaves and brush. A black bear made its way carefully to the creek. "I see it!" I whispered

11

excitedly.

I tried to sit still on my dad's shoulders. I knew, even then, that wild animals would run away from humans. It was difficult to remain silent, but my efforts were soon rewarded by an unexpected sight. A smaller bear moved out of the brush and sidled up to the larger one. My mother stifled a gasp of delight. "A cub!" she whispered up to me.

From my tall perch I could see the two, mother and baby, as they drank from the stream. The cub slapped playfully at the water, splashing its mother. I remembered my television commercials. "Is that Smokey's family?" I wanted to know.

Mom's green eyes sparkled with amusement as she looked up into my face and smiled. "No, honey," she said, shaking her head so the brown locks swished across her face.

The bear cub caught sight of a butterfly and reached out to bat it with a paw. The insect easily evaded the swipe and fluttered tantalizingly just out of reach. Following its prey, the cub shuffled down the stream, stopping to bat at the creature now and again.

Finally, the butterfly flew out over the water. The cub lumbered into the stream, raising itself on its hind legs. As it reached overhead, the cub lost its balance and tumbled into the water. It moaned in frustration and rolled awkwardly to its feet. The mother bear, which had followed her infant's hunt with a watchful eye, now hurried to its side. It was a tender moment as the mother licked her cub and led it out of the stream.

Suddenly, the bear's head came up. We heard it, too—the sound of hikers on the trail ahead of us. As they approached, their talk and laughter grew louder in the still forest. The mother bear turned and padded into the woods, her cub following quickly and without complaint.

"Beautiful!" my dad whispered in awe. "Weren't they something?"

"I liked the cub," I answered, "but I'm glad he didn't catch the butterfly."

The group of hikers, probably in their twenties, passed us on the trail, waving and calling friendly hellos. We greeted them, still standing where we had watched the bears. After they moved out of sight, my parents turned and headed up the trail again.

"That baby bear was so cute, Daddy," I began. "Does he have lots of friends in the forest, like Bambi?"

"Maybe so," my daddy answered thoughtfully. "If he did, who might they be?" That was all I needed. I began to name all the cub's animal friends: raccoons, bunnies, foxes, deer, a skunk, and many more. I prattled on for at least another mile. My dad asked me questions about the cub's imaginary life and I spouted answers as if I actually knew what I was talking about.

We did that a lot. We always had a story about everything and everyone we saw. We shared a remarkable world of make-believe. And our real world seemed just as magical.

I was always fascinated by Dad's worn toolbox. All he had to do was open it, take out his tools and something wonderful appeared. He could make anything. He built chairs, a deck, a boat, and even a swing set for me. He often carved wooden animals and sold them in one of the shops in Providence. But that was just his hobby; by trade he was an accountant.

I wondered, when I grew a little older, why he didn't make his living with his woodworking skills. That's when I learned how much he enjoyed accounting. "I don't know how to describe it, Katy, but working with numbers can be so relaxing to me."

"Just make sure you don't get too relaxed and fall asleep," my mom commented wryly.

Dad reached across the dinner table and playfully ruffled her hair. "That's why I hear all that snoring from your office. I was wondering what that was."

Mom grabbed his hand and pretended to bite one of his fingers. "You!" She stopped and kissed it instead.

They held hands for a moment, gazing tenderly into each other's eyes. I knew, even then, that was the look that made our home so happy. My parents loved each other deeply and never seemed embarrassed to show it. Still, I was impatient with what I termed "the mushy stuff."

"Daa-aad! Are you still going to the store?" I stood next to them, my plate in my hands. "Are you going to get me chocolate ice cream?"

Mom and Dad both looked at me with mock exasperation for breaking the spell of the moment. They smiled. I always loved their smiles, especially when they did it together. Somehow it seemed more beautiful that way, like two rainbows in the sky.

Dad pushed his chair back from the table and rose, saying, "You're right, Katy. I do need to get to the store."

Mom hurried to check the list. Handing it to him, she paused. "Oh, and I forgot we're all out of tissues."

Dad tapped his temple, making a mental note. "Got it."

I put my plate in the sink with a clatter and ran over to my dad, almost dancing around him. "And ice cream. Chocolate ice cream!" I shouted gaily.

He stooped to give me a hug. "And chocolate ice cream for my little Katydid!"

"I'm not a bug!" I pretended to pout.

He patted me on the head. "I don't know about that. You seem just about the right size." I giggled.

Dad kissed my mom on the cheek and walked to the door. "Now, no wild parties while I'm gone!"

Mom grinned. "Of course not. We'll wait 'til you get back!"

He laughed and pulled the door shut behind him. I could still hear his laughter as he made his way down the walk to the car. That was the last time we ever saw him.

I thought he was home when the doorbell rang. Instead, a big policeman with a serious face was standing there when I opened the door. The smile froze on my childish face. Fear gripped at my throat when Mom called out to me. "Who is it, honey?"

I remember her nervous steps when I told her, "It's a policeman." I ran behind her and held onto her belt. She put her hand back as if to protect me from what the officer had to say. I think she knew what it was when he started with, "I'm sorry, Mrs. O'Brien…"

CHAPTER TWO

Something in my mother died that night. I'm not sure what it was, but I still miss it. All I remember about the next two days is her face, red and swollen from crying. I never saw it like that before or since. The grief that tore her heart was incomprehensible to me at that age. I didn't really understand the finality of death. Dad was gone and wasn't coming back. I would cry when I thought of it. But then I would go out and play on the swing he had made for me. There was much to occupy a little girl—to protect me from the raw hurt that robbed my mother of sleep for months afterward.

I hated going to the funeral home. The smell of formalin made me wrinkle my nose and complain bitterly to Mom. "What's that awful smell?"

Mom frowned. "It's the chemical they use to..." She hesitated, obviously uncomfortable. "To preserve the bodies," she finished with a whisper and started to cry.

I took her hand and held it to my cheek. "It's okay, Mom. Dad never minded those smells when he painted. He'll think they're fixing things here."

She sniffed and tried to smile. It looked hard to do, though. "That's right, Katy. I know he won't mind."

Hand in hand we walked into one of the rooms. At the far end, surrounded by huge flower arrangements, stood an open coffin. My dad didn't look real as he lay there in that artificial pose. I could feel my mother stiffen beside me. "Oh, God!" she whimpered, putting a hand over her mouth. She turned away, struggling with tears, her face contorted with a failing attempt to control her emotions.

"Mommy?" I looked from Mom to the coffin. Why were we coming here if it was going to make her cry again?

"I'll be okay, honey. Just give me a minute." She leaned on the back of a chair. I had already made my decision. I turned and walked resolutely up to the coffin and planted my feet. Hands on hips, I stood and gave the whole scene a good, long look. The coffin and flowers made it seem as though my

15

father were part of some kind of bizarre centerpiece. His face, once so alive with movement and healthy color, looked pasty; it reminded me of an old doll I once had. I had never liked it.

"This isn't right," I muttered to myself. I stepped around to the other side of the coffin and pushed on the lid. It shut with a bang that echoed through the room and out into the hall.

Mom turned, startled. For a moment I thought I would be in big trouble, then my mother's shock transformed into a sheepish grin. She wasn't trying to control sobs anymore; she had clapped both hands over her mouth to keep from laughing out loud. Thinking back on the incident now, it probably was not really funny to Mom. But in such an odd circumstance, laughter had to be the only response she could come up with. She was determined to stay strong for me. Besides, Dad would have preferred her laughter to her tears.

Of course the man that rushed into the parlor and slipped on the rug was not at all amused with my action. He lay there a moment in his neatly pressed suit and muttered something under his breath. "How did that happen?" he spluttered, as he struggled to get up in a dignified fashion. Looking from my mother, to me, to the closed coffin and back to Mom, he gasped and shook his head.

Finally he decided I was the perpetrator and fixed me with a stern look. "Did you do that?" he demanded.

I watched him a moment. His coloring had changed from purple to red as he began to recover from his initial shock.

"That's not my daddy in there! My dad is in heaven! He's not that…that…thing over there." I stood there, defiant of him, of my loss, and of death itself.

"I'm sorry," my mother interposed, trying to diffuse the situation. "This is…very hard—for both of us."

He relaxed and took a deep breath. "Of course. I was just a bit—uh—surprised," he began, never taking his eyes off me for an instant. He shook his head. "I'll take care of it."

He glanced at the coffin and walked toward it, brushing past me with an air of efficiency. As he reached for the lid to lift it back into place, I screamed. "No!" Running up to him, I grabbed his arm. "Leave it alone! It makes Mommy too sad!"

The man turned in surprise. I thought he would get angry with me, but he simply lowered his arm and patted my hand. He looked at my mother, the question plain on his face.

"Yes." My mom's voice sounded unusually calm. She straightened into a posture of authority. "Please leave it as it is. Kate is right. We wish to remember him as he was, thank you." Overcoming her grief for a moment, she smiled at me. "You're right, honey. That's not Daddy."

"Certainly," he responded politely. "I shall be in my office if you need anything." Giving me one last pat, this time on my head, the man turned and walked quickly from the room.

I ran to my mom and grabbed her around the waist, clinging tightly. She held me while I sobbed, her tears mingling with mine. "It's all right, Katy. We're going to get through this."

All during the funeral I gripped her hand in mine, barely hearing the minister. He didn't know my dad, so I knew he really couldn't say anything about him. He kept repeating things like "He was a good father" and "He was a faithful husband." But he never knew that Dad could throw a Frisbee across three yards in our neighborhood or that he liked to play pranks on his buddies at the office.

The cemetery stood on a hill against a bright blue sky. Over our heads a green canopy fluttered lightly in the breeze. I thought it odd that we stood on a carpet made to look like the grass, little knowing that it covered the grave that lay hidden under the coffin, which was, in turn, almost completely shrouded by the flowers draped over it.

I noticed the headstones near my dad's grave. On a new grave was the name of a man born in 1901. His daughter's stone stood next to his. She had died when she was only four. I kept thinking how sad he must have been to lose his little girl. I knew he would have understood what I felt that day when I finally turned away from Dad's coffin and walked with my mother back to the car.

Two weeks later we moved to Virginia. Mom told me we had to make a fresh start. So we got a new house and I went to a new school and made new friends. I guess I adjusted pretty well. But Mom still had a hard time and I would sometimes hear her crying alone at night in her bedroom. I would pad softly into the room, climb into bed and give her a hug.

"What would I do without my Kate?" she would say, before kissing me on my forehead and sending me back to bed. "You need your sleep. It's a school night, you know."

Those nights grew less and less frequent until finally they stopped altogether. I think I was nine by then. Mom had already gotten a promotion at her new job and life had settled into a contented routine.

I did ask my mother about Dad's death when I was older—seventeen, I think.

"There's not much to it, Kate. He walked into the store and a few minutes later..." She shook her head. "That was it."

"Why didn't they catch the killer?"

"They never found him." She poured me another cup of tea.

"Are they still looking?" I asked as I picked up the cup.

Mom refilled her cup and set the pot down on the table. "I suppose they are," she murmured, almost to herself.

Mom continued to work at the accounting firm until I finished college. Then she quit and moved to Blacksburg in southwest Virginia. She had finally decided to pursue a long-cherished dream of becoming a veterinarian. When she enrolled at Virginia Tech I found it amusing to visit her at school. I even went down for the big Parents' Weekend that fall. There I was, with all those parents, visiting the campus and getting the royal treatment.

"I just love this place, Kate!" She exclaimed, gesturing to the gray, stone buildings around her.

"I don't know, Mom. It looks pretty somber to me—all that gray."

"Oh, hush!" she cried, giving me an affectionate slap on the shoulder. "I happen to like it. It's...it's very dignified!"

I smiled. "Just like you, Mom."

She laughed.

We ate dinner with a couple of her classmates, Karen and Julie, and Julie's father. The two girls were a lot younger than Mom but it didn't seem to matter. The three of them giggled like teenagers when they were together. I felt more like a doting parent than a daughter.

"Melinda just loves this place," Julie was saying. Her cheeks glowed with the brisk weather we had just escaped. "Loads of vegetarian stuff."

Julie's father took this opportunity to politely ask about my schooling. "So you graduated from Mary Washington?"

"Yes."

"What was your major?"

"English," I responded automatically.

He leaned forward, his elbows planted on the table. "So what do you do with it, an English degree, I mean?"

What should I say to this guy? I leaned forward. I could tell he expected some wonderful answer, that maybe I taught English to inner city kids or was a published novelist. I hated to disappoint him. He seemed like such a nice man, too. "I wait tables," was my answer.

I could see that he didn't want me to notice the surprise in his look. He tried to put the situation in a positive light. "Oh. Uh, any special place?"

"No, just some cheesy dive in downtown Fredericksburg."

Mom couldn't stand any more. "Kate's also a writer, Tom. She's been published in the paper up there." I glanced over to catch the pride in her eyes. Leave it to Mom to toot my horn in front of strangers. I have never been any good at it.

Blushing, I tried to put Mom's words in perspective. "I write a little on the side, but there's not much money in it yet."

"But you are a writer," Tom emphasized in a tone close to triumph. The smile that had slipped from his face earlier in the conversation was back.

Ah, he's got me labeled now. I nodded reluctantly. I didn't feel I deserved that particular title yet. I felt more comfortable with 'waitress.' When people learn you're a writer they start developing all sorts of false expectations. But, then again, maybe I found it easier to live up to the waitress label than the writer label. Accepting the challenge the latter offered was a thing I hesitated to do. The brassy little girl I had been had somehow grown up into an insecure woman. How had that happened?

CHAPTER THREE

When I returned home, I settled back into my usual routine of working at the Lucky Dog Cafe, researching and writing. Every day, without fail, I sat down at my computer and wrote. It didn't matter what it was, as long as I was writing. I churned out short stories and newspaper articles. I even toyed with the idea of writing a novel, but I kept convincing myself I wasn't ready for that.

I had plenty of ideas but very little confidence, which did not improve as my file of rejection letters from magazines grew large enough to warrant buying another folder. As long as I was out, I could stop and pick up a pair of jeans; I was wearing the only pair without holes.

My old station wagon lumbered down Route 3, the main artery through Fredericksburg and the only way to get to the mall. I pulled up into a long line of cars waiting at the light. A homeless woman was walking down the median. She was one of the many faceless, nameless people who wandered the streets of the city. I watched her with a writer's eye for detail; she could be an interesting character in a future story.

Then I was struck with her unusual manner. Unlike other homeless I had seen panhandling at intersections, she did not wear an expression of shame. Instead, her tanned features seemed lit with a brightness from beyond this world. The web of wrinkles covering her face leapt into high relief under the spring sun when she smiled. Her worn body moved with difficulty as she made her way down the line of cars that stood trapped at the red light. And I was trapped right along with them.

She smiled kindly as she passed each car, looking for an answering kindness in any of their occupants. Her cardboard sign read: "Homeless, need money for bus fare to Indiana." Everyone ignored her, shut off behind metal and glass. Maybe they thought her world would only be real if they met her gaze. Drivers averted their faces as her eyes sought theirs, but she smiled, unconcerned, continuing her walk down the median.

I wondered if I should give her money. Would I only be encouraging panhandling, just adding to the problem? All I had with me was a single dollar bill. Would that be enough to help? She looked into my windshield and I smiled; at least I could acknowledge her humanity even if I could give her nothing.

She passed on, continuing to display the sign announcing her modern leprosy. I watched in the rearview mirror as the woman stopped, turned around and began to trudge back to her station. Dickens' words flashed into my mind, "Are there no prisons? Are there no workhouses?" and I quickly grabbed my wallet, fumbling for that last dollar. I rolled the window down all the way and called out, "Ma'am."

She stopped and beamed her angelic smile at me as I reached out with the folded bill. When she clasped my hand in both of hers, a loving energy passed between us. "Thank you, my dear! God bless you!"

Looking into her eyes, I felt an odd sense of deja vu. The touch of her hand and the intensity of her look stirred an old memory, so vague I could not recall it to mind. I just knew there was something familiar about this woman and our exchange.

Around us several drivers honked their horns indignantly, disapproving of my gesture, I supposed. The woman moved away toward the light, which had just turned green. She waved at me as I passed on my way through the intersection. I struggled to regain the memory that lurked just beyond my reach. Was it happy or sad? I couldn't even remember that.

I splurged and bought two pairs of jeans and a blouse; I hadn't bought new clothes for myself in quite a while. Shopping is not my favorite pastime.

The bookstore beckoned as I hurried through the crowd. I don't believe in walking slowly through the mall. Get in and get out is my motto. Crowds make me nervous, anyway.

But there it was, a treasure house of knowledge and I had some money left in my account. Hemingway's *Islands in the Stream* jumped into my hand. I was surprised they had it. I decided a book of poetry would balance that out—yes. I only had one book by Maya Angelou— I needed another one. My trek to the mall was now complete.

I walked out into the parking lot and slipped behind the wheel of the station wagon, shutting the door with a hard pull. I sat thoughtfully, leafing through the book of poems. I liked her style—bold, yet full of compassion. We all need compassion.

A red Camaro pulled up into the space beside me, rap music pounding hard enough to make the whole car shudder. The sound stopped suddenly and the young driver got out, looking over at me with a curious expression. I put the book down and started the car. A puff of blue smoke shot from the tailpipe.

    Eyes forward, I drove out of the parking lot. As I drove through the intersection I noticed that the woman no longer stood at her post. Perhaps she had gone to another spot, or maybe she had gone home or wherever she went to spend the night—a shelter or something. I tried not to think anymore about her. I had to go to work that night anyway.

CHAPTER FOUR

The restaurant was busy as it always was on a Saturday night. It was a quaint little place in the historic section of Fredericksburg. The people I worked with seemed pretty nice, all in their twenties and waiting tables until they found what they really wanted to do in life, just like me.

I seemed to have the most in common with Jenny and Nick. We all were ready to split when our ship came in. Jenny—a religion major—had graduated from my alma mater and was saving to go to grad school in D.C. or somewhere else up north. Nick played in a local band and usually worked days, but came in on the Saturday nights when he didn't have a gig.

We had a lot of fun, except when we were "slammed". That happened around holidays or when there was some event at the college that brought many of the students' parents to town. Then the adrenalin would pump, the kitchen would go into overdrive and we would hardly be able to talk to one another, much less go out for those surreptitious smokes out back. I didn't smoke but I liked to go out under the starlight and talk with the other "servers", as we were more correctly called these days.

That night was not one of those nights and so we had plenty of time to talk. "Well, Kate, I now understand how you feel about all those rejection letters." Jenny inhaled deeply and tipped her head to blow smoke at the full moon just overhead.

"C.U. didn't accept you?" I asked.

She shook her head and took another drag. "Nope. 'Thank you for your application, but you're just not the right combination of grades, money, and good background.'"

Nick smiled at her. "You had the grades, though."

"Yeah, but nothing else."

Jenny was an interesting study: she was passionate about her research into world religions—so passionate that she had tried quite a number of them. Now she had a wide repertoire of religious practices that spanned the spectrum from Buddhism to Santeria. I found it a unique combination.

"There are other schools," I reminded her.

"Yeah, Jen." Nick ground the end of a spent cigarette into the pavement. "What about your other applications?" He drew another one from his shirt pocket.

Jenny sighed. "I don't know. Maybe I should move to India and take up with a guru."

"Or live in a cave in the Himalayas," Nick added. "I hear some of those guys never come out again."

"Only if they'll keep me stocked with cigarettes and beer." She laughed.

"Right," I said, tossing the rest of my diet cola into the adjoining alley. It had gone flat and the ice had melted. The slight aftertaste bit into my tongue, drying it out.

Jenny smashed the end of her smoke into the brick wall. "Break's over. See ya." She turned and made her way back into the alley. We heard the screen door creak open, then slam shut as she walked into the kitchen.

Nick blew a stream of smoke downward through barely parted lips. "I don't think she really knows what she wants. I better go, too. Damn." He dropped the cigarette and ground it with his foot. "You coming back in?" he asked.

"Yeah, in a minute." I looked up into the night sky, drinking in the moonlight. I sighed and rose from the trashcan where I'd been sitting. My feet hurt and I felt tired from the long day, a day that had started at seven AM with a quick two-mile run, followed by three hours of research at the library for a new article I was writing for the local paper. And all of that had preceded my shopping trip to the mall.

By the time I got home from work it was two in the morning. I hated closing on Saturday night but it came with the territory. My housemates weren't home yet so I enjoyed the quiet as I showered quickly before slipping into bed. I must have fallen asleep almost immediately because I don't remember anything after I pulled the quilt up over my shoulders.

My dreams were filled with troubling images of homeless people and dumpsters in dirty alleys. An old man held out his hand as I walked down a dark street. I was about to give him a sandwich, but I saw he held a diamond that glittered in the cold moonlight. The gem held my attention. It grew in size until the woman I had seen that afternoon walked out of it.

Now she held a different sign: "Need money for trip around the world."

It didn't seem strange at all. I took her hand and we walked down the street together into a meadow filled with flowers and sunlight. She turned to me and patted my cheek, smiling with crooked yellow teeth. Then she simply faded from sight.

It rained on Sunday, so I got caught up on my laundry and housework. I tried not to think of the homeless woman during that next week. I wanted to get my article done and in to the paper. My editor liked my work, probably because it was always neat and on time. Those may seem to be pretty basic requirements for a writer, but freelance writers didn't always follow them, at least not in his experience.

I completed the third rewrite of my short story and finally felt ready to show it to my mentor, a published novelist and non-fiction writer who had moved here from New York when he had retired. Now he divided his time between gardening and a handful of writing students who had been lucky enough to discover him in their midst. I looked forward to my meeting with him the next day.

Friday morning dawned orange and pink as I pulled on my running shoes and laced them up securely. I slipped out the front door of the small, two-story frame house I shared with two other girls. The morning air felt cool on my bare legs and arms. I walked quickly down my street and turned right on Augustine. I loved walking through the neighborhood on my way to the track. Each of the houses had character—no cracker boxes here. Some were brick, others had real stone facings, and the rest bore simple wood or vinyl siding. Each seemed well cared for, complete with small lawns and flower gardens. Azaleas predominated as the shrub of choice, blooming in a variety of pinks, reds and purples, all accented by bushes overflowing with white flowers.

I paused to gently stretch my legs. The fresh spring air invigorated my body as I inhaled it deeply, almost greedily, into my lungs. I savored the scents of wisteria and other flowers, of the green growing things all around me, as I would savor the bouquet of a good wine. My legs, warm and flowing with energy, felt eager to move. I strode up a hill and broke into an easy trot as I turned on to Brent Street, which led directly through the college gates. I turned again before reaching them, however, and loped across the next intersection. Suddenly I stopped and gazed down the sidewalk along William Street. There she was, toiling up the steep hill, carrying a cardboard sign.

The woman looked up at me as I stood on the corner, poised to continue my run. A smile broke across her face and she raised a weathered hand to wave a greeting. I waved back, slightly hesitant. For a moment I considered turning away, but something kept me from leaving. I'll never know what prompted me to do it, but the next thing I knew I was padding across the street and part-way down William to meet her.

"I know you! You helped me last week. So, here you are out getting your exercise, and so early!" She fondly took my hand in hers and peered into my face.

That same feeling of vague memory came over me again. I laughed nervously. "I like to run in the morning while the air's still fresh."

"Oh, and it is so beautiful today!" She looked from me to the college across the street. "Are you a college girl?"

"No, ma'am. I graduated from there five years ago. Now I'm trying to make it as a writer." She let go of my hand tenderly and continued walking up the street to the corner with me. One of the college trucks accelerated past us on its way to the playing fields where the track waited for me. We crossed to the other side and I stopped to indicate I could accompany her no further.

"I think you are a fine young lady and I do hope you become very successful. I was, once, but now I have nothing left. I just live one day at a time."

"Well...uh...I'm sorry..." I trailed off, not knowing what to say. At that point I felt very uncomfortable and she must have seen my expression.

"Don't be." She patted my hand. "My name is Caroline Rose, dear."

I smiled with more confidence. "I'm Kate, Kate O'Brien."

She paused a moment, a thoughtful look creasing her brow. Peering into my face, she relaxed and resumed her cheery appearance. "Such a pretty name, child. And you look Irish, too."

"Yeah. Well, I am. It's nice to meet you, but I really have to go now. I've got a lot to do today." I felt impatient to be off.

She nodded understanding. "Of course you do. Have a good day, dear."

"You, too, Ms. Rose."

"Caroline sounds so much better to me, if you would indulge an old woman."

"Caroline," I corrected, relieved to get on my way. "Take care." I turned and jogged down to the end of the street. Before crossing to the playing fields, I looked back. She was gone, but somehow I felt a strange kinship with this woman whose warm smile could not be erased by the miseries of her homeless existence.

CHAPTER FIVE

My writing teacher and mentor lived downtown on Caroline Street in one of the smaller historic homes. He kept the house in pristine condition, always adding historically based touches here and there. The grounds were better manicured than my nails, and in the back yard he had constructed a walled garden. He called it his "secret garden", taken as he was with the book by that name.

I always felt a little self-conscious parking my dilapidated Ford in front of such a beautiful house, but Walt wasn't bothered by it. He told me that, although he felt obsessed with neatness in his own home, he never expected others to follow suit. "We all have our own forms of madness," he would say.

I slammed the car door and walked around to the sidewalk where I was met by Java, the neighbor's West Highland Terrier. I thought it a totally fitting name for the creature that yapped at my ankles until I relented and treated her to a luxurious tummy rub. "Java, you nut!" She wriggled and snuffled in sheer delight. "OK, off with you now. I've got an appointment." Knowing that was all the attention she would get until I was finished with my business, she rolled onto her feet and trotted off, wagging her tiny stub of a tail.

As soon as I rang the doorbell Walt opened the door, the chimes sounding behind him. I must have looked rather startled because he burst out laughing. "Come in, come in! I know; I should be careful of how I use my psychic abilities, but sometimes I can't help myself!"

For a moment I almost believed him. At twenty-seven I was still a rather gullible person, though I hoped to gain a healthy sense of skepticism in time. "Then you didn't hear Java demanding her usual tummy scratch." I smiled, hoping I looked worldly-wise. Walt just laughed again.

"For a writer, you're awfully innocent. Didn't your mother teach you not to believe everything you hear? Come, show me the story," he said as he strode to the elegant cherry-wood table in the dining room and pulled out a chair for me. He sat down, the smile fading into his customary working scowl. He had the ability to move from laughter to serious business and back again at exactly the appropriate times.

I pulled a green folder from my canvas pack and handed it to him. "My query letter is on top." He picked up his reading glasses from the table and put them on with one hand as he opened the folder with the other.

As he read he began to nod. "Good. Good. That should do very well," he said without looking up from the pages. "The college literary magazine—that can be helpful to mention along with the articles in the paper—hmmm... Yes, good." He glanced up at me over the tops of the lenses. "What about that short story contest you won last year? You should put that in, too."

"Well, it was just a local newsletter. I didn't think—"

Walt interrupted me. "Well, you should. And how do they know what kind of circulation that publication gets? You've got to sell yourself to these people, Kate! You have to convince them that they need your work in their magazine!"

"Yes, sir!" I answered smartly, with a mock salute. He smiled and shook his head. Putting the query letter aside, he adjusted his reading glasses and began looking over the rewrite of my story.

"Make yourself at home." He waved absently in the direction of the kitchen. "There's coffee in the pot and soda in the fridge."

I stood up. "You want anything?"

"No, not at the moment," he said, as he continued to read.

In the colonial kitchen I found a fresh pot of coffee sitting in the very modern coffee maker. I opened the glass door of the cupboard and reached for my favorite mug, the one with the Tibetan flag. Walt Cleary was an ardent supporter of the Free Tibet movement, even though he was Episcopalian. Religion didn't matter to him; he championed freedom for all peoples. He made that quite evident in his books, which ranged in topic from the plight of small farmers in America to the tragedy of Tianamen Square.

I sat in the cozy breakfast nook that looked out over the walled garden. Through the screened window I could hear the gurgling of the Greek-style fountain. A child stood on an open oyster shell playing aulos from which the clear water streamed. Dark green ivy, interlaced with morning glory vines, climbed the wall behind the fountain. Green and white striped hostas enclosed the bowl before giving way to evergreen periwinkle, the small-leaved vinca minor, with its bluish-purple flowers. The serenity of the garden calmed my restless mind and I slowly relaxed from the busyness of the day.

I turned my head to see Walt striding into the kitchen. His tall, lean frame filled the doorway as he passed quietly through to the coffee maker. He poured himself a cup and stopped at the refrigerator to add milk.

I watched his movements expectantly, waiting for him to speak. He raised his mug as if in salute. "You've done it, girl. You're ready to send it off!" He grinned proudly at his relieved student.

"Thanks. I really appreciate your help on this," I said gratefully.

"Happy to help, but now I've got some more work for you." He slid a pile of papers, newsletters, and magazines from the end of the table over to me. He was doing research for a new book detailing the plight of the Tibetan people under Chinese rule. "Give me a synopsis of this material, highlighting the main points of interest."

"OK. When do you need it?" I asked, dubiously eyeing the stack.

"No hurry. Can you have it in a couple of weeks?"

"Sure. That should be enough time." I rose from my chair and reached for the pile. "I better go now. Looks like I've got my work cut out for me!"

"How's the article?"

"Oh, I brought it in on my way here. If Pete likes it we should see it next week." I hefted my bundle.

"Nice biceps for a girl," Walt teased.

"Thanks." I glanced at his muscular arms, set off quite nicely below the cuffs of a royal blue golf shirt. "You back to working out?" I asked.

"Yeah. I finally got over that tennis elbow."

"How's your backhand now?" He never could play tennis.

"Very funny," he commented wryly, getting up from the table to see me to the door.

Java ran up just as I stepped out onto the front steps. She wriggled and panted, hoping for more attention from me. "Sorry, girl. My arms are full." I looked back at Walt. "Thanks again."

"Give me a holler if you run into any trouble with the research."

"I will," I replied, turning toward the car.

"Behave yourself, Kate."

I grinned, indicating the papers in my arms. "I won't have time to do anything else!" It really was a pretty good deal we had made. He helped me with my writing and I assisted him in researching the occasional book.

He hadn't given up writing entirely. I didn't believe he ever could.

Back at the house I busied myself reading the material Walt had given me. I had just finished reading an article about a Buddhist nun who had been imprisoned and tortured for having a picture of the Dalai Lama in her possession. As the incarnation of the Buddha of compassion, Chenrezig in Tibetan, he was a central figure in Tibetan religious beliefs. Tibetans treasure his picture as Catholics treasure the crucifix or a picture of the Sacred Heart.

I stopped reading and rested my chin in my hand, staring out the window. There was too much injustice in the world. One person couldn't do very much, if anything.

I thought of Caroline Rose and wondered if she had eaten today. What had happened to bring a woman like that from wealth to abject poverty?

I realized that I felt as much curiosity as compassion. My news sense seemed to have been activated, too. There might be an article in this for me. I didn't want to admit it, but my motivations were not as pure as I would have liked. Besides, I rationalized, letting people know about the homeless was a good thing. Journalists got awards for this kind of story.

The local homeless shelter was listed in the white pages. I dialed the number, not exactly sure of what I wanted to say. A volunteer answered. I wondered what she would think of my query. "Hello, uh, my name is Kate O'Brien and I'm doing research on the homeless in this area. I was wondering if you could give me a little information on the services offered by the shelter."

"Sure." She began to explain that the shelter offered a place to sleep for up to three months—but only seven days for transients. Dinner was served every day to anyone who needed it, as long as they weren't inebriated, unruly, or on drugs.

"What about the people we see carrying those signs?"

"The people who stay here aren't allowed to do that. The ones you're seeing don't even come here except maybe for dinner." She spoke with some regret in her voice. "We don't have the resources to help everyone out there. We do what we can."

I described Caroline Rose and asked her if she had seen her. "No, I don't remember a woman like her, but a lot of people come for dinner. I might have missed her."

Thanking her for her help, I hung up thoughtfully. Perhaps Caroline was a transient with Fredericksburg as one of her stopping points along the way.

The germ of an idea entered my mind. I pushed my chair back from the wooden desk, glancing absently into its scarred, painted surface. The desk was a yard sale purchase and still carried the Ninja Turtle stickers some child had proudly placed on its top and drawers. I felt rather fond of them myself, since they went well with the purple paint.

Not sure of what I was going to do next, I rose and grabbed my canvas pack. Pulling the keys from the front pocket I slung the bag over my shoulder and ran down the steps to the front door.

"Going out, Kate?" one of my housemates called from the kitchen.

"Yeah. Need anything?"

Holly stepped into the living room, saucepan in one hand and dishtowel in the other. Her curly red hair hung in a fiery mist around her face and shoulders. Her green eyes danced as she smiled. "Could you pick up some eggs and milk? Oh, and Andy wanted some more Killian's."

"Sure, but I won't be back for a few hours." I readjusted my pack, eager to leave.

"That's fine. She'll be at the library all day anyway."

I grinned. "That term paper she was supposed to be working on all semester...some of us work best under pressure!"

"If that's true it'll be the best she's ever done!" Holly laughed, not unkindly. We were both amazed by our third housemate, Andrea, or Andy, which she preferred. She was one of those people you wanted to hate in college but couldn't quite bring yourself to do it. She could party and play almost the whole semester then turn out incredible papers and ace every exam. Keenly aware of her brilliant potential, her professors never gave her an inch. She played hard and worked even harder, while the rest of us looked on with envy.

My thoughts returned to the homeless woman as I drove down Route 3 towards the mall. I watched the side of the road for any sign of her. As I slid into the turn lane for Spotsy Mall, the light turned red. Caroline Rose began her walk down the line of cars. I took a deep breath, and strengthened my resolve as she approached my car. "Caroline!" I called out the open window.

"Kate! How nice to see you!" Her face brightened with that same angelic smile.

I leaned out over the door. "I was wondering if I could take you to lunch today." With that innocent invitation I set in motion a series of events that would bring me face to face with a past I had tried to forget, and that would forever change my life.

"Why, I'd love to, sweetie!" With that, she happily made her way around the front of the car to the passenger side. The light turned green as she painfully pulled the door shut. "This is so nice of you!"

I smiled over at my elderly guest, trying not to wrinkle my nose at the smell that had entered the car with her. "My pleasure, Caroline. What are you in the mood for?"

"Oh! Anything will be just lovely!" The years seemed to fall from her shoulders as she looked forward to lunch with childlike anticipation. I wondered when she had eaten last.

CHAPTER SIX

I took Caroline to the nearby cafeteria so she would have plenty of choices. Besides, I was on a budget. We settled down at a table in the non-smoking section. It was a little quieter there, set off in a room adjoining the main dining area. Now we could relax and talk.

Caroline had taken very little: some salad, corn, and a piece of barbeque chicken. "I won't have any room for dessert," she confided, as we passed the shelves of pies, puddings and cakes.

She folded her hands above her plate and closed her eyes for a silent blessing. I sat politely with my hands in my lap until she had finished. I usually said only a quick, silent mantra my mother had taught me from her Buddhist practice.

Caroline seemed in no hurry to eat as she unrolled her napkin and arranged her silverware on the table around her plate. She gazed at me, a grandmotherly smile on her weathered face. "This is so sweet of you, dear!"

My heart skipped a beat. I was touched deeply at her appreciation of a simple lunch. My eyes misted over and I dabbed at them with the cloth napkin. "The smoke still gets in here, I guess," I murmured unconvincingly.

"Oh, you poor thing. Would you like to move to another table?" Her face showed genuine concern.

"No," I smiled. "I'm fine here." Her solicitous manner reminded me of some of the wealthy matrons native to this city. I had occasionally accompanied Walt to their parties. They prided themselves on their hospitality, and rightly so. Those hostesses made certain their guests were happy, with plenty to eat and drink. Sometimes they even filled plates and glasses personally, the enjoyment of their guests being paramount to their own.

As we began to eat, I noted that Caroline's manners were impeccable. Suddenly I felt self-conscious. I must look like a slob eating next to her, I thought. I recalled our first conversation at the stoplight. She said she had been wealthy before she had lost everything, everything except who she was and, apparently, continued to be.

"What are you writing now, dear?" Caroline asked with interest.

"Well," I paused, considering the idea that had come to me at home. "I've been writing freelance articles for the paper. I was wondering..." I trailed off, looking deeply into her bright blue eyes. "I wondered if I should write an article about the homeless." I searched her face for a reaction.

She paused thoughtfully for a moment, before nodding her approval. "Yes. That is a splendid idea. There are so many people in this country who have nothing. They have no one to turn to in their need. I'm one of the lucky ones." I choked on a mouthful of lettuce and cucumbers. "I've made a lot of friends and we help each other out as best we can. But most homeless people have no one."

She nodded again. "Yes, dear, that would be a good idea." Her answer heartened and amazed me at the same time. How could she say that she was lucky?

"I also wondered if you would be willing to help me out—if I could interview you." I felt strange asking for her help.

She looked away, gazing across the noisy dining room, and then turned her eyes back to me. Resolve added strength to the lines in her face. "Yes, I will help you. I would be happy to do that for you."

Caroline wanted to know more about what I had written in the past and what I planned to do in the future. I answered her questions as well as I could, telling her about Walt and the story I had just finished. She seemed impressed.

"I enjoyed writing stories myself," she explained. "My husband was away a lot. I traveled with him on business until my pregnancy; then it became more difficult." She told me she had been confined to bed for the last three months before their baby was born. "Oh, but he was the sweetest baby! I didn't even think of it as any trouble once I got to hold him in my arms for the first time."

She seemed to look far into the distance, into the past. "My sweet little Kenny." The blue eyes dimmed with tears that she quickly wiped away with her fingertips. "I'm sorry, dear."

"Please, don't apologize." Moved by her emotion, I put my hand over hers. "Maybe we should go somewhere else to talk," I suggested.

"Yes," she agreed. "Let's go to that lovely park. It's just off Route 3. Oh, what's it called?" Her thin brow wrinkled in mild annoyance. "I just can't remember things like I used to."

"Alum Springs?"

"Yes, dear, that's it." She brightened a little. "Let's go there if you have time."

"Of course, I've got the rest of the day off." We rose and made our way out of the restaurant amid many curious stares. I guessed that the other diners wondered about the old woman in her ill-fitting clothes and faded red kerchief. She didn't smell very good, either.

Caroline seemed delighted with my old station wagon. It was the largest model they made back in '75 and I appreciated its roominess. "This old car takes me back," she said, settling herself comfortably into the ample seat. "My Kenny was born in the '70's. Those were such happy times for us."

Her eyes softened with a dreamy look. "We were living on Long Island at the time. For the baby's sake, Neal and I decided to move to Newport. He had just opened a branch firm there."

"Newport? I lived in Providence when I was a child."

"Oh?" The thin eyebrows rose over the blue eyes. "Providence?"

"Yeah. My aunt still lives there." As I watched Caroline's features an odd look of consternation passed briefly over them. "What's wrong?"

She shook her head, the oily hair moving stiffly about her ears. "Nothing." She had already resumed her customary smile. "So you are familiar with Newport?"

I nodded eagerly. "Yes! I still visit every time I go up to my aunt's place. I absolutely love it there!"

"Then you must have some happy memories up there as I do."

"Yes. But I'm sorry. I've interrupted your story. Your husband was a lawyer, then?" I asked.

"No, a stock broker." She sighed. "It was such a lovely place, Newport. Our house looked right out over the ocean. I still remember the sound of the surf whenever we opened the windows..." She trailed off into quiet reverie and I drove on in silence. At least, I thought, she could enjoy her memories in peace.

I turned off the highway and drove past the clusters of apartments. We had to ford the creek to enter the park. Wisps of steam seeped out of the hood as cold water met the hot engine block. When we wound up the road to the parking lot, I noticed only one other car. The children weren't out of school yet so we had the park pretty much to ourselves.

As we shut the car doors three ravens took flight from a nearby oak tree. Their wings shimmered blue-black as the sunlight splashed on them. "Beautiful birds, ravens," Caroline said with admiration. She watched them fly off to another tree across the park. "Even though they do remind me of Poe's poem. He was such a troubled man."

"You like Edgar Allen Poe?" I asked, interested.

"Oh, yes. I've read almost everything he wrote. It gave me the chills, but that was part of why I liked it." She ambled slowly under the old trees, the dried loam whispering and crackling under her worn tennis shoes.

"Do you still like to read?" I asked awkwardly, wishing I hadn't. How could a homeless woman get books, I wondered.

"I did until I lost my glasses." When I didn't respond she explained. "I had a pair of used reading glasses someone gave me. I used to go to public libraries and spend part of the day reading."

"Oh," I made a mental note to stop at the drugstore on the way home for a new pair of glasses for her. No, I shouldn't get too involved, I reminded myself. Just be a reporter.

We made our way to one of the benches by a tall, rusted swing set. For a few moments we sat in silence, breathing the forest scents and drinking in the sunlight that shimmered through the leaves high overhead.

"I love staying here in the good weather," my new friend began.

I glanced around the park. "Where do you stay?" I asked, recalling the comforts I knew growing up in a family that camped with the most modern equipment. In all of our travels Mom and I rarely stayed where there was no running water. I couldn't imagine what Caroline had to do to take care of her basic needs.

Her eyes glowed with the joy she so obviously felt in the beauty of nature. "Oh, sometimes I just find a nice spot away from the trails and settle down in some leaves." She looked pointedly at me. "I do have to watch out for young hooligans on weekends. They're out for mischief. They'll come back in the woods and drink and do whatever drugs people do these days. I've seen dealers, too."

I shook my head in disgust. "Have they ever bothered you?"

"No. I stay clear of them."

"Do you mind if I ask you a very personal question?" I wanted to know, but I wasn't sure how to ask.

"No, dear. If I don't like it, I just won't answer!" She stated this matter-of-factly, but not unkindly.

"Well," I began, hesitating. "How do you take care of your...uh...personal needs out here. Or anywhere else, for that matter?"

Caroline smiled, chuckling softly. "That is a good question. How do you think?"

I felt unsure of how to answer so I tried a little humor; it usually worked for my mom in awkward situations. "I guess you have to be careful what kind of leaves you use."

She laughed at this, patting my knee and rocking back and forth. "That's right, honey! You learn that pretty quickly!" She inhaled deeply and tried to sound more serious. "I shouldn't laugh, though. It did happen to an acquaintance of mine down in Louisa County. He suffered for weeks with poison ivy! Too proud to go to a free clinic to get any of that lotion...whatever that stuff is called."

"Calamine?" I offered.

"That's it. No, he just wouldn't get any help. Didn't want anyone to see that part of him." She grinned at the memory. "Oh, he had a terrible time with that!"

The humor faded from her face as another memory filled her mind. "Sometimes, just after dawn, I'll find a pool along this creek, here." She pointed toward the stream that wound through the park. "And once I make sure no one's around, I'll strip and bathe in it. It's as cold as the devil," she said, hunching her shoulders at the thought, "but it is invigorating!"

"That's a good word for it, invigorating," I agreed, almost shivering myself at the thought of the icy cold swimming holes I remembered from my childhood.

"Of course, I can only do that in the warm weather. It chills these old bones so!" She opened and closed her withered hands. "Even then it gets into my joints sometimes and pains."

"I'll bet it does," I sympathized.

She continued with her answer to my question. "When I'm not near a creek or a river I'll usually go to the restroom in a fast-food restaurant and give myself a little 'bird bath'." She turned toward me and rested her arm on the back of the bench. "I do what I have to, dear."

She sighed and took a long breath, as though closing that topic. "What else do you want to know?"

I had many questions but the most tantalizing was why this woman had become homeless in the first place. I gazed off into the treetops, seeing the sunlight shining through the spring green leaves, bringing their veins into high relief. The activities and tragedies of human existence were of no concern to them. They budded, lived and died in their arboreal world while we moved like ants below, bound to the earth and our own concerns, our own sorrows.

I gazed into Caroline's face, recognizing the lines of suffering there. I returned her ever-present smile and continued the interview, asking her general questions about other homeless people and how they lived. She had met many of them in her travels. Often she would go down to the river to visit with friends she had made.

"A lot of homeless try to camp in the woods around the Rappahannock," she explained. "As long as the police don't see them they might actually sleep through the night. When they need shelter there are some big drainpipes nearby. They call them 'the tubes'." She shook her head thoughtfully. "Oh, but it's so much harder on families. Some won't go to the shelter even though they can stay for three months."

"Why not?" I asked.

"Because they separate the men from the women. Only the younger boys can stay with their mothers." A pained expression creased her forehead. "They'll live in cars or abandoned buildings or any other place they can find. Even if the parents find work they can't afford the rising costs of housing around here.

"At least they can get food and other necessities from the food bank. The Salvation Army runs that." She brightened. "I've met the people there. They really want to help but, like the shelter, funds are so limited."

"I don't understand, though. How can unemployment be down if the homeless population is growing?"

Caroline looked sweetly at me as if I were a child. "The percentages only reflect the people registered with the unemployment offices. They don't tell us how many people have run out of benefits and still can't find work. And many are simply unemployable."

I realized that I would have to do a lot of research for this article. I felt completely ignorant of the complexities of the poverty around me. Caroline's insights jarred me into a reality I had never faced in my sheltered suburban life.

The spring sun declined into the west, its pale light angling through the lush growth around us. I had to get home and work on Walt's research. Caroline stood up stiffly, a glimmer of pain in her eyes. "Where can I take you, Caroline?"

"Actually, I'd like to go downtown. There are some friends I'd like to have supper with at the shelter. Dinner at six, you know."

As I dropped her off downtown we made plans to meet in a couple of days to continue the interview. By this time I was interested in more than an article for the paper. Her story intrigued me—and something was nagging at my subconscious. I felt convinced that there was a much deeper tale beneath her surface.

CHAPTER SEVEN

I arrived early for my meeting with Walt on Thursday morning but he was out, so I opened the wooden gate to the garden and stepped inside. Sitting on the wrought iron love seat opposite the fountain, I breathed in the heady scents of the flowers mixed with the sharp odor of new mulch.

I had known Walt for three years now, ever since he had taught a couple of summer workshops at the college. I had taken both. He had impressed me with his deep knowledge of the English language and how to use it effectively in writing. I admired him as a teacher and as a human being. He was always courteous and never tried to make anyone feel bad about mistakes.

The birds chirped excitedly around the garden. Two squirrels chased each other through the trees overhead. Nature's cycle of birth had begun wholeheartedly in this city. Tourists were already streaming in to view the various historic homes and gardens. Walt's would be on the Historic Garden Tour this year. I couldn't remember when he said it would take place, but he was just about ready.

I recognized the sound of the Suburban slowing, then stopping out in front of the house. Rising quickly I stepped down the flagstone path to meet him.

"You're early," he observed, pulling two bags of groceries out of the truck with him.

"I wanted to be sure I was on time. You shouldn't keep a master waiting." Despite the joking tone, I never seemed able to conceal my girlish admiration for Walt. He was sensitive enough to take it well, knowing I looked at him as a father figure.

"Ah, so, Grasshopper," he answered in his best Chinese accent. "You are eager to learn the secret ways. But can you catch the key that will open the door?" He tossed the house key to me. I plucked it out of the air and turned to open the front door with a flourish.

As I helped Walt put the few groceries away I remained thoughtful, wondering if I should talk to him about my friendship with Caroline Rose. Before I could decide to broach the subject Walt stopped, leaned against the sink and peered at me a moment.

"What's up, Kate?" he asked, his keen intuitive gaze almost boring a hole through my skull.

"I can't hide anything from you," I exclaimed in mock exasperation.

He smiled kindly. "Kate, you are as easy to read as an open book. It's a good thing you're not a spy."

The tale tumbled out of my lips in a rush of words. Walt listened patiently and with interest. I expressed my fears that maybe I was getting too involved, that maybe I needed to show a journalist's detached approach. He smiled sadly and shook his head.

"We're human; of course we care about the suffering of our fellow beings. If we don't...we've lost our own humanity." He shifted his weight against the sink and stroked his smooth chin with his fingertips in that thinking gesture he always used when talking about issues of import. "No, you have to follow the prompting of your own heart. And your heart, Kate, is a kind one. Just don't over-reach what you, as one person, can do."

"I wish I could offer her a place to stay, food to eat." I felt frustrated with my inability to help in any substantial way. "A hot shower!" I blurted out.

"Offer her whatever you feel you can give, but respect her choices, her wishes for her life. She may not want anything from you except a friendly ear."

I studied the tiled floor with its blue and gold cornflower pattern. When I raised my eyes to meet his gaze I saw his face filled with deep compassion and concern. He had taken on his fatherly role out of genuine love for a needy young woman. I felt safe in his presence, my confidence renewed. "Thanks, Walt. I knew you would understand."

"I don't think I've actually given you an answer, but...you're easy to please." He grinned, revealing a perfect set of teeth. I liked how his laugh lines drew attention to the deep-set, green eyes. They were honest eyes, eyes you could trust—yet filled with mystery. If I could have chosen one man in this world to be my second father, it would have been him.

"You must be working hard at the research to have something for me this soon," he commented, pulling out a chair for me at the table.

"Well, the material is fascinating, in a disagreeable sort of way. The Chinese remind me a bit of the Europeans who destroyed the culture of Native Americans. They seemed to use similar tactics: killing, discouraging the native tongue, destroying the religion, and replacing the population with their own people."

"An effective and time-honored method to conquer a people," he said with an edge of sarcasm in his voice.

Walt glanced through my research notes and nodded his approval. "This will do very nicely, Kate. I like the timeline of the invasion and occupation by the Chinese in Tibet. That encapsulates a lot of data for me."

"I'm glad you like it. I have more material to go through but I wanted to make sure this was what you had in mind." I felt pleased, even flattered, that he liked my work. I tried to put my whole heart into whatever I did. His approval validated not only my efforts, but also me as a person.

Walt shuffled the papers together into a neat stack. "Can you find me some more detailed maps of Tibet and the area surrounding it?"

I shrugged my shoulders. "I suppose so."

He eyed me with a peculiar seriousness and said pointedly, "I'll need the most updated map of Lhasa that you can get." Lhasa was the capital city of Tibet. It contained the Potala, the seat of government where the Dalai Lama used to live before he was forced into exile after the Chinese invaded.

"I'll get it," I assured him, wondering why he had become so serious.

"Good," was all he said, as he turned back to my notes.

We discussed further avenues of research. I had called a number of organizations that supported the Tibetan cause and they were sending me more information. One of them was in D.C., only an hour away. I suggested we visit and interview the staff. They had seemed eager to help in any way they could.

When we finished discussing the project I made ready to leave. As I packed my notes into my backpack, I happened to glance over at Walt. He was watching me with a strange expression on his ruggedly handsome face.

"What's up?" I asked, spreading my hands in a quizzical gesture.

He cocked his head, looking sidelong at me. "I don't like to see you have to work as a waitress. You're a good writer and a fine researcher."

I wondered why he seemed so concerned. "Thanks. That's quite a compliment. But I don't mind the job. It pays the bills."

"How would you feel about working for me?"

"I am working for you."

"I have a lot of projects in the works now. I could really use your help full-time. Besides, I'm not teaching you enough to repay you for all you do now."

I didn't know what to say. I knew Walt had plenty of money. I felt unsure of his motivation. "Why do you want to hire me, really?" I emphasized the last word.

"I just told you. I have a lot more work and I could accomplish more with your help." He waited for my answer.

"Wow. You mean I don't have to put up with surly customers anymore? It sounds good to me," and I relaxed into the chair.

Walt quoted me a salary that would more than cover my living expenses. Since I had to give notice to the restaurant, we agreed to meet after my last day to discuss my assignments.

Still dazed from this new development in my professional life, I hoisted my pack to my shoulder and prepared to leave. "You know, I thought you were retired. What is all this work you're doing now?"

He grinned at me sheepishly. "I just can't give it up yet. I love it too much."

"You're too young to retire, anyway," and I finally understood. He had thought he might enjoy a more relaxed schedule in retirement, but he was the kind of person who had to be completely engrossed in his craft. We were, in some ways, a lot alike.

CHAPTER EIGHT

I met with Caroline on Friday morning. She was sitting on a bench outside one of the quaint shops on Caroline Street. I thought that rather fitting and I smiled to myself. The day was warm already. She had tied her jacket around her waist. The sleeveless, flower print blouse revealed thin but sinewy arms. She needed that strength.

"Good morning," I called. My friend rose to greet me with an engaging smile.

"Good morning, dear. I was just sunning myself. It's such a gorgeous day!" And it truly was one of those perfect spring days when the sun shines with a contented warmth and the sky is a soft, deep blue.

The shops were just beginning to open up and down the street. Once town homes built in the 1800s, each was painted a different color. On this end of the street some of the buildings stood vacant, so the hustle and bustle of the historic district barely touched here.

The coffee shop across the street was open and we crossed over. At the door of the Java Hut stood a suit of armor, intriguing shoppers to venture into this less-traveled area. Java, the terrier that often greeted me at Walt's house, was named for this establishment by one of its most devoted patrons.

Inside, the black and white floor tiles gave the place an air of casual sophistication, an invitation to relax from the rigors of a hectic world. We took a corner table so we could talk more freely. The proprietor greeted us with an amiable smile and asked for our order.

I turned to Caroline. "What would you like?"

"Oh, the Swiss chocolate almond looks delicious to me!"

I nodded. "And French vanilla for me."

The man hurried off to make our coffees.

After exchanging pleasantries for a few moments, I broached the topic

45

of her origins. "Where did you grow up, Caroline, I can't place your accent."

"Well, we traveled a lot when I was a child. My father was in the Foreign Service for a while, so we lived in Egypt, France, and England. We finally settled in Washington, D.C., when I was fifteen. I lived mostly with my parents until I got married." Our coffees arrived and we sniffed the rising steam approvingly.

Raising my cup to my lips I sipped cautiously; it was hot but delightful. I smiled over at my companion, who was enjoying her coffee as though it was the best she had ever tasted. Somehow I knew it was not. She had to have sipped some rich delicacies in her lifetime. I wanted to understand the cruel blow she had been dealt in her past, but at the same time, I didn't want to seem intrusive.

"What was Neal like, if you don't mind my asking?" I probed gently.

"I was so lucky to find him, or, rather, he actually found me. Neal made me feel like a wonderful person, which I was not," she added, shaking her head for emphasis. "But he worshipped me...and I him. He was tall, quite well built with a strong, handsome face. He treated me with such gentleness, as though I were a queen." She savored the memories of her husband along with another sip of coffee.

"Where did you meet him?"

"My father opened a brokerage firm in D.C. and it did quite well. I was in my late twenties and living with my parents at the time when Neal had just signed on with the firm. My father gave a grand party for his associates and their families. Neal came alone. I still remember watching him walk into the ballroom. He was so handsome!"

Caroline's face took on a youthful blush as she recalled her first meeting with the man who, two months later, had asked her to marry him. He told her he knew she was the one for him the moment he saw her in that blue, satin ball gown with her blond hair piled high on her head.

"'Just like a princess', he told me. He said I looked like a princess from a fairy tale. And he swept me off my feet—just like a prince!" She gestured gracefully with her hand as though to demonstrate how.

"It sounds like you had an ideal marriage," I commented, wondering where the fairy tale had gone wrong.

"It wasn't perfect, but we had such a deep bond." Her eyes dimmed slightly with tears. She looked straight into my eyes and said with deep feeling, "He was the best friend I ever had. I told him everything, even..."

She hesitated. "I never felt a need to keep anything from him."

All I could manage to say was, "How wonderful for you."

She paused to regain her composure, sipping her coffee daintily. Then she resumed her story. "Neal was also a fine father. I loved to watch him playing with our son. Kenny would play peek-a-boo with his blankey and end up throwing it over his daddy's head and say: 'Daddy all gone! Where Daddy?' and Neal would jump up out of the blanket and roar like a monster. Kenny would squeal and laugh and do it all over again!"

Caroline struggled to control her emotions, taking a few deep breaths. "Now Daddy is all gone." She covered her mouth with a thin hand. "Oh, and Kenny, too!" She looked out the window to subdue the rising tide of her memories. Her eyes shone bright with suppressed tears.

"It's okay, Caroline," I said awkwardly, patting her arm gently. "You don't have to tell me about it." She forced a little smile, and then looked down at her coffee as if to read something there. "I'm so sorry." I spoke softly, feeling a vague sense of guilt. "I had no idea this would be so difficult for you."

Finally recovered, Caroline smiled affectionately at me and said, "It's all right. I like talking to you. You are a good listener. I'm sorry to be so emotional." Then she eyed me with a glimmer of mischief in those old eyes.

"Now," she said in firm tones that were not unkind, "it's your turn. Tell me about you," and she pointed a crooked finger in my direction.

I shrugged my shoulders. "I haven't been alive that long, so there's not much to tell. I was born in New Haven. We moved to Providence when I turned two. My dad died when I was seven so it was just Mom and me. I guess Mom didn't want to deal with all the memories up there so we ended up in Northern Virginia."

At least I got through that without melting into a sorrowful puddle. I was getting better at suppressing my own pain.

"I came down here to go to college," I continued, more cheerful than I actually felt, "and they haven't been able to get rid of me since!" I laughed at my brief synopsis of my own life. It's funny how you can describe twenty-seven years in a matter of seconds.

"How terrible for you, Kate," Caroline chimed with sympathy. "Every life is so full of pain." Fixing her motherly gaze on me, she asked quietly, "Do you remember much about your father? Memories can be so comforting."

My mind traveled back to those happy times when our family was still whole. I told my new friend about how my father used to let me help him repair and build things around the house. Her eyes lit up as I recounted the beautiful carvings he made.

I could almost smell the fresh wood again as I remembered standing nearby while he sawed into its lovely, firm flesh for some new project. My father made me a swing when I was four. He had hung it from a sturdy beam fixed between two trees. I practically wore out its wooden seat swinging on it so much.

When he died, I spent hours hanging between earth and sky, remembering his gentle ways. The tears that trickled down my face dried in the air as I moved through it on my swing, back and forth, lost in memory.

My memories were all I had left of my father. Caroline was right; they were comforting.

My thoughts returned quickly to the present as the proprietor came over with our bill. He had waited discretely out of view at the coffee bar during our emotional exchanges. His brown eyes were filled with compassion as he placed the bill in front of me. "I'll pick that up whenever you're ready." He had obviously heard some of our conversation, but we didn't mind. He seemed a kind and sympathetic man.

I paid for our coffees and bought a few chocolates for Caroline—as well as some of Walt's favorite cherry cordials. "Nothing for you, Kate?" she asked, as I took the bag of candy from the cashier. "All of this lovely chocolate and you aren't even tempted?"

I shook my head. "No temptations for me."

"I've never met someone who didn't like chocolate, and I've met a lot of people in my life!" She laughed. "Allergy?"

"Yeah, something like that," I muttered vaguely and opened the door.

Walking out into the sunshine we both breathed the spring air with gusto. Caroline glanced at me. "You've been so kind to me, dear. I just wish I could do something for you."

"Well, you're helping me with my article."

"No, something more than that." Suddenly she gave me a look of triumph. "Kate," she said firmly, "I'm going to Bloomington next week. Would you like to come with me? I'd love the company and...there is someone I want you to meet."

For a moment I hesitated, mentally checking and rearranging my schedule. "That sounds intriguing," I replied thoughtfully. "I'm just not sure I can plan it that soon." She seemed a little disappointed so I reassured her. "Well, I'm quitting my job at the restaurant in a few days. When would you be leaving?"

Caroline explained that we could get a better rate on our bus tickets if we left between Monday and Thursday. I told her about my new job working for Walt. I knew he would be flexible, especially in this case. I just had to check with my boss at the restaurant.

As we continued to discuss the trip I became more and more interested. I really should go, I thought. It would be a great way to get to know this woman better, to hear more of her story; and I knew there was much more to hear. I sensed a great mystery behind her tale.

We walked down Caroline Street and crossed under the railroad tracks by the old refurbished train station. A train passed overhead, clicking rapidly along the tracks on its way to D.C.

We passed blocks of historic homes, making our way to the city dock, a modest wooden structure. A few elderly men were fishing there and a riverboat sat quietly in the water. I had heard that the boat offered tours of the Rappahannock River with dinner and dancing some evenings. But now she sat at her moorings, the placid water moving slowly past her.

The Rappahannock usually seemed quite serene. Its Algonquin Indian name simply meant "back and forth water," belying its dangerous nature. Every year it claimed a number of lives with its deadly undercurrents, hidden beneath the dark, gently rippling surface.

As we walked, Caroline grew quiet, obviously enjoying the spring sunshine. I accompanied her in silence, watching the water with its reflections of blue sky and leafy trees clothed in their new spring garments. The sounds of birds echoed around us while the river lapped lazily at the shore with a comforting murmur.

Caroline looked down the shore and suddenly caught her breath in excitement. "There's someone else I want you to meet," she exclaimed, pointing toward two men sitting downstream on a couple of fallen trees. As we quickened our steps down the path to meet them, they noticed us and rose unhurriedly to greet us.

"Why, it's Caroline!" said an elderly black man, obviously pleased to see her. As he grinned, the few teeth he had left gleamed yellow in the bright sun. He offered his hand to Caroline who took it warmly in her both of hers.

"Jonas. It's so good to see you! I want you to meet a new friend of mine, Kate."

Jonas took my hand and squeezed it firmly. "Nice to meet ya, Kate," he said. "Any friend of Caroline's is a friend of mine."

"Thank you," I replied, touched by the warmth and friendliness of his manner.

"And this here is Charlie," Jonas said, turning to the other man. Charlie was a middle-aged white man with a long, partly graying ponytail hanging down his back. His face was pitted and his lip bore an old scar under the thin moustache. He offered me his left hand. The right arm was missing almost up to the shoulder.

"Nice ta meet ya," was all he said. He had a strong grip when he took my hand, causing me to wince slightly as I nodded to him in greeting.

"Glad to meet you, too," I said, trying not to look too long at the blue-checked sleeve he had pinned up under his missing limb.

Caroline beamed up at me. "Jonas and Charlie are inseparable. Sometimes we call them 'Mutt and Jeff.'"

"Please, sit down," Jonas invited, as though we were in a house. He gestured to the fallen tree trunks that formed a semi-circle like some sort of outdoor living room, which, indeed, it was to him.

Caroline was first to speak. "Kate is a writer. She has written articles for the paper and is going to be published in a magazine!" She seemed quite proud of me.

"Well, we don't know that yet," I interjected, my face becoming suddenly warm.

"Oh, of course it will. Think positive, dear!" She patted my knee reassuringly and continued. "Kate is writing an article about homeless people and I hoped you would tell her your stories."

Jonas rubbed his chin thoughtfully, and then leaned forward in my direction. He looked deep into my eyes. "Don't see no harm in it and it might do some good, I s'pose. Just make sure ya change the names to protect the innocent, ya know," and he winked.

"Of course I'll do that," I assured him. "I really think people need to hear what you have to say."

"People don't care," Charlie exclaimed. "Why should they? It don't mean nuthin' to 'em." I was surprised at the deep bitterness in his voice. But at the same time, I couldn't blame him for feeling that way. Suddenly I wondered why Caroline and Jonas didn't express the same anger over their plight.

Jonas took a deep breath and leaned back. "Yep. I ain't worked steady for thirty years now. All I could get was seasonal work, handyman work. I been homeless that long. Now, I can't get no work at all."

To have been living this way for thirty years was unthinkable to me. Of course, I hadn't thought about the homeless much before. The middle class lifestyle was all I knew. Now my research was taking me places I wasn't sure I wanted to go. "How did you survive all this time?" I asked.

He glanced over at Caroline, then back at me. "Ya do what ya have ta. Ya stay alive any way ya can, beggin' at the back door of restaurants, goin' through the trash just to find some old food nobody else wants." He nodded his head, gazing at the ground. "Ya do what ya gotta do."

My heart ached as I looked at this man, who seemed a good, decent soul, stooped with age as well as the unspeakable difficulties of life on the street. His skin seemed as tough and dry as old leather; his old fingers were knotted like twisted tree roots. A grimy cap, its logo long faded, covered his gray, close-cropped head.

Caroline broke the brief silence. "Jonas is right. We have to do a lot of things most people wouldn't dream of doing just to survive. I've eaten out of dumpsters, too. Sometimes it's that or starve."

Jonas looked up again, brightening with Caroline's confirmation. "Yep. Amazin' what ya can find in them dumpsters, too. Friend o' mine found a whole lobster behind a seafood restaurant. He said he felt like a king, just like a royal king, eatin' that lobster."

Charlie began to look exasperated. "It's a shitty life, bein' homeless. It's shit. It's eating shit and living in shit. These old people are too nice to even admit what it's like!"

Caroline turned to Charlie, a stern look on her face. "You don't have to talk that way. Besides, Kate needs details, not just how you feel about it."

"He's right to feel that way," I added. "It's important for people to know the indignities of this life—how it makes you feel. Some people want to romanticize homelessness, or even say that people choose to live this way. That can't be true."

"She's right," Jonas rejoined. "I'd never live this way if I coulda got reg'lar work. Never in a million years."

Caroline looked encouragingly at Charlie. "Tell her your story," she urged. Charlie looked out over the river, his stubbly chin resting on his fist. Suddenly he stood up, shifting nervously on his feet.

"I didn't ask for this life, ya know," he blurted out to no one in particular.

He stared off again. I followed his gaze, knowing that he saw something besides the river and the newly green trees. He stared back into another time, another place, before misfortune had brought him here.

He began his story, speaking softly but clearly. The years seemed to fall from his begrimed shoulders. "I fought in 'Nam. They told me I was serving my country. I killed people. I don't regret it—most of it, anyway. 'Cept we couldn't always tell who the enemy was. You'd walk into a village and maybe it could be a trap. You never knew where the Viet Cong were.

"Sometimes they were waiting for you there. Sometimes they weren't but we didn't know 'til we'd killed a lot of innocent civilians. Even the kids could be enemies. Sometimes they had bombs and threw them into our trucks. They'd kill a lot of guys, truckloads of soldiers. Viet Cong told the kids it was a good way to die." He shook his head. "I dunno. I just did what I was told so I could go home agin."

I nodded towards Charlie's missing arm. "So you were wounded in combat?"

Suddenly he threw back his head and laughed. "Naw, I was one of the lucky ones that came back in one piece." Gesturing with his stump he explained, "Lost my arm in an accident fifteen years ago. Down on my place in Louisa. Well, what used to be my place.

"After I came home from 'Nam I bought me an old farm down in Louisa. I farmed a bit and did odd jobs for other farmers: harvestin', mowin', tillin', whatever I could find."

I thought I detected some past happiness in his voice. "You enjoyed farming?"

He nodded. For the first time he actually smiled, a thin smile, but it was there. "Yep. My family used ta be farmers. I always loved bein' on the land—workin' with the equipment." The smile disappeared.

"I was runnin' one of them ol' corn pickers." He shook his head. "Ya know, they stopped makin' that kind some years ago 'cause so many farmers lost arms and feet to those things...Well, I was just plain stupid. Some of them mornin' glory vines got caught in the works and stopped it up. I got down and reached in to pull 'em out—didn't even turn the damn thing off. I picked more 'n corn that day. Yeah, I went and picked me an arm. My own damn arm!" He paced nervously back and forth a few times, and then continued.

"After the accident I started havin' flashbacks from 'Nam. I'd wake up screamin' and fightin'. The old lady didn't stay around. Can't blame her for leavin'. She was sleepin' with me when I had one of those dreams. I beat her pretty bad before she could wake me up." He sat back down and rested his chin in his hand. His eyes were bright with repressed grief; his shoulders sagged as with a crushing weight.

Quickly he wiped away a tear. "I started drinkin' more and smokin' hash. I didn't care about workin' any more. I was finished. I lost my farm, my equipment, every bit of money I'd ever saved."

"He come up here," Jonas continued his friend's story. Charlie had covered his face with his hand and seemed unable or unwilling to continue. "We met under the train station, 'fore they fixed it up."

He turned to Charlie and clapped him on the back, remembering old times. "Yeah, that was a mess down there! It smelled somethin' terrible. Whew! We stayed down there on cold nights. Men usin' the corners for toilets. But it was outa the wind."

"So, how did you meet Caroline?" I asked politely, hoping to get on to more cheerful topics. I felt extremely uncomfortable with Charlie's story. His pain was too raw for me to handle.

When Jonas smiled I relaxed. A nice story would smooth over my discomfort. In the back of my mind it occurred to me that my readers might like it, too. "Met down here by the river. We were fishin' one mornin' when she came along." Jonas chuckled at the memory. "Takin' her mornin' stroll, she says. Jess as fine a woman you ever wanna meet. She stopped to ask us how the fishin' was going."

Caroline joined in, "And they had caught some beauties, too. I gave them a couple of chocolate bars someone had given me and said, 'Here's some dessert.'"

"She said, 'Those fish are so gorgeous they deserve a nice dessert afterwards.' That's what she said," Jonas added, the incident as clear as if it had happened yesterday. I smiled at the fond memory shared by these three unlikely companions.

We talked a little longer before I politely took my leave. I shook their pain from my mind, like a cat might shake a dainty paw after getting it wet. Besides, I had to go to work that afternoon.

As I drove to the restaurant, I wondered if I could get the time off to go to Indiana with Caroline. I needn't have worried. The owner of the restaurant was a very understanding woman. I appreciated that, especially when I went into her office on my break after the evening rush.

"Well, Kate," said Mrs. West as she leaned back in her leather chair. "I can see that congratulations are in order." She smiled pleasantly as she continued. "This is progress on your path as a writer, and I know how much you enjoy research."

"Thanks, Mrs. West. I knew you would understand." I sat opposite her slight, almost childlike figure. She only stood about 5'1" but her personality seemed much bigger.

"Do you think that Mr. Cleary will have enough work for you?" She glanced down at her desk covered with bills and canceled checks, and then she looked back at me. "I'm sorry; it's none of my business. I just worry about my kids." She always looked out for the young people that worked for her. She knew just how vulnerable they could be, many out on their own for the first time. Sometimes we called her "Mama West." I think she liked it.

I tried to reassure her. "I'll be fine. You don't have to worry." I brightened with a new hope, "Besides, I'm starting to earn money as a writer, too, what with my articles and the story I sent off. Walt is sure they'll be interested."

She didn't seem reassured, but she was happy for me. It turned out that some of the part-time help were asking for more hours, so I was able to leave immediately. I was glad to be done with waiting tables. Most of the people were nice, but it had gotten old fast. I was eager to get on with my career. At that moment life seemed very promising.

Goodbyes have never been easy for me. Tears sprang to my eyes as my fellow "servers" wished me luck. Jenny hugged me tightly. "Good luck, Kate. I hope everything works out for you!"

"And if things don't work out," Mrs. West said in her solicitous, southern accent, "you'll have a place here." She clasped my hand warmly in both of hers.

"Give 'em hell, Kate!" Nick kissed me on the cheek. "Don't forget to come back and visit, even when you get to be a famous writer." He winked.

"*If* that happens," I corrected, with a modest blush. "And I won't forget."

CHAPTER NINE

As our plans came together for our trip to Indiana, I wondered if some special destiny awaited us there. Time would tell, I thought to myself.

I invited Caroline to stay at my place the night before our departure. She hesitated, but finally gave in to my enthusiasm. "All right, dear," she conceded. "It is very kind of you to ask me, but please," and she looked deeply into my eyes, "let's not make this a habit. You are not responsible for me."

"I understand," I claimed, even though I didn't. "But this will make things easier and you can prepare for the trip in relative comfort." I lowered my voice to a whisper as we walked up to the house. "You haven't seen the house yet!"

"I'm sure it's lovely, dear."

"Only if 'lovely' is a relative thing," I said, giving her a sidelong glance. She obviously did not know how messy three busy young women could be.

I introduced her to my housemates, who were very polite. I had explained the situation and, with characteristic sympathy on their part, they had accepted Caroline's presence without the least hesitation.

"Kate's told me wonderful things about you both," Caroline exclaimed as she offered her hand to Andy.

"Then she left out a few things," Andy returned, laughing.

Caroline smiled up at her, peering into her lovely brown face. Andy was very dark-skinned. With her high cheekbones and long braids she looked like an exotic, Nubian princess. "Oh, my! You have the most beautiful skin, dear!"

Andy laughed again and glanced at me, a twinkle in her tawny eyes. "I really like you, Caroline. You can stay here anytime!" She gave Caroline an enthusiastic hug.

Holly hugged her, too. "And you have such lovely red hair, dear!"

"Thanks," Holly replied, blushing to the roots of that red hair.

We ate a simple dinner and Caroline decided to take a shower afterwards. I never realized how delightful a shower could be to someone who could not always indulge in such a luxury. Caroline sang lustily while she bathed. Once in awhile she would punctuate a chorus with exclamations of "What a wonderful shower!" or squeal and sing, "Lovely warm water!" I was glad the landlord had just replaced our old hot water heater.

An hour later, she emerged wrapped in my bathrobe, her hair and eyes sparkling. "Look what I found under all that dirt!" she proclaimed happily. She smelled her hands. "And I smell so clean, too!"

I smiled and nodded. "You smell great, that's for sure!"

"I think that's the thing I dislike the most about being homeless—the dirt and the bad smells." She sat on my bed and dried her hair with a towel. Pulling a comb out of her pocket she held it up for me to see. "And I washed my comb, too." She pulled it through her thin hair, grinning as drops of water fell from the grey strands.

Caroline enjoyed playing my CDs as I packed for our journey. Holding the box on her lap, she looked at each one as if it were some incredible treasure. With her legs dangling over the edge of the bed, she reminded me of a girl at a sleepover.

"Let's play this one!" she cried as she dropped a CD into the player. "Oh, I've always loved Bach, but his Brandenburg Concerti are my favorite works!"

"Why is that?" I asked.

"My father used to play them a lot. He loved to put them on whenever he made a particularly profitable sale on the stock market. He was so savvy with his investments and he made a lot of money for his clients."

"What happened to his company?"

"He sold out to a bigger firm when he retired—health problems—otherwise he would have stayed in the game, as he called it. Two years later he died of a heart attack." Caroline's face clouded with sorrow.

"I'm sorry." I knew what that loss was like.

Resuming her usual cheerful demeanor she said, "I guess he would have lived longer if he hadn't retired." Picking out another CD she exclaimed, "Debussy! He was Neal's favorite!" She slipped the recording of *La Mer* into the machine and basked in its romantic French sensuality. I listened quietly along with her, imagining a younger Caroline dancing with her debonair husband.

My mind turned to what it would be like to have such an idyllic partner in life. Would I ever find someone like Neal? Suddenly annoyed by the thought, I quickly put it out of my mind. I had a great career ahead of me. That would be enough, I concluded. It would have to be.

The next day we walked to the bus station; it was only a few blocks away, very convenient for the college students. The bus arrived fifteen minutes late in a cloud of distressing diesel fumes. One of our fellow travelers was pregnant and, apparently, very sensitive to smells. She turned pale and put a hand over her mouth and nose.

"Ugh!" she groaned, as we waited to board. Caroline patted her on the shoulder.

"Are you all right, dear?"

The woman turned to my companion, grateful for her concern. "Yes. I just get nauseous from strong smells. Even perfumes bother me."

"When are you due?" Caroline asked with genuine interest.

The young woman answered with a patience only pregnancy can bring, "Two months from today." She indicated her already large belly. "I can't imagine getting any bigger, though." She gave us a smile as she stepped with effort up the steps into the bus.

We found seats toward the rear. Caroline settled next to the window and looked out with an almost childlike eagerness. I wondered what charm Bloomington held for my friend, who had just embarked willingly on a nineteen-hour bus trip. I had never been fond of taking the bus anywhere, but this was a newer one and the seats seemed quite comfortable.

Watching Caroline as she gazed out the window reminded me of traveling with my mother as a child. While Mom drove we would often spend long periods in silence, just enjoying the scenery and the movement of the car down the highway. I used to look out the window at the houses and farms rolling steadily by and wonder what those peoples' lives were like. I would see fathers outside doing yard work and think about how it might feel to grow up with Dad around.

Mom always enjoyed pointing out the farm animals and wildlife. She loved animals and had studied biology in college. After her first two years she intended to go on to vet school but then she met my dad. She helped him with his accounting business, even after I was born. When Dad died she got her CPA and continued with accounting. It was a good living and she had shown an aptitude for it.

The bus sped up the interstate toward its first stop in D.C. I thought back to our meeting with Jonas and Charlie. "Caroline," I broke in on her reverie. "What is Jonas' story? Why can't he get the help he needs?"

She turned to me thoughtfully. "Well, Kate, he's got a lot of problems."

"He seems like a decent soul," I said.

"Oh, he is. He has a heart of gold. Jonas would give you the shirt off his back if you needed it, but...I know you want to understand, but I hate to speak ill of anyone, especially my friends." She gazed out the window at the tree-lined highway. "He used to be a big drinker; that's one reason he couldn't get steady work."

"He didn't seem drunk or anything like that," I interposed.

"Well, he's cut back some—a lot—compared to what he used to drink. But I've found him dead-drunk more than a few times since I met him five years ago." She looked sharply at me. "Kate, things are not what they seem in this world. People don't want to associate the homeless with substance abuse or mental illness. They want to believe that it's just bad luck that makes people chronically homeless."

"Well, isn't it sometimes that, or a lack of opportunity?"

Caroline's face softened again. "I guess you haven't finished your research yet."

"Well, I've read some newspaper and magazine articles. And I've got a couple books on order from Interlibrary Loan."

"Good. You should read the different studies. You'll find that the majority of chronically homeless are plagued with alcohol or drug problems or mental illness. Sometimes a combination of those things."

She patted my hand gently. "Jonas is eligible for help, but he doesn't think he has a drinking problem. He refused to go to counseling or AA meetings," she continued, sorrow plainly showing in her deeply lined face. "I understand that attitude. I've been there myself."

"You have?" I asked, astonished.

She nodded. "After Neal and the baby died I didn't want to live. I drank heavily and took tranquilizers. I thought seriously about suicide." She paused to wipe a tear away.

"Then one day I went on another binge. I meant to succeed in killing myself this time." Caroline looked up into my face, all hint of tears gone. "I ended up in a state hospital and then in de-tox. All my money was gone. I was completely ruined."

I inhaled sharply in surprise. "Caroline! I'm so sorry!" It was all I could say.

"One night I dressed, put my few possessions in my coat pockets and left without telling anyone." She gave an embarrassed laugh. "I've never been back since."

My mind reeled with the tragedy of her story. So that was how it had happened. "But, didn't your family know what was happening? Didn't you have relatives or friends who could have helped you out with your problems?"

She resumed looking out the window. "Not those problems." Her words sounded ominous but before I could ask for an explanation she quickly changed the subject to music. I understood. The discussion was over for the time being. Instead, we talked about our favorite classical composers, and then Broadway shows. Apparently, she had seen quite a few of those before becoming homeless.

We stopped first in D.C. then in Pittsburgh, where we had an hour to get some dinner. Neither of us was interested in looking around the city, so we returned to the station. We sat quietly, watching people come and go. I considered what Caroline had told me about her misfortunes but I didn't ask her any more questions. Perhaps she would reveal more of her story later, in her own time.

By evening we were on our way once again. We could see the last of the sunset fading through the mountains. I told Caroline about the times my mother and I had spent hiking in the mountains of Virginia and West Virginia. Often we would bring our friends with us and camp in the National Parks. We always felt those were the best places to camp, surrounded by great tracts of forested land. We studied and photographed the abundant wildlife on our treks. Occasionally we even gathered wild foods for meals.

"It sounds like you had such happy times with your mother!" exclaimed Caroline enthusiastically. "She sounds like a wonderful person."

I smiled, nodding in affirmation. "Yes, she certainly is."

The bus rumbled down Interstate 70 toward Columbus. I mused about my companion; she did not seem to fit the profile for a homeless person. I wondered what might be missing from her story and why.

"Caroline," I began thoughtfully, trying not to probe too deeply into her privacy. "I see you as a strong, intelligent human being. I still don't understand why you haven't been able to get back on your feet, or," I added, with no small admiration, "where you get your strength to go on living as you do."

She pursed her lips in thought for a moment and then smiled, almost to herself. "Perhaps I will answer half of that question." Her eyes brightened with deep feeling and gratitude as she explained. "God gives me strength and keeps me going, dear. Faith in Him and in His will for me helps me. God let me lose everything so I could learn some very hard lessons. Now I live for Him and do the things I think He would have me do."

I nodded my head; I'd heard these kinds of sentiments before. "And what is it you have to do?" I asked, wondering how homelessness could further God's plans in her life.

She gazed out into the darkness as if she looked deeply into her own pain. "To love and protect those in greatest need," she answered slowly.

For a moment I was dumbfounded. Perhaps she, too, had a mental disorder that only now revealed itself to me in these enigmatic words. I hesitated, fearing that I might offend her with my question. "Just how can you protect someone when you, yourself, are in so much need?" Suddenly, I felt I had said the wrong thing.

She bit her lip and continued to gaze out the window. "With all I have," she answered, almost to herself.

For a little while we did not speak. The bus continued moving through space along the dark highway. My curiosity grew, but I no longer felt comfortable asking questions. Caroline carried so much pain. Questions might only bring her more.

"Do you believe in God?"

I started, her question breaking into a quiet that seemed lost in time. "I'm a Buddhist," I replied, waiting for the shocked silence or condemnation that often met my answer to that query.

But it did not come. Caroline turned to smile fondly at me. "Then you, too, must be dedicated to love and compassion for all living beings. That is what Buddha taught."

I began to relax. "Then it doesn't bother you that I'm not Christian?"

"Why should it?" came the surprising reply. "I believe it pleased God to create variety in the universe. It was His skillful way to bring all peoples to His light."

I laughed gently at my understanding companion. She was either quite mad or profoundly wise. "So, you don't think I'm going to hell?"

It was her turn to laugh. "Of course not, my dear!"

"I don't know if I should believe you." I smiled. "A great many people have told me that's where I'm bound!" Now I felt even more comfortable in her presence.

"If they believe that then they must not know the extent of God's love."

I smiled at her answer. "Caroline, perhaps you are too kind to think of anyone as deserving of hell."

She nodded, her eyes twinkling and said, "You are right. I could never condemn anyone to hell. Can a human woman be kinder than the Almighty?" She raised a gnarled index finger to emphasize her words. "Tell me, dear, what merciful God would condemn anyone to eternal punishment for a temporal choice?"

I took a deep breath and sighed, "None that I know, Caroline. And none that I would care to know."

The wheels hummed as the road spun out from under them. Caroline dozed off, her head resting on the jacket that she had balled up to make a pillow. I closed my eyes for a moment, perhaps to shut out the realities of the world. The bus was quiet except for the low murmur of sleepy conversation.

Nearby I could make out the sweet voice of a mother singing her child to sleep. I could barely hear the tune or words, but the tones were filled with love. I thought I could hear the hopes this mother had for the darling of her heart. What hopes had Caroline nurtured for herself and her baby?

I began to muse about what she had said, "To love and protect those in greatest need." What could she possibly mean? And she would do it with all she had—what in the world did this woman have with which to protect others? Was this some sort of strange noblesse oblige on her part? Did she feel obligated to help the poor precisely because she had once been so privileged herself?

It just didn't make sense to me. Wouldn't she be better equipped for the task with wealth than without it? There had to be more to the story. Or, maybe she suffered from some delusional disorder. Perhaps the story she had told me was a fiction that she, herself, preferred to believe instead of the truth. But I knew one thing, she must have been raised in wealth; her manners and speech testified to a high class past.

Suddenly I felt that I was being watched. I looked quickly at my companion, who smiled sleepily. I hoped her sharp eyes had not picked up my line of thought from my expression.

"So, what kind of Buddhism do you practice, dear?" she asked.

"Tibetan."

"Ah," Caroline nodded. "What an interesting people, the Tibetans."

She seemed quite alert now. "I remember reading a book by that French woman who traveled there—oh, what was her name?"

"Alexandra David-Neel?"

"Yes! The very same! You've read her books, of course? They called her the 'Lady Lama' I recall." Caroline certainly demonstrated a knowledge of the author. Where had she gained that, I wondered.

We began discussing the Tibetan culture and how it was being systematically decimated by the Chinese. "They are such a peaceful people. It's a crime what the Chinese have done to them," Caroline exclaimed.

"They had no interest in technology or commerce," I said. "Their only desire was to practice their peaceful religion, to develop compassion for all sentient beings and gain enlightenment for the benefit of all. But that was what made them so vulnerable. Easy pickings for the Chinese."

Caroline nodded and then cocked her head. "I remember an interesting custom of theirs. They would feed their dead to the vultures."

I smiled. "Yeah, to us it seems pretty disgusting, but they felt that they should let the animals use the body, since its inhabitant no longer needs it—a parting gift."

"Yes, I liked the idea of that. It doesn't sound very pleasant but it seems a good thing to do in principle. The people in charge of carrying out that detail are called the 'body breakers', aren't they?" she asked.

"That's right." I thought a moment about what kind of task that would be.

"It seems," she mused, turning to me, "that the Chinese have become the 'body breakers' for the entire Tibetan nation."

I caught her thought and carried it to its logical conclusion. "And they have scattered them over the earth, to be swallowed by other countries, other cultures."

We both sat quietly for a few moments, reflecting on the plight of an innocent people. Caroline broke the silence. "Then, they, too, are homeless."

CHAPTER TEN

We pulled into Bloomington about mid-morning. Earlier we had snacked on leftover crackers while the sun rose over Indianapolis. The skyline had appeared out of the darkness like some fairy-tale city in the pinks and purples of dawn.

Bloomington itself was a college town surrounding Indiana University, an impressive school boasting about 20,000 students. Despite its large population, the city seemed to exude a small-town atmosphere,

We walked from the bus station down the main street crowded with cars. In the downtown section we passed restaurants and charming little shops. We saw more college students here than actual residents. Caroline walked leisurely, but purposefully, along these obviously familiar streets.

Crossing the main thoroughfare we made our way through an area of shops and modest homes. Caroline's step quickened as we neared a little cafe with green awnings.

"He's open, of course," she said in animated tones. We walked up to the glass door, which I pulled open and held for her to enter. Inside, the cafe was half-full of customers seated at tables with pressed green cloths. They chatted amiably, sipping coffee and eating bagels or fresh pastries. Most seemed to be college students in jeans, with characteristic backpacks slung over chairs or flung carelessly to the floor. The other patrons appeared smartly dressed for business.

"Caroline!" came a glad call from across the room. A portly, middle-aged man hurried to greet us, his red face beaming in welcome. "How wonderful to see you!" he cried as he engulfed my small companion in a great hug.

Caroline laughed happily and returned his enthusiastic embrace. "Franklin, my dear! You look well!" I guessed that this must be the "someone" she had wanted me to meet in Bloomington. They obviously shared a deep friendship. How they had met and become friends I simply could not guess, but I felt sure Caroline would fill in the details later. For now, I simply grinned at this joyous meeting, which did not seem to perturb any of the patrons of this quaint establishment.

The two turned to me, smiling. "Frank, this is Kate." Caroline gestured elegantly as she introduced me. "She's a writer and...a dear friend." Frank put out a strong hand to me. I offered him my own, which he clasped warmly.

"So nice to meet you, Kate. Any friend of Caroline's is a friend of mine." He beamed happily at her, exclaiming, "I owe this woman everything, but she won't let me pay her back for her help."

Caroline's face blushed pink as she tried to make light of his statement. "I just did what any decent human being would have done. You don't owe me a thing."

Even his balding head seemed to glow with love and gratitude. "I do—you're just too proud to admit it. Besides," he added with deep sincerity, "I've never met anyone since who would go to that much trouble for a stranger." He turned his head to me. From under a pair of bushy gray eyebrows gleamed large, hazel eyes. In their depths I perceived a past of immense suffering.

"Have I got a story for you, young lady. If you're a writer you'll be interested in this one—all about despair and redemption." Frank put his cheek down on Caroline's white head. "And this lady right here is the star." He kissed the top of her head while she playfully pushed him away.

"Enough, already. I don't have a halo to shine yet!" Caroline seemed pleased at the attention yet embarrassed at the same time.

"First, though," Frank added, "let me get you ladies some breakfast, on the house, of course!" He joyfully handed us each a small menu card. "Shall I get you coffee while you're looking that over?"

Caroline settled gratefully into the wooden chair with its green padded seat. "I'd love some coffee, and one of your fresh croissants," she sighed.

"Of course. Today's coffee is French vanilla. I think you'll like it," Frank offered.

"Yes," agreed my companion, leaning back and rubbing her temples with her thin fingertips. "That would be lovely!"

"And you, Kate?" Frank asked.

"The same, please," I responded with a weary smile. I hadn't realized how tired I was until I sat down. The green decor soothed my eyes. The nagging tension in my neck began to relax.

Frank bustled off to fill our order, checking with some other customers on the way. I looked forward to hearing his story. He seemed a very successful man now. I could hardly believe his intimation of past despair, with redemption at the hands of the unassuming woman before me.

"He seems like a great guy, Caroline," I began.

"Oh, he is, dear." Her face glowed with warmth. "Every time I come to town he insists on providing all my meals. He won't hear of me staying anywhere else but in his home. He treats me like a queen."

I looked across the table at her, absently smoothing the green linen tablecloth with my hand. "Sounds to me like the queen deserves it."

Caroline said nothing more until our host had brought the coffee. Then she began to tell me about Bloomington and how she had been coming here to visit for many years. She spoke with animation about the university and how she enjoyed going to the observatory there when it was open to the public. "Usually it's open Wednesday evenings, that is if the night is clear. I love looking through that big telescope they have! I've seen the rings on Saturn and the red spot on Jupiter!"

She seemed as excited as a little girl. I couldn't understand what brought her to Bloomington year after year, especially before she had met Frank. "What is it that attracts you here, Caroline?" I asked, puzzled. "It seems pretty far to go to look into a telescope."

She gazed down at her plate where flakes of her croissant lay scattered. She studied them for a moment as if to divine her answer there. "I like being here." She looked up at me again, nodding her head. "I just enjoy it."

I did not press her further. I didn't think she had really answered my question completely. Maybe she just didn't feel ready to reveal herself. I would have to respect her desire for privacy.

The customers trickled out of the cafe until only Caroline and I were left. Frank dried his hands on a green-checked dishtowel and walked around the counter to join us. He pulled a chair well out from the table and settled back, tired but happy from the morning's rush.

"Well, I hope you ladies enjoyed your breakfast. Do you need anything else?" he inquired.

"No, we're fine, Frank," Caroline answered. "Just rest yourself now."

I turned to our host expectantly. "Well, what's this story you promised me?"

Frank sat up. "Once upon a time," he began, his eyes twinkling with the excitement of a storyteller. "There was a successful stock broker..." Suddenly he became quite serious. "I was really very good at what I did. I had the big house, expensive cars, the vacation home."

His eyes gleamed wistfully as he continued. "I had a beautiful wife and two young children. I had everything and then, one day," he gestured with his hands and shrugged his broad shoulders, "I lost it all." This story was beginning to remind me of Caroline's past. I cocked my head to listen.

"Well, it didn't happen in one day." Frank shook his head. "My family died in a plane crash. They were going ahead of me to our vacation home. We always took a small plane—more privacy, no lines." He rested his elbows on the table, knotting his fingers together in front of him. "I had more work to finish up so Rita, my wife, said she'd take the kids to get things ready for me to join them."

He paused, the emotion telling on him now. He brought his forehead down to his fists and shook his head, trying to regain his composure. Caroline reached a sympathetic hand to his shoulder, rubbing gently, reassuringly.

"The police came to my office to tell me," Frank continued, now in control. "Apparently several witnesses heard an explosion and saw the plane drop from the sky in flames." He took a deep breath, still maintaining control. "My boss was there at the time. He told me to take as much time off as I needed." He looked directly at me. "I never saw him again. In fact, the only thing I remembered seeing for the next five years was the bottom of a bottle."

The words came with obvious difficulty as he continued to recount his decline into depression and alcoholism. "My brother and his wife tried to help me for a few years, but they had kids to raise. I was so stubborn. I refused any treatment. After a while they didn't have the energy to haul me home out of whatever gutter or alley I had made my own after another binge. It wasn't good for the kids to see me like that either."

He looked over at Caroline. In his glance I caught deep admiration as well as gratitude. This was no dysfunctional bag lady. She was his queen, he, her vassal. Perhaps in another life that may have been their relationship, I mused silently.

"Then this angel of God rescued me from certain death at my own hands," Frank stated evenly, without the emotion I knew he felt.

"Maybe," Caroline responded slowly, resting her chin in her hand. "I found him in the bus station in Indianapolis, sobering up after one of his bouts." She clasped her hands in front of her. "He was muttering to himself in a corner. Oh!" she exclaimed. "Was he a mess!'

Frank continued, "There I was, babbling some nonsense in the station, and I didn't even know how I'd gotten there." He gestured toward Caroline, "And this woman starts listening to me. I mean really listening."

My companion continued, "He was talking about stocks—broker talk—and I recognized it. I'd been around brokers all my life. I asked him what had happened. He told me the whole story."

Frank gently took her hand in his own. "I spilled my guts, and something even more disgusting, I'm afraid." Caroline shrugged her shoulders as if to say it didn't bother her. "Anyone who'll hold your head while you're throwing up in a bus station has got to be a saint. I have never found a truer friend in my life," he added quietly.

"She wiped my face and helped me out of the station. When I was able to walk she took me to a shelter. They wouldn't take me because I was drunk, but Caroline got a referral to the nearest AA."

Caroline continued the tale. "The AA referred me to a treatment center that actually took some indigent patients. I knew he had to detox and it wouldn't be easy. Like so many other homeless he needed professional help."

I asked, perplexed, "Don't the shelters offer those kinds of services to the homeless?"

"Very few," Frank responded. "They sometimes can refer substance abusers to help, but not many shelters can actually take them. They're too disruptive."

"But aren't those the ones who need help the most?" I shook my head at this new revelation.

"Those are the people who are usually screened out from homeless programs, Kate." Caroline spoke gently but her words hit me hard. "Caring for the mentally ill, drug addicts and alcoholics takes more commitment than a few months-worth of band-aid solutions. It may even take years of treatment. Many of these people require some type of professional help for the rest of their lives."

"Caroline committed to seeing me through the entire process of rehabilitation," Frank continued. "It took several months just for that. Then, when I was finally sober and going to regular counseling for the depression, she started encouraging me to get a job. If she had left me then I would probably have gone back to drinking. She helped us both get by until I found work in a grocery store. When she was sure I could handle a steady job, she recommended that I open a savings account. It was after I found a room to rent that Caroline decided to take a short trip."

"Well, I knew you needed to start living on your own." She smiled at me. "It was time to push him out of the nest, so to speak."

Frank's amazing story moved me. I could understand why he held his friend in such high esteem. I began to look at this woman with new eyes.

Later, Caroline had encouraged him to invest on a small scale before she left on her next trip. She came back to check on him often, just to make sure he was continuing to make progress and did not fall back into despondency.

In a few years Frank, who had been working two jobs, had saved enough to open a small business of his own. When he sold that one, he had enough to open the cafe. Eventually he became a silent partner in a number of businesses in the Bloomington area. His life had turned completely around after several years of continued encouragement from his friend.

"So that's my story," he said, patting Caroline's hand fondly.

"You worked very hard to rebuild your life, Frank." She stood up stiffly and excused herself for a few moments.

Frank turned to me and said, almost in a whisper, "She's so stubborn, though. She would never let me help her in the same way. I can only manage to slip her some cash before she leaves. And she does accept my hospitality while she's here."

"Why," I managed to ask. "She helped you get back on your feet; she's an intelligent, worldly woman...why does she remain homeless?"

He understood my quandary and patted me on the shoulder. "That, my dear Kate, is something Caroline will have to tell you." He added pointedly, "Believe me, she has her reasons."

We both heard the sound of a door opening and closing down the hall. Caroline's light but measured steps heralded her return. I glanced up at her over my coffee cup in the most casual manner possible, and then set the cup back down on the table.

Frank stood up and admitted jovially, "Yes, Caroline, we were talking about you."

"You must have been; my ears are burning," she joked. "Don't tell all my secrets now, Franklin!" Her tone was teasing, but she gave him a quick look that suggested no small amount of seriousness in her statement.

We left the cafe with Frank. He wanted to show us to his house and settle us in comfortably. He had a small but cozy cottage just down the street from his business. The guest bedroom looked out over a few gray stone buildings on the huge I.U. campus. Students walked the tree-lined lanes in small groups, the ever-present backpacks slung casually over their shoulders. I had only graduated from college five years ago, but already the college kids seemed much younger to me.

Frank gave us a key to the front door and hurried back to the cafe. "Really, I trust my manager completely, but I still hate to be away too long," he explained. "We'll be serving lunch soon. I'll fix something special for you both. Just come on down when you're ready."

"Thank you, Frank. We'll stop in around noon, if that's all right with you," Caroline returned graciously.

"Of course. That'll be fine." With a smile and a nodded good-bye, Frank tripped down the stone steps and walked quickly up the street. He moved rather lightly for an overweight fellow, I thought. But life had become good again for this man who had once given up hope. The bounce in his step reflected a satisfying life with an optimistic future.

Caroline and I took turns showering. Apparently, Frank always made sure there were fresh clothes for his benefactress. When I stepped out of the bathroom, Caroline looked like a completely different person. She had put on a soft blue denim skirt and a silk, flowered blouse. Frank had even provided new tennis shoes to match.

"You look great, Caroline," I exclaimed with enthusiasm.

She smiled shyly, her cheeks reddening a little. Perhaps I should have disguised my surprise a little, but I just wasn't good at masking my feelings.

"Thanks, dear." She seemed almost embarrassed to wear nice clothes. "Frank loves to spoil me when I'm here. I do think he goes a little overboard at times."

I dressed quickly in black jeans and white cotton blouse. I topped off the ensemble with a tapestry vest, a gift from my mother last Christmas, along with matching boots. I certainly didn't mind wearing nice clothes when I could afford them—afford being the key word for me.

Caroline wanted to show me a little of the campus. We took a leisurely walk under the great trees, whose branches were filled with twittering birds and squirrels scampering after one another. My companion took my arm and looked around with delight. "I so love it here, all the stone buildings and trees! It feels so peaceful."

I inhaled the spring scents, savoring them slowly. "Well, why don't you stay here?" I asked. "I'm sure Frank would be delighted if you did."

She stiffened. "Oh, no. I...I couldn't stay. I can't do that."

"Why not, Caroline?"

She let go of my arm and began to walk more quickly. "I...I just can't." She raised her arm and pointed down to a group of buildings. "There's the art gallery...and over there the Lilly Library." She turned to me, speaking with an enthusiasm I didn't think she felt. "They have some of the smallest books in the world there, some no bigger than a pinprick. It's amazing how they make them. I can't ever imagine making something so tiny!"

With that, she deftly closed the subject of staying in Bloomington. I didn't understand her at all. The possibility that she suffered from a mental illness loomed again in my mind. This time I could not dismiss it. Perhaps she had even fooled Frank into believing in her sanity. I found myself wondering if I could get help for her back in Fredericksburg.

As we walked, Caroline asked me more about my own life. She wanted to know how I had liked going to college in a small town and what I wanted in the future. I had a lot to tell her. I could have babbled on for hours about my college years. As it was, I think I only took ten minutes.

"I don't know, Caroline. Things just seem to get better for me all the time. College was great fun, but now life is even more interesting."

Caroline gave me an indulgent smile. "Of course, dear, that's as it should be."

I told her I wanted to continue my freelance work for the newspaper, but my big dream was to write novels. "Hopefully bestsellers!" I laughed at my own vision. I could see myself becoming a famous and, of course, rich novelist. Not a realistic dream, but I enjoyed thinking about it.

Caroline nodded, commenting almost to herself, "Yes, just like your friend. What's his name again?"

"Walt," I replied quickly.

"Yes, just like your Walt," she mused. Did she emphasize that word, "your", or was that my imagination?

My Walt? What was that supposed to mean? Yes, I did model myself after him, of course. I admired him a great deal, but her tone implied something more. However, I had no time to ask what she meant or to consider it for myself. We had arrived at the cafe for lunch.

CHAPTER ELEVEN

The scents of soups, grilled chicken, onions, and a variety of quiches greeted us as we entered the restaurant. Gourmet coffees mixed their sweet and spicy aromas into the milieu. I realized then that I was hungry and my stomach grumbled that I had not heard its messages before now.

We took a corner table, out of the way of the servers hurrying back and forth among their customers. The cafe hummed with conversation and occasional laughter.

"Franklin must be in the kitchen," Caroline explained. "Oh, how he loves to cook! And he's so good at it, too!"

A young woman stepped up to our table to wait on us. She looked like a college kid to me. Her face looked fresh and healthy, without any lines. Was I really that much older than this young thing, I asked myself. I'd already noticed the laugh lines deepening around my own eyes. She must be a freshman.

"Hi! My name is Angela. I'll be your server today. What can I get you ladies?" Her smile seemed genuine and her manner was buoyant.

We ordered lunch and the waitress turned to go. On a whim I caught her attention. "Angela."

She turned back, smiling. "Yes?" she answered politely.

"I hope you don't mind my asking," I began, a little sheepish now at indulging my curiosity. "Are you a student at the university?"

She seemed pleased at my question. "Yes! It's my first year and I just love it!"

Caroline took an interest now and asked Angela her major. "Well, I haven't decided," she admitted, blushing.

"You have plenty of time, dear," Caroline assured her.

Lunch was lovely. Frank's cooking did not disappoint us. We both declared it the best quiche we had ever tasted. We decided to splurge and order dessert as well. Caroline got the cheesecake and I, the Irish Cream pie. Neither of us could finish them but they certainly tasted heavenly.

Frank came by after the rush and leaned on the back of an empty chair. Caroline daintily wiped her mouth and sighed approval. "My dear Franklin, you have outdone yourself!" she proclaimed, with still another sigh.

Frank acknowledged her praise with a gallant bow. "Why, thank you, dear lady." He winked at me, then asked, "Is there anything else you would like?"

I shook my head with a contented smile. Caroline grasped his hand. "No, thank you, dear. Not a thing."

"Looks like it'll be clear tonight," Frank commented.

"It's still open Wednesdays at nine?" my companion asked.

"Yes," he answered, then turned to me to explain. "Caroline loves to visit the Kirkwood Observatory whenever she comes to town. It's open to the public on Wednesdays if the skies are clear."

"Oh, yeah. Caroline was telling me about it earlier."

Caroline turned to me, her face animated. "There's a wonderful astronomy professor who sometimes gives talks on whatever it is we're looking at." Glancing over at Frank she asked, "What will be visible tonight, Frank?"

He shifted his weight, thinking. "I believe it's Jupiter tonight. Yes, that's it."

"Oh, I love looking at Jupiter!" Caroline's enthusiasm for that planet seemed a little odd to me, but people have to find joy somewhere in their suffering. I supposed Jupiter to be an interesting sight for an obviously educated woman like my friend.

We left the cafe and walked around the downtown shops. There were a lot of unique places selling crafts or oriental curios. I bought a little brass Buddha for Walt, who had an interest in Buddhist art. In another shop I picked out a bamboo flute. The instrument had a sweet, rustic tone to it. I would add it to my modest collection of folk instruments back home. I might even play the thing once in a while.

We ate a delicious dinner at the cafe and returned to the house to freshen up. Caroline told me that the evenings were usually cooler here, but tonight we only needed light jackets.

We walked up the street toward the campus. My companion guided me unerringly along woodsy paths that I could barely distinguish from one another. She had obviously trod them many times in the past. When we stepped out from among the trees there stood a round, two-story building. I felt a bit disappointed at its size. I had expected something more impressive.

We walked around to the door. Inside, the dim light glowed dully off the pale walls. A few students stood at one of several lighted displays. I glanced at one with information about the moon and its phases. Caroline made her way to the circular stairway. Two young men were just coming down out of the darkness above.

My companion smiled and wished them "Good evening." They mumbled politely and walked toward the door. She turned to me, saying, "Now be careful, dear. It's dark up there, but if we go up slowly, our eyes will adjust."

I nodded absently, peering up the dark staircase. From the room above I heard the low murmur of hushed voices. I followed Caroline, gripping the steel handrail and stepping carefully. She was right; it was almost completely dark up here. The only light came from the room downstairs and the campus lights that filtered in through the large windows. I stood quietly while images slowly came into view, my eyes adjusting to the semi-darkness.

Several shadowy figures moved around the long, thin shape of a telescope, which angled up and out of a window. I heard an authoritative female voice giving directions to what must have been a student aide. Caroline made her way carefully to that voice. I followed, not knowing what to expect. This was nothing like the Naval Observatory that I had visited in D.C.

From the end of the telescope came a sharp intake of breath. "Oh, I can see it! It's beautiful!" exclaimed a young woman. The voice of authority added something inaudible in distinctively French tones. The younger voice said, "Yes, there it is. I can see the spot!"

Caroline turned to whisper in my ear, "The woman standing by the telescope is Dr. Therese DuVal. She's one of the astronomy professors."

We made our way under the scope and around to Dr. DuVal, who was watching her student intently. In the semi-darkness I could barely see the tall, slender figure of the professor. A mass of curls hid the side of her face. All I could make out was a pert, upturned nose and gently curving chin.

She noticed our approach and turned to peer into our own shadowy faces. "Is that you, Ms. Rose?" Dr. DuVal asked in a luxurious French accent. I started at her words. Did everyone know Caroline? The plot only seemed to thicken as I continued to learn more about my friend.

"Yes. Good evening, Dr. DuVal," Caroline said in a half-whisper. "Is it Jupiter tonight?"

"Yes, and it's particularly clear. You can see the red spot. Here," she said, motioning the student away from the telescope. "Come look."

Caroline ducked under the end of the scope and climbed carefully up the ladder to reach the viewing end. She peered through the eyepiece. "Yes! I can see it clearly!" I heard her exclaim in wonderment. "And the rings! I can see them better than ever!"

"It seems to be a very special night, Ms. Rose. I'm so glad you are here for it." In the shadows I could just make out a smile crossing the professor's features. She, too, shared my companion's feeling of awe at this celestial sight.

For several minutes Caroline looked through the telescope while I basked in the cool night and the euphoric energies of dedicated stargazers. I glanced occasionally at Dr. DuVal. She carried herself with an almost regal bearing, yet she readily shared a childlike joy in studying the night sky with all of its fascinating splendor.

As Caroline stepped cautiously down the ladder, she beckoned to me to take my turn. "Kate, you must see this!" Now I climbed up the four rungs and settled myself for a look through the telescope.

The sky was clear. I could see Jupiter with its bands, and as I continued to gaze, I could just make out a tiny red spot. Scientists still didn't agree what the spot was—a giant storm, perhaps. It mattered little to me. I simply enjoyed this private moment between the great planet and me. In the stillness, through the medium of the telescope, I felt a strange connection with this heavenly object. For a moment I felt I could reach out and pluck it from the sky. I half wondered if I should try.

Reality returned as more students arrived in the darkened sanctuary of the stars. I stepped down to relinquish my turn.

At my side Caroline whispered, "Wasn't that impressive?"

I nodded. "Yes, it really was."

Caroline turned back to the professor and began asking her about the other planets. I drifted away from their conversation and walked out one of the open doors to the small balcony that encircled the observatory. Leaning on the wrought iron rail, I gazed up into the velvet sky. Jupiter shone brightly, a great white light among the scattered stars.

I roused from my reflections as Caroline and Dr. DuVal walked out to join me in the night air. Caroline introduced me to the professor, who clasped my hand warmly.

"Kate, I am so very happy to meet you. Ms. Rose has been coming here for years. I feel that she is a friend."

She asked me a little about myself. I carefully avoided mentioning how I had met Caroline, uncertain if she knew of her homelessness. From her conversation, I guessed that she did not. Just as well, I thought.

Dr. DuVal told me she had grown up in France. Her father was a Frenchman who fell in love with an American woman. Tragically, she died suddenly after the birth of their daughter. He had returned to his home in a small village outside of Paris, and there Therese had grown into her teen years.

"My father wanted me to go to a big American university," she continued. "I missed my home, but I loved America very much, almost right away." She leaned her tall frame back against the stone wall. "I attended two years of high school to acclimate myself to American schooling. Then I went on to college and graduate school. When I was offered a position here I took it eagerly. I had always wanted to teach about the stars and planets. So," she said simply, spreading her hands in a gesture that took in the campus around her, "I am here."

I nodded, almost envious of her sure path through life. I still wasn't certain where my future would take me. "You must really enjoy what you do," I affirmed politely.

Her smile showed a perfect set of white teeth that gleamed in the starlight. "Yes," she agreed. "I really do enjoy it."

Caroline patted her happily on the arm. "And you must be a very good teacher, too, my dear," she added.

Therese raised her eyebrows in a doubtful expression. "I don't know about that," she said. "I do hope so."

The student aide called to Dr. DuVal for help with the telescope so she said her goodbyes to us, wishing us a safe journey home. As we left the observatory, I noticed that Caroline looked back wistfully at the modest stone structure. Then she turned, took my arm and led me down the path.

During the walk back to Frank's house she seemed very far away. I did not disturb her reverie. I hoped my friend was finding comfort in old memories, as I often did. Perhaps the observatory reminded her of some past happiness.

Looking up into the vastness of space and watching Jupiter as it glowed silently in the dark, turned my mind to a broader perception of reality. My own challenges dwindled in the face of the awesome power and beauty of the universe. It was billions of years old. How that unfathomable period of time dwarfed our own tiny span of days. We appeared for no more than an instant upon this planet, while the stars gleamed quietly out in space for aeon upon aeon.

Frank opened the door for us as we strode up the brick walkway. He greeted us warmly and insisted on hearing every detail of our visit at the observatory. Caroline had returned to her usual enthusiastic self and spoke with animation about seeing Jupiter and speaking with Dr. DuVal, who she obviously respected as much for her knowledge as for her warm personality.

The conversation eventually turned to current events and the recent political maneuverings between Congress and the White House. I offered little comment myself, preferring to sit and absently finger the wooden beads I had pulled from my pocket. I had a lot on my mind and holding the small mala, Buddhist prayer beads used for counting prayers, soothed my fretful spirit.

I wondered how Walt was doing and if my mother was busy preparing for her exams. It seemed odd to have my mother going through the familiar college activities while I was now a graduate trying to make my way in the world with what I had learned.

Of course, Mom still seemed young to me. She fit into college life rather well, but she would. My mother had the enviable ability to feel comfortable in almost any situation. She credited her calm, centered approach to years of meditation. I wished it would rub off on me, and, occasionally, I confessed as much to her. Mom would just smile and tell me that it would come, in time, from my own practice. "The monkey mind can only be tamed with patient effort," she often told me.

A light touch on my arm returned my "monkey mind" to reality. Caroline had risen from her chair and come over to wish me goodnight. "I'm off to bed. We older folks need our rest, dear." Her face showed traces of weariness mixed with a certain joy of being among friends. Frank and I wished her pleasant dreams as she walked upstairs, leaning on the banister for support.

I watched her go, wondering at this woman's odd lifestyle. Except for the fact of her homelessness, she demonstrated no overt signs of mental instability.

Frank stood up, stretching his tired legs. He had been on his feet all day. He looked over at me, the usual warm smile on his face. "Would you like some decaf coffee or tea?" he asked kindly. He could not stop playing the gracious host. His was a genuine vocation.

"Yes, I would, Frank," I answered appreciatively, slipping the beads back into my pocket. I followed him down the hall. It did not surprise me to find an ultra-modern kitchen here. After all, he was a gourmet cook.

The place gleamed immaculately, from the blue-and-white tiled floor to the white stucco ceiling. I wondered how he kept that last so clean. All the appliances were brand new. At the top of the wall someone had stenciled an intricate pattern of blue and gold flowers with pale green stems and leaves. The kitchen exuded cleanliness as well as charm.

Frank offered me a chair in the breakfast nook in front of a bay window. I sat down, admiring the unique, honey-colored wood of the table and chairs. Beautiful patterns swirled under a lustrous silken finish. "That's Oregon myrtle-wood," he said, noticing my interest. "Beautiful stuff. I commissioned the table myself." He ran his fingers over its surface.

"It's gorgeous," I agreed wholeheartedly. I stared at the wood, unable to ask what I most wanted to know about my traveling companion. Frank busied himself fixing some aromatic decaf for us. He must have guessed my thoughts. As he sat down he broke the ice with characteristic sensitivity.

"She's an unusual woman," he began, offering me some half-and-half.

I nodded and stirred my coffee, the dark liquid swirling into the light creamer. "Yes, she certainly is." I looked into Frank's gentle eyes and then out the window into the darkness. "Frank," I began, hesitating. "Is Caroline...does she have any...uh... mental difficulties?"

A broad grin spread across his features for a moment, then he became serious. "No, Kate. She is quite sane. Maybe more than anyone else I know."

"Then why does she live the way she does? Why won't she accept help?"

Frank absently turned his coffee cup in his hands. I recognized that the pattern on the cup was the same as the one stenciled on the walls. He drew a deep breath, answering slowly, "I would help her in any way she would allow. Hell!" he exclaimed, in what could only be frustration. "I have enough money to give her a house of her own if she wanted."

"Then why?" I asked, now even more mystified at the situation.

He stared into the depths of the cup as though it might hold an answer for him. "She pulled me out of my own puke and forced me to live again, and I love her for it. She lost her own family—car accident is what she told me. That's what drew her to me in the first place."

He met my eyes for a moment and continued. "She probably did not tell you that after the funeral her personal business manager proceeded to embezzle her money out from under her. She didn't notice. She was drinking heavily by that time and taking God-knows-what-kind of drugs: uppers to get up in the morning and downers to go to sleep. When she woke up in detox the manager had left the country without a trace. What he had left for her was a pile of overdue bills and no money to pay them."

My eyes widened at this revelation. "So, couldn't she declare bankruptcy and start over? Surely someone could have found him and brought him to justice."

"Well," my host began, shrugging his powerful shoulders, "Caroline felt ashamed of what had happened, but she also had good reason to fear. The man had threatened to kill her if she tried to find him. She wouldn't even tell the police the whole story."

Now I finally understood. Of course she wouldn't dare draw attention to herself by staying and attempting to rebuild her old life. She had chosen to slip away and remain anonymous. Yet something still bothered me about the story. It seemed too radical a step to take just to protect her life.

"Somehow, Frank," I said after a long pause, "I think I would rather take the risk of having this guy kill me than live such a terrible life."

Frank stood up and began gathering the cups and saucers. He glanced at me for an instant as though to speak, then turned to carry the dishes to the sink. "Not everything is as it seems, Kate. Caroline doesn't think of her life that way."

He began washing the dishes, his back turned to me. I rose and excused myself. I felt tired, but I wanted to read a little while before going to bed.

"Kate," Frank called as I was about to walk out of the kitchen. I swung around in the doorway to face him. He picked up a dishtowel from the counter and began drying his hands. "Don't judge her until you really understand what she's gone through."

I smiled sadly. "I'm no judge. I just want to be a friend—to do what's right."

Frank nodded, "That's good. Just remember, she's made the only choice she felt she could. We have to respect that."

I sighed, nodded in agreement, and wished him goodnight as I turned to go upstairs.

CHAPTER TWELVE

Our stay in Bloomington came to an end three days later. We had spent a lot of time walking around the downtown section and peering in various shops. We visited the University campus, spending time in the library, the art gallery, and a small cultural museum. It felt like a normal vacation. I didn't ask Caroline any more questions about her life and she didn't volunteer any more information. We simply enjoyed each other's company, as friends often do.

Frank brought us to the bus station when it came time to leave. He had tears in his eyes as he said good-bye to Caroline. "Be careful, now."

"I always am." She pinched his cheek. "And I won't take any wooden nickels!"

Frank shook his head and laughed, wiping his eyes with his fingers. Then he turned to me and gave me an almost bone-crushing hug.

"Take good care of my friend."

"You bet," I promised, knowing she would never allow me to do that. We moved slowly away from him toward the waiting bus.

"And drop me a line once in awhile," he called, waving a stout hand.

"We will," I answered. I had his phone number and address tucked into my pack so I could keep in touch with this new friend.

Caroline waved to him from the window as the bus pulled away from the station in a cloud of black smoke. Then she settled contentedly into the seat, a wistful smile playing over her features.

Frank had insisted on sending her back to Fredericksburg with a new outfit: a comfortable pair of tan, brushed denim slacks and a white cotton blouse with tiny yellow flowers. Now she had a sturdy pair of walking shoes that gave her feet better support and more comfort than her sneakers.

We passed the time talking, watching the scenery or reading. Caroline loved books and had been delighted when I had presented her with a new pair of reading glasses before the trip home. As a parting gift Frank had pressed a copy of Dickens' *Great Expectations* into her hands. She had read almost half of it by the time we pulled into Fredericksburg nineteen hours later.

Caroline stayed with me that night because it was late, but she insisted on returning to her old ways. She did not want to be a "burden" to me, she said. The next morning I asked if I could drop her anywhere, but she politely refused any more of my help. I gave her my phone number; at least she could get in touch with me if she needed any help. But would she?

"Please, don't hesitate to call me," I told her. I'm sure I couldn't hide my concern from her. It must have shown plainly in my face.

"Of course, dear. Thank you for everything." She smiled and patted me reassuringly on the cheek.

I watched with vague regret as Caroline walked down the street and turned the corner out of my sight. Eyes downcast, I shut the door. Now it was time to catch up on my backlog of research. I stayed quite busy with my work. It kept me from thinking too much about Caroline during the next several weeks.

I only saw her one other time that spring. She called to tell me she was going on another trip, this time to see friends in Northern Virginia. We met at a favorite downtown haunt of mine. The dim lighting glowed warmly from the wood paneled walls and accented the antique tin ceiling. I treated my friend to lunch and we sat happily with each other, getting caught up on the latest events in our lives.

I noticed her clothes showed signs of wear, though the material was of good quality. She seemed animated about her trip. Several years before she had stayed at a shelter in Arlington and met a group of homeless people who had begun to rebuild their shattered lives. They had banded together and formed a community whose sole purpose was to help others like themselves. She loved to visit them and spend time helping out.

"It makes me feel good to be needed," she told me, with a sincerity that tugged painfully at my heart.

"I'll bet it does," I answered, masking my concern for her own welfare.

"You would be amazed at the work they do there. So many success stories!" She grinned and took a bite of her sandwich.

I ran a fry through a pool of ketchup on my plate. Popping it into my mouth, I picked up another and stirred the pool into swirls. When I looked up I found her watching me, a peculiar expression on her face.

"You're such a pretty girl, Kate. You must have your pick of the boys."

"Huh?" I dropped the fry. "Oh, well, not really. I don't date much."

"Why not? What about Walt? You seem to like him a lot." She fixed me with her piercing gaze.

"Oh, no! It's not like that! He's just my mentor and, I guess, my boss. Oh, no, no, no. He's so much older than I am..." I sputtered to a stop. My face grew very hot. I picked up another fry and started swirling it in the thick ketchup as though trying to mesmerize myself.

Caroline chuckled. Shaking her finger at me she gave me a knowing smile. "I know what that means. 'The lady doth protest too much!' I think that a certain gentleman has stolen your heart."

I shook my head, almost violently. "No. I just don't date much, and I'd rather maintain a professional relationship with him." I looked at her with a mixture of embarrassment and frustration. "I'm just a kid to him. That's all."

She patted my hand with a motherly tenderness that, in that moment, I almost resented. "Maybe he does and maybe he doesn't. If he's smart he won't let you go on thinking that."

It felt confusing to talk that way about Walt. I wanted to keep our relationship manageable, clear of any romantic entanglement. I couldn't allow myself to think of Walt as any more than my mentor and friend. If our relationship changed I feared I would lose what we had now. Maybe I was just afraid of losing him altogether, just as Mom had lost Dad.

We finished lunch, chatting amiably. In the back of my mind the questions Caroline had raised about my relationship with Walt nagged at me. There should be no questions, I kept reminding myself.

Outside the restaurant, Caroline hugged me good-bye. "Thank you for a lovely lunch! You are such a dear!"

"Have a safe trip, Caroline." I found it difficult to let her go. "Let me know when you'll be back in town."

"Of course, dear. Good luck with your writing."

Now I focused on my research and writing. In June the newspaper published my article on the homeless. A handful of local residents had bantered back and forth about the issue in the "Letters to the Editor" for about a week, but nothing else came of it. Even donations to the shelter stayed about the same. What did I expect, anyway? Meaningful change takes more than one article. I took the money I received from the paper and brought it down to the shelter.

"It was a good article, honey," the volunteer told me.

"Thanks. But it didn't do much good, I guess."

She smiled at me. "I don't know about that." She gestured to the check I had given her. "It did bring us a new donation."

"Well, I wish it was more, but I don't have very much."

"Every little bit helps, honey."

I walked away unconvinced and buried myself in my work again.

In August I received three rejections of my story. "But this one took the time to write you a note," Walt pointed out to me.

I felt too upset to let the editor's words cheer me. He had written "Good writing. Just not what we're looking for right now."

"It's still a rejection, Walt." I took the letter from his hand and slipped it into my pack.

"Yes, but there are rejections and then there are rejections that tell you you're getting closer to publication." He pointed to my pack. "Soon, Kate. Believe me, you will get published."

I did not share his optimism at this point but I kept writing. One day Holly brought the mail into the kitchen where I stood heating a frozen dinner. "Well, Kate, it looks like another magazine letter." She handed it to me. With hardly a glance at it I dropped it on the table.

"Aren't you going to open it?" she asked, peering into my face.

"I suppose." The microwave beeped and I popped the door open. "Ouch!" I exclaimed as I tried to pull the plate out with my fingers.

"It gets hot, too, you know," Holly pointed out, grinning.

Grabbing a couple of paper towels I used them as potholders to take the plate out of the oven. Setting it on the table I took another look at the letter. Walt had felt this magazine would buy my story. Well, I supposed I would prove him wrong again.

"Want me to open it?" Holly asked helpfully.

"Nah. I'll do it." Resigned to remaining a wannabe writer, I picked up the envelope and tore it open. I read the letter once, then twice. "I can't believe this! They actually want my story!" I beamed at my housemate. "They want to publish it in the next issue!"

I grabbed Holly and hugged her. We started to dance around the tiny kitchen. If anyone had seen us, they would have thought we were crazy, or, at least, very poor dancers. We attempted to end with a flourish, but I tripped on a chair and Holly fell into me. We ended up sprawled against the cupboards, laughing like we would never stop.

Holly put a hand over her mouth. "I suppose we'll both be bruised tomorrow."

I didn't care. Nothing mattered except my first real triumph as a writer. I felt as if I had won a Pulitzer.

I waited to tell Walt in person. I knew he would be proud of his student.

"What's up, Kate? You look like you've had a visit from Ed MacMahon."

"Well," I said, drawing out the word as I walked into the house and turned to face him. I couldn't say it I was so excited. Whipping the letter out of my pack, I shook out its folds and held it up for Walt to see.

A broad grin lit up his handsome face as he reached for the paper. He walked over to the window and read it in the light. I could see his lips move as he read each and every word.

Nodding his head, he looked from the letter to me and back again. He folded it with care and placed it in my outstretched hand. "Well done," was all he said, but I could hear the pride in his tones. "Well done," he repeated, then indicated the table. As proud as he might feel, there was still work to be done.

I settled myself in a chair and we began. No celebration, just work. That was his way. But working with him was celebration enough for me.

In September I began work on my first novel. It seemed difficult to start. At first my writing felt stiff and formal, as though all my old English teachers were glaring at it over my shoulder. This was to be a great novel, damn it! But as I became more involved with the story and the characters I had created, the story took on a life of its own. Great or not, it was mine.

When I shyly showed the first few chapters to Walt he said, "You have something here. Don't worry about going back to change anything right now. Just keep going until the first draft is finished. Then I'll have more to say."

He grinned encouragingly at me. I detected a glimmer of pride in his look. I supposed it must have felt good to have a student follow in his footsteps. Too often his other private students wanted to talk about writing, but when it came time to work, they didn't have the determination to do it. That kind never stayed with him long. He didn't have the time to waste with people who weren't passionately involved with their craft he once told me.

Of course, I knew what he meant when he said, "I'll have more to say." He liked the story idea but my writing would need a lot of reworking. That was okay. His approval of my work validated my desire to become a novelist. It would take practice, like any other art, but I felt confident that my skills would develop with time.

When October arrived with its colorful foliage and crisp nights, my thoughts turned more and more to Caroline Rose. I wondered where she might be and how she was doing. Perhaps we had developed a psychic link with each other because she called a few days later. I met her downtown and we walked to a local deli for lunch.

She looked a bit more careworn than usual. She had found some warmer clothes before leaving Arlington. They had already seen good use. "Just enough to be comfortable," my friend commented.

Her eyes grew animated as she sat across from me describing the work she had done with the volunteer group. Most of their activities centered on getting homeless substance abusers to regular treatment and counseling. They made the rounds every day in donated cars, transporting people to their appointments on time or taking them to pick up their medications. These simple services meant the difference between staying homeless or becoming more functional members of society.

"Not all of these people will be able to enter the job force, but they will learn to cope better, get them well enough to make use of whatever social services are available to keep them off the streets and out of jail. At least they can have more of a life than they had before, and that, in itself, is progress," Caroline concluded with a smile.

"Well, I'm impressed," I said between sips of my soda. "Are there many programs like this in other cities?"

My companion shook her head, "No," she answered regretfully. "Shelters may refer people to counseling or treatment for addiction, but too often the homeless patient is left to find their own way there."

Whenever she spoke on this subject she always seemed outside of the problem herself. Of course, she didn't live the typical homeless life. She had places that she could temporarily call home. No, she was more of a gypsy than a homeless woman. And it seemed she lived that way by choice.

We both reflected in silence for a few moments, then I changed the subject. "Caroline," I began. "I'm going to visit my Aunt Maggie in Providence next week." I watched for her reaction. "I was wondering if you might like to come along."

She looked at me sharply, and then her eyes softened. I continued before she could turn me down. "You know, since it's been so long, I'm sure no one would recognize you." I paused. "If that's worrying you."

Caroline studied her hands as they lay clasped in front of her on the table. She spoke slowly, "I have never gone back, not even to look at their graves. I wonder..."

"I asked my aunt already," I added quickly. "And she said she would be happy to have you as her guest. How 'bout it?" I encouraged her. She couldn't turn me down. I felt she should come, but I didn't really know why; somehow we were linked.

My eyes pleaded silently. She lifted her head with a resolute look. "Yes, I think I would like to go, dear. Thank you for asking me."

As we parted that day I felt a sense of elation that she would accompany me. My Aunt Maggie had given her consent just that morning. She possessed a kind heart. I had counted heavily on her generosity and had not been disappointed.

My father's sister was my only living link with him. I tried to visit at least once a year, and Maggie was always happy to see me. She had no other family herself. As an English teacher, she heartily approved my goal to become a writer and had often given me helpful suggestions on my papers in high school and college. I looked forward to visiting her and bringing Caroline to see her old home in Newport. Once she had told me that in all her travels she had never visited a city she could love as much. I only hoped I was doing the right thing.

We began our trip on a clear but cold morning. The pungent scent of dry leaves mingled with the clean air. I kept my window half open as we swept up the interstate. The smell reminded me of countless autumn days when I had wandered in the woods near my childhood home, now and then jotting down ideas for poems or descriptions of nature to use later in stories. I had always felt happiest in natural settings.

Caroline had brought a battered canvas bag containing a change of clothes she had picked up from Goodwill. She sat beside me, snuggled into a used, quilted coat in her favorite color- purple. On her head she sported a pink, knit cap into which she had tucked all but a limp fringe of white hair. She seemed in high spirits. She told me she was eager to see how things might have changed since she left over fifteen years ago.

The trip went smoothly. Traffic was rather light, since it was a Tuesday. We stopped for meals during the rush hour times. Caroline wanted to know all about my aunt.

"She teaches advanced high school English in a private school," I told her. "She is very strict; not many students make 'A's' in her class!"

Caroline nodded approval. "Kids need to be challenged these days. Standards have lowered a great deal since I went to school. We had much more schoolwork and we had to memorize poems, passages of Shakespeare..." She shook her finger to add emphasis. "We were well educated in those days!"

I grinned. "My aunt is going to love you!"

"I'm sure she will." Laughing, she added, "If she can get past the fact that I'm just a vagabond."

We arrived at my aunt's quaint cape cod at around seven that evening. Caroline fell in love with the tiny blue and white cottage on the outskirts of the bustling city of Providence. Every shrub seemed perfectly placed and pruned with English precision.

Aunt Maggie hurried down the steps to greet us as we got out of the car. She was middle-aged and a little stout. Her gray hair fell to her shoulders in wiry curls. Once it had been black like my father's. Maggie's green-flecked eyes sparkled behind the silver, wire-rimmed glasses, their round frames accentuating the roundness of her pleasant face. She threw up her hands at the sight of my old Ford.

"You came all this way in that old rust bucket? You're lucky it didn't fall apart on the road!" She extended a hand toward my friend in warm acceptance. "You must be Caroline," she stated the obvious in New England accents.

My companion clasped her hand in gracious greeting. "Yes. So nice to meet you, Maggie. It is so kind of you to have me."

Maggie glanced quickly at me, then back at her guest. "Any friend of Kate's is more than welcome in my home," she added, as if to reassure us of her sincerity.

She turned to me and nearly smothered me in a warm embrace, the smell of homemade cookies still fresh on her clothes and in her hair. "Maggie! You've been baking!" I exclaimed with anticipation.

"Well," she explained, "I don't see you very often and I know you like my cookies."

"Only the best in the world, Aunt Maggie!" I had very fond memories of those cookies, and the scent of the kitchen just after they came out of the oven.

Aunt Maggie led us into the roomy cottage, directing us to set our things in the living room for the time being while she hung our jackets on the antique coat rack. We followed her gratefully into the black-and-white tiled kitchen. I noticed the cookies cooling on the counter— big, round ones with plenty of juicy raisins. The spicy scent of cinnamon tickled my nose. I wrinkled it with pleasure.

"Please sit down," my aunt said, indicating an oval, wooden table by the window. We made ourselves comfortable while Maggie bustled around the stove. With her baking spatula she carefully dished cookies out onto her best dessert plates and brought them to the table with a flourish.

"Oh!" Caroline exclaimed with delight. "They smell wonderful!" She picked up a cookie and took a delicate bite. "And they taste delicious!"

"Thank you!" Maggie beamed with pride. She loved to hear praise for her baking. Of course, it was always well deserved. "I hope I didn't put too much cinnamon in them."

Caroline shook her head. "No, not at all. They're perfect!"

I had already started on my second cookie. They were soft and warm and as good as I remembered.

Aunt Maggie prepared tea and brought it to the table on a silver tray that had once belonged to her mother. She poured tea for us and finally sat down. "So, you had a good trip?" she asked.

"Yeah. No problems." I took another bite of cookie.

"It was enjoyable, for the most part." Caroline set her teacup on the saucer. "But going through Connecticut... Oh, my! I've never seen cars go so fast!"

I chuckled. "Really! It's like the Autobahn there. And you'd better keep up, too, or you're toast!"

"They must have been going 100 miles an hour!" Caroline picked out another cookie.

"It wouldn't surprise me in the least," I added. "They sure did zip past my old car—warp speed!"

We spent a quiet evening with Maggie, watching the news and sharing the latest events in our lives. My aunt very pointedly did not ask any questions about Caroline's past. By eleven o'clock we had retired to our rooms to prepare for bed.

I had always loved the room Maggie kept for me. On its walls she had hung some watercolors my father had painted before he had married Mom.

He had made the frames himself out of driftwood he collected on forays to the beach. I ran my fingers along the soft, weathered wood, remembering past visits to Aunt Maggie's.

Though we had lived in Northern Virginia, Mom and I had visited regularly after Dad died. Maggie would take us on tours of Newport, with its charming shops, and the fantastic historic mansions of wealthy families like the Vanderbilts and the Astors.

Not yet sleepy, I sat in the tapestry-covered chair near my bed, reading. The book was my dad's favorite—the poetry of William Butler Yeats. Some of the poems evoked very dark images, but, being of Irish heritage, I enjoyed it thoroughly. The Celts took their laments quite seriously.

When I finally did turn out the light, I slept well—a little too well. My aunt came in a couple of times to try to wake me up. She had to go to school and wanted to make sure I knew what to fix for breakfast—as if I couldn't have figured it out on my own. But that was Aunt Maggie; everything had to be just so in her house. I had ceased to find it annoying and, instead, accepted her peculiarities. After all, she was a good-hearted woman.

After Maggie left I stole downstairs to prepare breakfast for Caroline and myself. I did not want to wake her, but, apparently, she had awoken when my aunt left. She made her way down the steps soon after I did and greeted me with a bright and wide-awake smile.

"Good morning, dear! Did you sleep well?" she asked solicitously.

"Yes, I did. How 'bout you?"

She sighed luxuriously. "Like a baby, Kate. Just like a baby!"

I brought her a cup of coffee and placed sugar and cream on the table in front of her. This seemed to please her and she exclaimed, "Real cream—what a treat!" She seemed just as happy when I brought her eggs and toast. Her heartfelt appreciation for the meal made it feel special and I ate with almost equal enthusiasm. Everything tasted better than usual. My mother would have said that I was experiencing a heightened awareness of breakfast.

We cleaned up the dishes in a leisurely fashion and decided to head south to visit Newport. It was a clear day and the city looked like a multifaceted jewel set between the silvery blue waters of Rhode Island Sound and Narraganset Bay. We drove through the older section of town and stopped at the famous "Cliff Walk" to stroll along the coast. From the sometimes rocky path we could view several of the "summer cottages" of the very rich who had made Newport a popular vacation spot.

The mansions were huge, some, with their walls of stone, looked more like castles. I couldn't understand why people would want to live in a place that appeared about as warm and inviting as a museum.

Opposite the homes, the sound shone like sapphire—calm, yet in constant motion. We stopped to sit on one of the stone benches and gaze out over the water.

Caroline looked far off, almost beyond the sound itself. "How beautiful it is still," she commented wistfully. "Oh, I have such wonderful memories of this place!"

"Can you share them?" I asked.

For a moment she continued to watch the water, then she began to speak of another time, another life she used to live. "Neal and I would come here often to walk along the cliffs. Sometimes we would leave the baby with the nanny and walk by ourselves. He would gently put his arm around my shoulders as we went along and we would listen to the water and the sea birds. They would call—just as they are now—while they dipped and skimmed over the sound."

Her face held a dreamy look. Somehow the wrinkles softened as she let her memories wash over her like lapping waves of silken water.

"Sometimes we would walk here in the moonlight while the water glowed pale below us." She looked over at me for a moment, then back out over the sound, back into the past. "People got used to seeing us here. They would smile that indulgent smile you give to young lovers...and we were so in love!" She patted my hand. "I must be boring you, dear."

"No!" I protested. "Not at all. I'd love to hear more."

"Well, if you say that you may be sorry! You might not be able to stop me." She laughed, a musical laugh that her husband must have found enchanting. "Neal and I enjoyed going into the mansions that had been opened to the public. We would look around, wide-eyed like children on Christmas Day! Everything seemed so fantastic! We were wealthy in those days, but we seemed poor in comparison to those families."

Her gaze turned down to the stones of the path. A smile played over her features. "We would pretend that we were getting ideas for decorating our house. 'That marble staircase would look wonderful in our front parlor' we would say. 'Yes, we should have a fountain like that in the back yard...'" She trailed off.

I broke the silence politely. "That all sounds wonderful. How nice to be in love like that when you're married. It seems so rare these days."

"Too rare, dear, too rare," she agreed. "But we knew how to help each other feel loved and wanted."

I knew that's what my parents had done for each other, too. I didn't want to think about that, so I moved on to another subject. Besides, I was curious. "Was your house around here?" I asked.

"Oh, no, not here!" she laughed. "Ours is...was off Ocean Avenue. Such a lovely place, too, a Frank Lloyd Wright design. It must still be standing. I don't think anyone in their right mind would tear it down."

"Should we go see?" I asked, trying not to show my eagerness.

Caroline nodded. "Yes. Let's go see if it's still there."

CHAPTER THIRTEEN

We drove down Ocean Avenue, admiring the beautiful homes that looked out over Rhode Island Sound. While they were not as impressive as the mansions, they still exuded their own ambience of wealth. Some were quite tastefully designed, situated to complement the landscape like the final artistic touch in a painting.

Further along the road, Caroline pointed to a large, gray home. Its design was characteristic of one of America's most renowned, yet notorious, architects. I pulled off the road onto the narrow shoulder and stopped the engine.

Yes, it was a lovely home. I could just imagine its high ceilings with exposed roof beams. The builder had effectively utilized both stone and wood to create the sense that the house had sprung naturally from the land itself. The large windows must have given its owners ample views of water and windswept, grassy hills.

"Wow! You must have loved living there."

Caroline gazed up at the house, hand to her mouth. I had no idea what memories engulfed her as she continued to stare at the place she had once called home. I expected an emotional response, but she gave none. She simply glanced over at me and said, "Yes. I loved it very much."

After one last look, she asked me to take her back to Providence. I started the car and we drove away in silence. I noticed that Caroline's face had taken on a more youthful look as she drank in the sights that had once been so familiar to her: the sea birds, the stunted trees, the sand and the water.

Maggie had arrived home shortly before we pulled into her driveway. She seemed tired—and with good reason. She had taken her class on a field trip to a local museum. I knew she hated field trips. Every year she told me that she found them quite trying and not very useful. Kids could see more interesting and educational places on computers and videos. However, the school required her to do one trip a semester; she had now done her duty, as she called it.

When we walked into the living room Maggie had her feet up on the sofa, a large glass of brandy in her hand. She looked the picture of a hassled teacher as she reclined on the quaint, velvet-covered couch sipping from the over-sized snifter.

"Great field trip," I quipped, as I sat in the rocker across from my aunt. She gave me a malevolent glance, before taking another sip.

Caroline greeted Maggie courteously and excused herself to go upstairs. I stayed, knowing Aunt Maggie would need to tell me all about how she had sacrificed her sanity to take a busload of ill-behaved cretins on an educational outing. Everyone has their way of dealing with stress.

Remarkably, she had very little to say about the trip, except that she was glad she wouldn't have to do another one for a few months. She really did love her students, but the classroom was where she felt comfortable. It was her kingdom, under her rule. The outside world was a different story. There she felt she could maintain but a tenuous control at best over teenagers bursting with hormones that conflicted with any rational messages from their developing minds.

I helped my aunt cook dinner that evening. We prepared roasted chicken, baked potatoes and broccoli. A vegetarian for philosophical reasons, I just ate the last two items. I didn't like cooking my animal brethren, but the poor creature was dead already. Besides, I couldn't leave all the cooking to my weary aunt.

Maggie broached the subject of homelessness that night. She tried to sound open-minded and kind, but she was of the opinion that there are two kinds of poor people—the kind that deserve help and the kind that don't. Caroline was very patient with her. Obviously she had heard these sentiments before.

"Well, if they want to drink or drug themselves into oblivion we can't stop them," Maggie was saying, justifying the scarcity of substance abuse programs for homeless addicts. "It is a free country. They can choose that life if they want."

Caroline pressed her thin lips together, biting back some choice words, no doubt. "Addicts from the wealthy and middle classes are viewed with more compassion simply because they can afford treatment. Their families and friends do not usually abandon them, but try to address the causes of the addictions. In fact, private treatment facilities have become very popular.

"When it comes to the homeless," she continued, quietly, but with passion, "it is up to us to help them with treatment as well as rehabilitation. What kind of people are we to toss them aside as so much refuse?" She spoke as though she were separate from the rest of the homeless population. I found her attitude puzzling.

"But the cost would be outrageous. Where would we get the money?" my aunt responded.

A sad smile spread across Caroline's features. "The bottom line, yes. That's the final argument, isn't it? But tell me, doesn't it cost more to send alcoholics and addicts through the revolving doors of band-aid solutions over and over again? Shouldn't we help as many as we can to get them off the streets permanently?"

Maggie mumbled a reply, questioning the possibility of my friend's suggestion. She had exceeded her level of comfort with the topic, so she quickly turned the conversation to more pleasant subjects, asking us about our day in Newport, and wasn't the weather perfect for sightseeing?

I had not contributed much to the conversation about the homeless, feeling that Caroline was a much more believable advocate. Now I chimed in with my impressions of Newport. Caroline let us do most of the talking at this point, preferring to add only polite, expected comments.

One thing I didn't mention was going to see Caroline's old house. Maggie didn't need to know about that, I decided. A rather private person myself, I felt that Caroline might prefer to keep some information to herself.

The evening ended quietly with Caroline retiring to bed first. I followed soon after, giving Aunt Maggie a firm goodnight hug and kiss. She stopped me a moment. "Kate," she said hesitantly as she resumed her seat on the sofa. "I really hope I didn't make your friend uncomfortable. I ..."

"It's okay, Aunt Maggie. Everyone has an opinion." I stepped over to her chair and kissed the top of her gray head. "She has a lot of respect for you. You took her into your home as your guest without question or hesitation. She can recognize a good heart when she sees one, regardless of whether or not she agrees with your point of view."

As I walked up the stairs I smiled at my aunt's concern. She was no more perfect than anyone else, but, even with all her faults, she was a loving person in her own way. That was something I had always appreciated about her.

I did sometimes marvel that she and my dad had actually been siblings raised under the same roof. He had become an extremely tolerant man, secure in his own identity. Quiet and gentle, he had never once raised his voice in our home. His eyes had spoken volumes. Sometimes, just a look from those clear, grey orbs had stopped me right in the middle of some mischievous act. He possessed a quiet power. Even as a child I recognized and respected it. I often wished I had inherited it from him.

The next morning began with a hopeful, rosy sunrise. The horizon awoke in purples, lavenders and pinks, imbuing the world around us with their soft tints. Caroline and I decided to do a little shopping and sightseeing in the old section of Newport. I had a few favorite stores along Thames Street that I hoped to visit. We also thought it might be fun to play tourist and stop by one or two of the mansions as well.

When we walked into my favorite gift shop, I felt compelled to look carefully through all their cases of jewelry. I admitted to Caroline that gemstone pieces were one of my weaknesses. She stayed at my side, offering suitably admiring phrases when I pointed out the ones I liked.

"I do love malachite with silver," she commented, pointing to an exquisite piece in the center of the case. I looked closely at the pendant, noticing the clear but fiery gem set on the top of the green-banded stone.

"What's that stone with it?"

"Water opal, I think," she answered. Her familiarity with the various gems spoke volumes about her past. Again I was hitting the brick wall between her past and her present lifestyle.

"You're right, ma'am." The saleswoman approached with admiration in her voice. "Would you like to see it?"

"Oh, no thanks," I responded quickly. Suddenly I felt that we didn't belong there. Well, maybe I didn't belong there. At one time Caroline could have bought that piece with her pocket change. We left and continued our walk. I looked over at my companion searching for signs of hunger. That was one thing I didn't want her to feel when she was with me.

We ordered lunch at the Newport Creamery, an old-fashioned diner famous for its sundaes, shakes, and other ice cream delights. As we ate our sandwiches, a little boy across the aisle peered at us with interest. He decided he needed to walk over to our table to show us the new teddy bear his grandpa had just bought him. His grandfather looked at us apologetically as he tried to coax the child back to his own table.

The boy trustingly put the stuffed animal in Caroline's hands. She smiled down at him then held the toy up to look it over with approval. "What a lovely bear you have!" she exclaimed, to the boy's obvious delight. Meeting his grandfather's eyes she reassured him, "It's all right. He's a beautiful child!"

Caroline handed the bear back to its owner saying, "Thank you so much for showing him to me!" The scene struck me as vaguely familiar, but I didn't know why.

"Come on, Pat. I'm sure the ladies would like to finish their lunch. They've seen your bear." Grandpa got up from his booth with some effort. He was a stout, elderly man and moved with a slight limp. Stepping over to our table he gently took his grandson's hand to lead him back. Suddenly he stopped and stared at my companion, a startled expression on his weathered features.

His mouth opened to speak, but for a moment no words came out. I could see Caroline stiffen slightly as she gazed back at him, before quickly looking down at her lunch. "I'm sorry, ma'am, but don't I know you?" he asked in subdued tones.

"I don't know how you would, since I don't live here," Caroline stated lightly. But I could feel the tension behind the words.

The old man glanced from my companion to me and back again, with an odd, puzzled frown. "I'm so sorry...but I thought for sure..." He grasped the little boy's hand more firmly. "Please forgive me ladies." Turning his gaze on Caroline once again he continued, "I thought you were someone I knew long ago. She lived along Ocean Avenue—a woman by the name of Carol Spencer Dawes."

At the name Caroline's face took on a strange expression. She pursed her lips and looked pointedly at the old man. "Then you are sadly mistaken, sir," she said with a thin smile. "As you see, I am obviously not wealthy enough to live there," and she chuckled at the idea. I admired her ability to act this part.

"She lost all of her wealth and was deeply in trouble," he went on. "I offered to help her but she disappeared." He seemed at a loss as to what to do next, but finally decided to introduce himself. "I'm sorry. My name is Burkette, former detective, Homicide."

I had just taken a sip of soda. I nearly spat it across the table at that last word. Caroline had not mentioned that kind of trouble. Quickly I brought my napkin up to my mouth in an attempt to cover my reaction. The soft drink tingled in my nose as I tried to swallow without choking. Detective Burkette had caught my response, despite my valiant efforts to repress it.

Caroline glanced coolly at me, before returning her gaze to the former detective. "Well, since I haven't murdered anyone here, how could I have met you, Mr. Burkette?" Once again she patted the boy on the head, saying to him, "You have a wonderful teddy bear. You must love your grandfather very much. He is so good to you."

Burkette still hesitated. Caroline smiled sweetly up at him and dismissed him, saying, "So nice to have met you both. My young friend and I have a lot of plans for the day, so you will have to excuse us. Have a good day!"

"Yes, of course. Sorry to interrupt. You have a good day, too." With that the old man turned and led the boy up to the cash register to pay for their meal. Caroline watched them go, her eyes narrowing. I realized that, despite her circumstances, she still possessed the power and presence of a wealthy matriarch.

I stared across the expanse of table at her, mouth slightly open, eyebrows raised. As my friend met my gaze I blurted out, "What the hell was that all about?"

Caroline looked down for a moment. Then she folded her napkin and carefully laid it beside the plate. "I was so afraid something like this might happen if I came up here." She looked into my questioning eyes with tears starting in her own.

"I have not told you the whole story. I wanted to protect you as well as myself," she admitted, heaving a sorrowful sigh.

"I'm ready to hear it any time you're ready to tell it," I tried to keep the concern out of my voice. Of course, I didn't quite manage that.

Caroline smiled to reassure me. "Don't worry. Even our detective friend is not sure who I am." Her expression became serious. "But I can't explain here. Are you ready to go?"

"Yeah, let's get out of here." I left the money with a generous tip on the table. I knew how hard it was to work as a waitress.

We made our way out to the parking lot and got into the car quickly. I noticed the former detective in his own vehicle. He looked as though he had stayed around just to watch us. He had not even started his car. I turned the key and the engine rumbled to life. With a last glance at Burkette, I drove hurriedly from the parking lot, eager to leave our new acquaintance behind.

CHAPTER FOURTEEN

We drove in silence for a while, until Caroline pointed to a small park ahead of us. "Let's stop there, dear," she said.

I pulled into the parking lot overlooking a rocky headland that tumbled out into the water. Caroline took my arm and led me across the street directly to it. She clung to me as we climbed over the rocks and out to the edge. She stopped, looked behind us, then sat down on one of the stones. I settled myself on another, facing her. Here the wind whipped the water into a spray that almost reached us with its clammy fingers. I pushed my hair under the collar of my jacket to keep it out of my face.

I looked expectantly at my companion. She had certainly chosen a private place where we could not be overheard.

Gazing out over the small whitecaps surrounding the rocks, she began her story. "Kenny was four when he died. He was not the target, Neal was." She turned her now tear-stained face to me. My heart beat slowly with anticipated dread of the words to come.

Caroline continued, wiping the tears with her sleeve. "When Neal opened the branch firm here he told me how surprised he was when he immediately landed a large account." She smiled at the memory. "He was overjoyed. We went out to dinner at our favorite nightspot. He told me about his new clients. They owned businesses all over New England and they wanted to invest with Neal's firm.

"I suppose we should have thought it odd from the outset, but we were so happy to have made the branch successful in such a short time. More new accounts followed quickly. It seemed that they had just been waiting for us to open in Newport. Neal worked quite hard for them and they all seemed so pleased with him."

Her face fell into lines of sorrow as she shook her head. "After two years I noticed a change in my husband. He became irritable, morose. He often walked directly into his study after coming home from work and would stay there for hours. I tried to ask what was bothering him, but he wouldn't tell me. 'Work', he'd say. For awhile I left him alone like that, thinking he just needed some time to adjust to the stress.

"One Friday, seeing he felt no better, I suggested we take a vacation. He blew up at me, telling me we couldn't go anywhere. He had too much to do. He had problems at the firm that he needed to deal with. I ran out of the room and upstairs to our bedroom, sobbing until I was exhausted.

"Neal finally came up and put his hand on my shoulder ever so gently. When I turned to him he held me for a long time, telling me how sorry he was. 'We're in trouble,' he said. I thought he meant financially. I tried to reassure him that it didn't matter. We could be happy, even without all the money and nice things. 'It's not that kind of trouble,' he told me.

"Now I pulled away from him and sat up, asking him what he meant. I remember feeling fear even then, before he had a chance to tell me. Maybe I felt his fear; I don't know."

I had lost all awareness of the water churning and splashing nearby. My eyes locked onto her features as if nothing else in the world existed but her face and the story she unraveled before me.

"He told me he had become suspicious a year after his new clients had come to him. When he checked out some of the companies they owned he found that they had just sprung into existence and were already showing unbelievable profits. He continued to dig further, as secretly as possible. But someone had discovered his inquiries. Two men he had never seen before came to his office and told him to stop. They gave him no explanation, just told him to stop delving into the records and to keep his mouth shut. That way, they said, no one would get hurt.

"Neal had already gathered enough evidence to know who he was really dealing with. He had never thought organized crime would take an interest in his business, but he realized he was investing laundered money." She paused, seeing my expression. I was finally getting a clearer picture of Caroline's past.

"Neal wanted out, of course. He tried to resign, but his biggest client sent a representative to discourage him from doing that. He felt trapped. He was afraid to go to the police. He was afraid to resign or just leave. At last he tried to contact the F.B.I. He again received a visit from the two strangers, who told him what a terrible mistake he was making. Obviously they had tapped the phone. Neal just didn't know what to do."

Caroline turned to look out over the water. I waited quietly, hardly breathing until she turned back and continued her tale. "Now he was finally telling me. I was so frightened! How could he escape from these people? I suggested he try the F.B.I. again, on a safe line."

She bowed her head. As tears dripped from her eyes she blinked them away quickly. "The next day he wanted us all to go into town together to run errands. I was busy writing invitations for a special tea I was giving for my friends. I told him to take Kenny and go without me."

Caroline looked, grief-stricken, into my eyes. Sorrow choked her words so that she could do no more than whisper, "How I wish I had gone with them. That was the last time I ever saw my family." Overburdened with her terrible loss she gave in to the tears, shoulders shaking as she sobbed in heart-wrenching despair. Without hesitation I took her in my arms, the tears flowing freely down my own face.

She wept for a few moments, while the birds cried overhead, as if in sympathy. After a little while she pulled away from me and wiped her face with the tissues I pressed gently into her hand. Now only the sound of wind and water reached our ears as we sat silently on the hulking gray rocks.

"They told me that Neal's brakes had failed," Caroline went on, her voice now clear. "He had hit an eighteen-wheeler at top speed passing through an intersection that ran down a steep hill."

I wished that I could say something helpful. All I could manage was, "I'm so sorry, Caroline. I'm so sorry."

She drew a deep breath. "I became hysterical when I had to identify the...bodies. Simmons, our personal business manager came with me. After he took me home he called the doctor, who prescribed something to calm me down and help me through the week of the funeral. I don't remember much about that week...except that Simmons seemed to be at the house with me a lot."

Shaking her head at the memory she said, "He made himself very helpful. Made sure I had my pills. But he also made sure I had plenty of vodka and brandy in my room...I had started drinking again."

I asked, delicately, "Again?"

"I had a drinking problem before I met Neal. But I was treated and thought I could never taste alcohol again." Caroline sighed, a deep and weary sigh. "But I-I just couldn't handle it. My life was everything I had wanted it to be until... All my dreams became my worst nightmares. And there was my business manager taking care of me, telling me to have a drink for the stress, handing me pills that seemed to take away the pain."

She revealed how she spent most of her time drinking in her bedroom, only coming out of her room when she noticed she was hungry, if she noticed at all. Her physical condition deteriorated quickly as the alcohol robbed her body of nutrients and her mind of any rational thought.

Meanwhile, Simmons kept the liquor cabinets, and her prescriptions, full. Caroline was no longer aware of reality or the passage of time. Simmons gave her drugs to wake up and drugs to go to sleep. She didn't even know what they were. She just focused on keeping her glass full to prolong her anesthesia.

Stumbling downstairs one day she arrived in the kitchen where Simmons was speaking to two men in dark suits. They wore sunglasses, which could not hide the mockery in their smiles.

"I hardly understood what they were saying," Caroline remembered sadly. "But I'll never forget their harsh laughter as one of them slapped me to the floor.

"Simmons was laughing with them. He told me that all my money was gone—that I could never get it back. He had embezzled everything while I had been kept drunk and tranquilized. I still remember his words, 'And you made it so easy, you pitiful bitch. So damn easy!' He kicked me so hard I started throwing up. That made him angry."

I saw her fists clench with futile rage as she told me how he had begun swearing at her, cursing her wealth and position, telling her she was nothing better than some bag lady on the street. "He was right about that, though. I was no better than anyone else. In fact, I wished that I were dead. I couldn't believe what was happening to me. Neal and I had trusted Simmons with our personal finances since we had come to Newport. How could he have betrayed and robbed me like that?

"He just laughed again and told me that Neal should have just shut up. His prying had caused his death and the death of my son. He said it was too bad that little Kenny had gotten in the way, but it was just as well.

"I remember looking up at him and asking him if he had killed my family. He just smiled, as though he was proud of what he had done. Neal had been nothing more than a pawn in a game involving millions in laundered money. He had been useful, but another could be found. Then he grabbed me by the hair and pulled my head back. I could see the cruelty in his blue eyes. He told me that if I reported what had happened, he would kill me and anyone who knew me. He made it clear that I was to disappear or die, and he didn't care which. It was no idle threat. I knew that. I was now completely sober."

Caroline's eyes glinted a cold blue. "Simmons was careless. Even his partner thought he'd said too much, that he should kill me because of what he had told me."

"Why didn't they?" I asked.

"Brad was arrogant. He had some perverse agenda regarding me. I sat on the floor, frozen in fear. I even wished he would kill me then instead of leaving me in doubt. No matter where I was, I knew they could find me, if they wanted to, and take my life on a whim."

To say I was shocked by her story would have been an understatement. I stared at her in disbelief, but her anguished features gave proof of the tale. I stammered something about going to the police. Caroline laughed bitterly. "Oh, yes. That was when I met our friend Burkette."

She told me that after the three men left the house she had called a friend. Though shocked by her appearance, this woman had the presence of mind to get Caroline to the hospital. That was where the police questioned her.

Vividly remembering Simmon's threat, Caroline was afraid to tell the truth. "But the officer was an astute man. He knew I was hiding something so he told his superior. In my condition, well, when he came I just couldn't remember the lies I had made up to pacify the police. The story changed every time I told it."

When the hospital discovered that she had no money they sent her to a state hospital. There a detective came to visit her every day. He introduced himself as Detective Burkette. At first Caroline thought he was only interested in her sudden loss of fortune. Then one day he told her that he not only suspected an embezzler at work, but he also felt that the deaths of her son and husband were no accident.

"'I think you know that, too,' he said, and he looked deeply into my eyes. Oh, at that moment I became terribly frightened. I saw no escape.

"He kept trying to get me to admit the truth. Apparently I had hinted at what really happened while I was much weaker. Now, I continued to deny everything in hopes that the good detective would give up and go away." She shook her head at the memories.

"But he kept asking as if to wear down my resistance. Finally, he told me he had talked to someone at the F.B.I. Apparently it was the same contact with whom Neal had spoken. The F.B.I. would put me in the Witness Protection Program if I would testify. They already had a list of suspects for both the murders and the embezzlement of funds from my accounts."

"Caroline," I interrupted, "you would have been safe and have probably gotten some of your wealth back!"

She glanced quickly back at the road, as if to be sure we were not being watched. She sat up straight. I perceived no little pride in her bearing. "No, dear," she said. "I might have been safe, but my friends—anyone who helped me—were threatened by these men. I knew I had to disappear in order to protect us all.

"I thought for a long time about what I should do. Then one day I saw the answer just outside my window." Caroline smiled. "There, on the sidewalk, sat a bag lady. As people passed her she held out a paper cup, begging for money. To my amazement, most of the people passing acted as if they did not even see her. Only a few paused to drop some coins or a bill into her cup. I realized that I had so often done the same thing—walked right by some homeless person and not even seen their face. These people were the most invisible when they were in plain view."

She chuckled at her own realization. "I knew," she continued, her eyes twinkling. "I knew then that I could escape. I would disappear into the ranks of the homeless, the human refuse of the streets. That way I would most likely never be recognized by anyone, even by those who knew me."

I nodded in sad agreement. "Yes, you were right." I could feel the gathering moisture in my eyes. It was not caused by the strong winds that blew around our stony retreat. "So that was when you became homeless."

"Yes, dear," Caroline answered, resignation creeping into her voice.

"And you started going by the name 'Caroline Rose'?"

"Yes. Rose is my middle name." She smiled suddenly. "My father used to call me his Caroline Rose. He liked to sing it to the tune of 'Second Hand Rose'." She glanced over at me, amusement lighting her features briefly. "Isn't that ironic? Now, almost everything I wear is second-hand." She looked away.

We sat together in silence, listening to the water and the wind and the sea birds calling overhead. I gazed down at the rocks. Here and there, in shallow depressions filled with water, lay stranded starfish, waiting for the tide to set them free from their watery prisons. What tide could rescue Caroline from her self-imposed exile? I could see no hope for her future.

She pulled the coat closer about her shoulders. "You're shivering," I said with concern. She nodded. "Let's go back."

"Yes, I think we should," she answered. She rose and took my arm. Together we made our way over the rocks and back to the car. The late afternoon sun, though bright, could not warm us.

CHAPTER FIFTEEN

Aunt Maggie had a faculty dinner to attend that night. I felt relieved that she had already left when we walked in the door. Caroline looked wearily up the staircase, pausing with her hand on the banister. "I just need to freshen up, Kate. I'll be down soon to help with dinner."

Putting my hand on her thin shoulder, I shook my head. "Don't worry about helping," I told her quietly. "I'll take care of dinner. Come down when you're ready."

"All right, dear." She sighed heavily. "Thank you."

I hurried into the kitchen as she trudged up the stairs to her room. Pulling the electric wok from its hiding place under the shelf, I set about cooking a stir fry with tofu and all the vegetables I could find and toss into the sizzling concoction. When it was ready, I set the cover on the wok with pride and looked around for my friend.

She had not yet come downstairs. I walked to the bottom of the steps, about to call her. Thinking better of making any loud noises, I padded softly up to her room. The door stood ajar. The soft glow from the bedside lamp spilled into the hallway.

Slowly pushing the door open, I confirmed my suspicions. Caroline had fallen asleep. With her feet still on the floor, she had slumped sideways, her head just resting on the edge of the pillow.

As gently as I could, I picked up her feet and knees to lay them on the bed. She stirred slightly, turning her head away in her sleep. Carefully I undid the laces of her tennis shoes and pulled them off. As I brought the blanket from the foot of the bed up over her sleeping form, I noticed some photographs that she must have dropped on the floor.

I stooped to recover the pictures from the carpet. They were worn and faded, two color photos and an old black-and-white. One showed a boy of around four years of age, Kenny, I guessed. Another was a family portrait. A smiling young Caroline held the same boy on her lap while a smartly dressed man stood protectively over them. That must be Neal. She was right; he was very handsome. And she, she was absolutely beautiful.

The third picture was a black-and-white photo of a baby in a christening gown. It was so worn I could scarcely make out the child's face. These tattered remnants were all that Caroline had left of her family.

I placed the pictures on the nightstand and switched off the light. Turning to go, I glanced back at the old woman sleeping so peacefully on the bed. I could hear the whisper of her breathing. The stress of remembering must have tired her more than I realized.

Walking softly out the door, I could smell the scents of soy sauce and cooked vegetables. I would have to enjoy my stir-fry creation by myself.

After dinner I relaxed into the rocker and picked up a Dickens novel I had enjoyed many years ago when I was still in high school. *The Pickwick Papers* took my mind off the events and revelations of the day. Of course, so did the red wine.

My aunt bustled in the door around ten o'clock that evening. She had grown tired of the political conversation after dinner and felt she had better things to do at home. I thought sleeping seemed foremost in her mind, since she went upstairs soon after arriving.

Our brief conversation must have awakened Caroline, who came down the stairs just after Aunt Maggie had gone up. She seemed refreshed by her slumbers and told me she was ready to try my cooking. "I'm sorry I fell asleep," she said sheepishly as we walked into the kitchen. I reheated dinner in the microwave for her. She ate with a healthy appetite. I always took pleasure in watching her eat. I guess that was when I got the feeling that I was actually doing something of substance to help. But somehow, I was also convinced that Caroline really didn't need my help. Maybe she didn't need anything. Her reality didn't seem to fit her attitudes.

I cleaned up the dishes, rinsing them in the steel sink before placing them carefully in the dishwasher. My aunt liked things done in a certain way. I had visited enough times to know that she always put the plates in the back part of the bottom rack, while other large dishes went in the front. Cups and small items belonged on the top rack. I tried never to misplace anything, knowing how irritated she would get if I did.

Closing the dishwasher, I started the cycle. "So, where would you like to go tomorrow?" I asked.

There was no answer. I turned around to see Caroline looking steadily at me. "What's up?" I returned her gaze with a questioning look.

"Well," she began, but stopped there.

I guessed her thought. "By your look I think you're telling me you don't want to spoil my trip, but you'd rather go back to Virginia."

Caroline grinned broadly. "Yes, dear, you've read my thoughts exactly. If you don't mind, I'd really like to leave as soon as possible."

"Of course," I replied easily. "I'll be happy to take you back home...I mean to Fredericksburg." Home was an unfortunate choice of words, I thought.

"Actually, Kate, I was wondering if you could drop me off in Arlington at Samaritan House. I like to help out this time of year before I head south for the winter." She laughed at herself. "I sound like a bird, heading south for the winter!"

"It's perfectly understandable. Besides, it's supposed to be a tough winter this year." A slight flutter of foreboding passed through my thoughts as I added, "I'll be relieved to know you're nice and warm down south."

She smiled reassuringly. "Don't worry, dear, I've survived many a cold winter. I will be just fine."

We decided to leave early in the morning. We had very little to pack so it would simply be a matter of eating breakfast and saying goodbye to Aunt Maggie. Caroline wanted to write a thank-you note to my aunt. I found some stationary and a pen. She sat writing while I went upstairs to shower and brush my teeth. When I came back downstairs, Caroline was just finishing her note.

"Are you writing a tome to Maggie?" I quipped.

She eyed me with mock annoyance and laughed. "It's been a long time since I've written a thank-you to someone. I almost forgot how!" She slid the paper across the table toward me. "How does that sound?"

It felt strange to be asked to judge Caroline's letter. I read it through, surprised by her flawless style. I handed the note back to her. "This is really quite good. Maybe you should be a writer."

She shook her head, chuckling softly. "Very funny, dear, but even if you were serious—well, I'm too old to start over again."

In the morning we told Maggie of our plans. She insisted on sending us home with bags of home baked muffins and cookies that she had stored in the freezer. I laughed good-naturedly. "Thanks, Aunt Maggie. It's a good thing we have all this food with us. After all, there might not be any baked goods between Providence and Northern Virginia."

She gave me a sharp look. "Not like mine, anyway," she answered, a smile twitching at the corners of her mouth. She hugged us both warmly. "Come back any time, Caroline." She winked slyly at my friend. "And you can bring this one along with you if you want," she added, indicating me with her thumb.

Caroline laughed and took my arm. "I will, Maggie. And I'll be sure to bring her along, too."

My aunt stood on the front steps as we drove away. I saw her wave until she was out of sight. Good old Aunt Maggie, I thought to myself. She was quite a trip.

I told Caroline we would have to stop for gas soon. Her lips tightened as she delicately asked, "Would it be possible to wait until we're...out of state?"

I understood her fear. "Yes, we have enough for that, although I'm sure we'd be just fine. Detective Burkette is probably still back in Newport."

Caroline nodded, settling into the seat with an expression of relief.

I refilled the tank just outside of New London, Connecticut. It took over eighteen gallons. I had waited until we were plainly out of danger to ease my friend's mind, even though the car had been running close to empty. I purchased a couple of coffees and we were on our way again down the interstate.

Caroline talked about the beautiful weather and the foliage. The changes of autumn had progressed much further here than in Virginia. The leaves shone brilliantly at the height of their color against the azure sky.

The conversation turned to Caroline's past. I wondered how she had managed to survive all these years. "Did you have any idea what it would be like when you first became homeless?" I asked curiously.

She shook her head, laughing a little. "No, dear. I had no idea. All I could think of was escaping the police and...the others. It's been a very difficult life. All I can do is live it one day at a time."

She paused for a moment, gathering her thoughts. "I remember how hard it was at first to beg for money or food. I took up with another homeless lady. She showed me where she ate. We would beg at the back doors of restaurants. When no one gave us food we had to pick through the dumpsters. You'd be amazed at how much food restaurants throw out. Once I got used to eating what I found...it wasn't so bad." She looked at me suddenly. "I hope that is okay to tell you. I don't want to upset you."

I reassured her that it was fine to tell me anything about her life. Inside, my chest tightened and my stomach felt queasy at the thought of what this woman had been through. I couldn't imagine eating other people's food, especially out of the trash. No, I just didn't want to think about that.

"Have you stayed in a lot of shelters?" I asked, glad to turn to another, perhaps more bearable, facet of her homeless life.

She nodded, looking out the window at the passing scenery. "Yes," she answered in far away tones. "I've stayed in more shelters than I can remember. Some were relatively clean; others...well, others seemed more like nineteenth-century mental wards—only terribly dirty. The smells in some of those places...ooh! They were just awful!"

Perplexed, I glanced over to her. "Mental wards?" I had to ask.

"Yes, people howling like animals all night long, Kate. You can't imagine what some of those places are like until you've stayed there. Rats, cockroaches, fleas...and God knows what other kinds of bugs. They were all over, even in the beds. People coughing and vomiting. And the smells..." she stopped. "Well, that's enough of that!

"I stopped staying in shelters unless I knew they were decent and safe. But mostly I haven't bothered with them for years. I like staying with the Samaritans. They have a group home for the volunteers, who used to be homeless themselves, and it's pretty nice. I just have to be careful not to settle in for very long."

"Settle in?" I wondered about her last statement. "Why don't you want to settle in there if you enjoy it?"

"It's too dangerous, dear. I can't risk being found. I must remain anonymous." Pointing out the window she quickly changed the subject. "Look at those beautiful trees!"

They were lovely. Caroline started talking about the fall color in the different states she had visited in the past. The patter helped clear my mind of the images of her eating out of dumpsters and staying in some of those shelters.

"You know, Caroline, I'd really like you to meet my mom."

She hesitated. "Yes. I'd love to meet your mother, dear. She must be an incredible woman to have raised you so well, and by herself," Caroline exclaimed, but the enthusiasm in her voice sounded hollow.

Maybe she was just tired. I prattled on, oblivious to her mood. "She's a great lady, Caroline. I know you'll love her the minute you meet her." A new thought occurred to me. "Hey, where will you be at Christmas? That would be a perfect time to bring you to meet her. She'll be on break then."

My mother and I always celebrated the Christmas season in honor of my father, who had been Episcopalian. I still remembered our last Christmas with Dad, when we had gone together to the midnight service. How I had loved the soft glow of the candles and the happy sounds of the choir singing old English carols. Every Christmas Eve, I felt my father's presence when I went to church in his memory. Yes, I thought, it would be wonderful to share our Christmas with my friend.

An ominous silence fell on the car. I glanced at Caroline, expecting some sign of joy or anticipation. Instead, she was looking out the window, her shoulders hunched as though to protect herself from some danger.

"Caroline?" Had I done something wrong? "If I said anything that bothered you, I'm sorry."

Her voice choked out into the oppressive silence. "Please, pull over."

"Are you okay?" I glanced at her with consternation. "Are you sick?"

"No. Just—please, stop for a moment."

I pulled off the highway at a small rest stop. What was going on, now? I sat very still and waited for Caroline to speak. She struggled for some minutes before she could begin.

"I can't see your mother. And when you hear what I have to say, you may not want to see me again."

"What could you possibly say that could cause that?"

She rubbed her eyes almost violently with her hands. "I...I almost feel responsible myself..."

"For what?" I asked, completely mystified. I began to fear for her sanity.

"For your father's death."

CHAPTER SIXTEEN

I caught my breath. What was she talking about? Maybe she was experiencing some sort of delusional episode. Caroline seemed to be battling a demon inside her. The usually calm face had become contorted with powerful emotion. I thought that I should try to calm her somehow.

"Now, wait a minute. You had nothing to do with his death, Caroline."

"How do you know that?" She whispered hoarsely. I tried to pat her hand but she pulled it away, fluttering it in front of her.

It took a lot of effort to hold my voice steady. "Because, my dad was killed in a robbery. One of those convenience store things."

She inhaled sharply. "Did they ever find the killer?"

"No, but it had nothing to do with Neal's murder..." I stopped. "I don't understand..."

"Neal was desperate. He needed to make sure of what was happening. He went to a private accountant he knew he could trust, your father, Sean."

I shook my head, almost angrily. "No! My mother would have told me that! You must be thinking of the wrong person!"

"It was so unfortunate that they found out." Her eyes were bright with tears. "When I read the newspaper account of his murder, I knew."

"But, the robbery..." My hand clutched the steering wheel. I wanted to run out of the car and get away. I steeled myself to stay put.

"It was faked—to cover up the hit." Caroline wiped her eyes. "I contacted your mother. I had to warn her." She fixed me with a steady gaze. "You were young, but you must remember."

Remember? That day, long ago, when I first saw those eyes and that kind smile. Yes, the haze surrounding those old memories cleared. My voice dropped to a whisper. "You were talking to my mother in the park."

I was seven and not very patient that day. "Just let me talk a minute, honey, then I'll take you home." I looked from my mom to the woman on the bench. She smelled funny. Why did Mom want to talk to her?

I nodded. "Okay. But can I feed the pigeons?"

"Sure." My mother reached into her coat pocket and handed me a package of peanut butter crackers. "See if they like these."

I snatched the packet from her hand and ran over to a cluster of pigeons. They started to flap off in alarm, but settled quickly when I opened the crackers.

"Want some?" I asked, holding them out. Their coos and murmurs answered me. I picked out one of the orange squares and sniffed it. The pigeons craned their necks, hoping to be the first to taste it.

"Sure smells good." The birds shuffled impatiently forward. "I don't know if I want to give it to you. Maybe I want it." I pretended to put it in my mouth. "Nah, you can have it."

I broke the cracker and threw the pieces out over the birds, which all strove to get to them first. Crumbling the rest of the squares, I tossed them into the flock. The birds scurried about snapping up every tidbit. When they were done they strutted away with pigeonly pomp. Without food I was of no interest to them. They went off to find new providers.

I looked over at my mom. She was talking earnestly with the woman. She listened for a moment, and then started to cry. The older woman put an arm around her shoulder. I wanted to run over and comfort her, but she soon stopped crying and stood up. Maybe it was time to go. I hoped so as I hurried to my mother's side.

The woman was speaking. "Everything will be all right, dear, I'm sure."

Mom nodded. "Thank you for...seeing me."

The woman smiled—a bright smile that made her blue eyes twinkle in the afternoon sun. "Of course." Turning to me she smiled again, only this time I thought I could see a touch of sadness. "You have such a lovely daughter." She reached out a hand to pat me on the head, but I hung back, clinging to my mother's coat.

She nodded in understanding. Instead she turned to the bench and picked up my stuffed bear. I had left it there to go feed the pigeons. "Don't forget this, dear," she said as she returned Gretchen Bear to me. I reached out to take the toy. Our eyes met and I saw kindness in her look.

I took the bear and mumbled, "Thank you." Working up my courage I asked, "What's your name?"

She glanced off into the distance and folded her arms across her chest,

111

as though suddenly feeling a chill. When she looked down at me again a tear rolled down her cheek. Then the smile, a sad smile this time, settled over her features. "My name?" This time I let her pat me on the head. "My name doesn't matter, dear."

As Mom and I walked away, I looked back at the woman. She waved to me before turning to walk in the opposite direction. When I looked again, she had disappeared down the path. I hugged Gretchen close with one hand and held my mother's hand in a tight grip with the other until we reached the car.

I closed my eyes as if to shut out the past. When I opened them I saw Caroline studying my face. "I got her number from your father's card," she said in a low voice. "I knew if it was that easy for me to find you, they wouldn't have any trouble." She turned away to look out the window.

"I wondered why Mom wanted to talk to you. I'd never seen you before." I paused while pieces of the past took on new meaning for me. "The move. It was really to get away, wasn't it?" I murmured.

"I thought it—your mother thought it would be best to leave quickly, before the police made the connection between the murders."

A vague feeling of fear grabbed at my solar plexus. "Do...do you think they ever did?"

She shook her head. "I don't think so. Not while I was there, anyway."

"I'll be back, Caroline. I just need... to stretch my legs for a minute." I opened the door and got out of the car. The air had a satisfying crispness to it as I inhaled sharply. I shut the door and stood there, breathing and watching the bright leaves as they tossed in the breeze.

Shoving my hands in my pockets, I walked along the edge of the parking lot. Why hadn't my mother told me these things? I could take it. I was an adult. Why protect me from knowing that my father was murdered by design?

Who did it, anyway? They still didn't know. What did it matter who did it? "He's still dead." I stopped. Had I said that last aloud? I looked around. Caroline sat in the car, head back, eyes closed.

At least I had one answer: why he was killed. It wasn't really helpful to know that. I supposed it wouldn't be helpful to know who killed him, either. Besides, nothing had changed. Nothing could bring him back or give me a childhood with him in it. I turned and walked back to the car.

The rest of the trip passed quickly. Caroline directed me unerringly along the crowded streets of Arlington until we turned into an old neighborhood. The trees were beginning to flame with autumn color. They stood tall and gnarled, shimmering with dying leaves moving in the breeze.

The houses were partly covered in ivy and almost every yard boasted huge shrubs. I recognized some of them. "This place must burst into color in the spring, with all those azaleas," I commented.

"Mmm, you should see them, Kate! Lovely, just lovely. Everyone here has a green thumb!"

I became absorbed in the beauty of the old neighborhood. Caroline brought me back to our purpose. "Here!" she cried suddenly, pointing to a street I was about to pass. "That's the street."

I slammed on the brakes. "Sorry, I wasn't paying attention. You okay?"

Caroline smiled ruefully. "Just a little jolt. I'm sure I don't have whiplash!" I could feel my face redden slightly.

I backed the car quickly and turned onto the street. At the end stood what must have been an old farmhouse. It was a big, but simple, frame home with white clapboard siding. Four brick chimneys rose from the slate-gray roof.

"Wow! What a great place! Is that Samaritan House?"

Caroline nodded, smiling. "Yes, it is."

I parked on the street and helped Caroline out of the car. She seemed a little stiff, probably from sitting so long. We walked, arm in arm, up the steps. I noticed ivy trailing up over the porch rail, ready to spill onto the gray floorboards at any moment.

The door opened and a spare young man stood smiling at us. "Caroline! Good to see you!" He hugged her and shook my hand. "Hi! You must be Kate."

"Yeah." His hand, though thin, had a strong grip.

"I'm Gaige. Nice to meet you."

We stepped into a spacious living room. The wood flooring needed some polishing but its warm hue exuded the casual comfort of a family home. The floorboards creaked softly under our feet as though in greeting.

Gaige gestured proudly around him. "Three floors of beautiful space for our residents."

"It's wonderful," I agreed.

"This is the original house from the farm that used to be here. They had to move it when they built the other houses. The old owners took real good care of it."

"Must be a lot of work." I glanced around, noticing the scents of old wood and a slight, sour smell of unwashed clothes.

"It is, but we're getting a special grant to help keep it up. We'll be able to afford some improvements then."

"And refinish this wood flooring," Caroline added pointedly.

At this, Gaige grinned and nodded. "Yes, and refinish the floors. Caroline's been telling us that since we first got the place, years ago!" He put a hand on her shoulder. "I promised her we would find a way to do it. And now we have!"

I liked Gaige. He seemed warm and personable. He loved talking about all the Samaritan House projects that he had in the works. I guessed he possessed a strong motivation, having known, first-hand, the anguish of being homeless.

Caroline and I embraced warmly as we said our tearful goodbyes. I tore a page from my memo pad and scribbled my phone number on it. Placing the scrap in her hand I said, "Please, Caroline, don't hesitate to call me collect."

Gaige gave me one of his cards at Caroline's request. I felt that we were creating a new kind of connection for her. She had lived so long dissociated from society. Now, she had exchanged telephone numbers with a friend. But it was thoughts of my father's murder that occupied my mind as I drove away from the house. In fact, I was so preoccupied that I wound up taking a wrong turn. When a few more wrong turns didn't take me anywhere familiar, I finally had to admit I was lost. Stopping in the middle of another old neighborhood, I pulled out my map of Northern Virginia. I had to study it awhile until I figured out how to get back to the interstate.

When I pulled into Fredericksburg I felt a sense of relief. At least I was home. I tried to think of all the work I had to do, but the same questions haunted me. Who would have killed my dad? I realized that I much preferred to think of it as a random act by frightened thieves. Caroline had shattered that illusion with her words. Now the motive was a much more sinister one, part of a plan to cover the tracks of a criminal organization. And wasn't it likely that they were still in operation?

CHAPTER SEVENTEEN

My mother had left a message for me on the answering machine. I waited until I had showered and relaxed a little before returning her call. She had never suggested any other explanation for my father's death than a robbery gone bad. Maybe Caroline was mistaken. Wouldn't Mom have told me if it were true?

Though past midnight, I knew she would still be up reading or studying. I often called this late knowing she kept a student's schedule. After I graduated from college, Mom had become more like a big sister than a parent. She had often told me her job was to see that I made it to adulthood in one piece with a good education. Once she had accomplished that goal she could finally enjoy her daughter as an adult. Of course, she still gave me advice; and I still listened to it. Then I did exactly what I wanted to do, if I could figure out just what that was.

I settled back into a worn, overstuffed chair—another thrift shop find. Covered with a quilt left over from my childhood, it was my favorite spot to relax. For a moment I hesitated, then, pulling my feet up into the chair, I picked up the phone and punched the numbers in their familiar pattern. After two rings my mother's calm "Hello" filled the receiver.

"Hi, Mom." I made an effort to sound equally calm.

"Kate! How was your trip?"

"Great. We hardly ran into any traffic. I was surprised."

"You must have just gotten back today. You sound tired."

"Yeah," I replied, breathing slowly to stay relaxed. "Actually, I got back around eight. But we had a good time, for the most part. We went over to Newport a couple of times. Hasn't changed much. Oh, by the way, Aunt Maggie sends her love."

"Is she well?"

I laughed softly into the phone. "She's fine, especially since that field trip is over!"

My mother's answering laugh sounded kind and musical. "Oh, good for her. We all need to stretch ourselves now and then." Her voice grew softer. "How did your friend like the trip?"

I took a deep breath, considering what I should say. "Well, actually, it was pretty hard on her at times." I recounted our forays into Newport, our meeting with retired Detective Burkette and Caroline's revelations on the windswept rocks. My mother listened intently. In fact, she became almost deathly quiet.

When I had finished the story I heard her sigh, breathing compassion across the distance that separated us. "Mom? On the way home Caroline mentioned Dad."

"She did?" Her tremulous voice carried an unfamiliar tone: fear.

"She told me Neal went to him with the evidence. She said Dad's death was related to Neal's and Kenny's." Only silence answered me, but it sufficed. "Mom, please tell me if she's right."

She sighed again. "Yes," she whispered. "Yes, she's right."

For a long moment I could not speak; anger welled up inside me. I struggled to remain calm. "Why didn't you tell me?"

"I felt it was best to leave you out of it. You were so young, and later—well, what was the use?"

"I can't believe this. Then you know who ordered his death. Why didn't you do anything?"

My mother had regained control over her voice. "There was nothing left to do except protect you. You were all I had left. Caroline said..." She trailed off, knowing she had said too much. "Oh, Kate." I could hear the catch in her voice that always told me she was close to tears. "When Caroline told me how these people had killed her family I became so afraid. I knew I had to protect you. We moved as soon as I could get a job in Virginia."

"But you let the murderers go free. What about justice for Dad—for us?"

"They had contacts even on the police force. They were too powerful to fight. We were still alive. I wanted to make sure we stayed that way."

Bitterness crept into my voice. "So, they got away with three murders."

"And we got away with our lives." My mother breathed deeply, a sign that she had returned to her patient calm. "Leave it alone, Kate. There has been enough suffering. Let it go."

I knew I could never let it go. I knew that this knowledge would eat away at the back of my mind until I took action. I wanted justice, but I would wait for the right time. That thought stored itself away while I pretended to let it go. "Okay, Mom. Still, Caroline suffers for it even now."

"I'm so sorry for her. I thought she would start a new life somewhere else. It doesn't make sense for her to live the way she does. I wish...I wish there were something we could do to help."

Now, trying to think only of my friend, I saw my opportunity and began, "Well, Mom, there is. Caroline hasn't celebrated Christmas in a home with a family since she took to the streets. I was wondering..." I let the question dangle, unasked. My mother knew me well enough to guess the next words, and I already knew her answer.

"Of course! Let's have her stay for Christmas!"

We talked excitedly then, making plans for a special holiday together. Mom would have almost a whole month off and we could spend a lot of time together.

The conversation spun off into other areas of our lives. I talked about the research I was doing for Walt. My mother shared the challenges of her first year of vet school. Starting college in her forties had proved more difficult than she had ever imagined. She seemed to have adjusted by her third year. There was actually a large population of middle-aged students with whom to commiserate. These days, going back to school in mid-life for a second career was not uncommon.

We talked for almost two hours. My ear felt sore where the receiver had rubbed it, but I loved sharing my thoughts with my mother. I had always felt that I could tell her anything—well, almost anything. I supposed her meditation training must have given her the serenity to see her through any trial, including those of motherhood. She never passed judgment on anyone, trying instead to understand the difficulties and motivations of her fellow human beings. Of course, sometimes I wished she would tell me straight out what she felt about some of my decisions. I knew she wanted to respect my judgment, but I wasn't always so sure about it myself.

Autumn passed quickly. The cricket song that had rung so insistently in August now dwindled to a lonely chirping, a dying song of the end of warmth and growing things. The sun's slanting rays caught the last of the whispering leaves, turning them to flames of gold and red. Autumn was a time of remembrance, of putting away the thoughts of summer's lazy pleasures, of preparing the ground for fallow sleep in the bitter cold of winter. I told no one of the revelations concerning my father. I went on with life as though I had never heard them. I could do nothing now. Besides, there were so many other things to occupy my time and my thoughts.

One November day I found myself sitting in Walt's airy kitchen discussing the Tibetan situation. "Actually," Walt was saying, as he stood and began pacing the immaculate floor. "I have connections in Dharamsala, India, who can also put me in touch with some people in Lhasa. We can get first-hand information, even pictures, to familiarize ourselves with both places before we go." He nodded and rubbed his chin thoughtfully.

"We?" I asked, surprised. "Is that a you-and-me 'we' you're talking about?" I felt a thrill of excitement, before the quick realization that I couldn't afford such a trip sucked the wind right out of my traveling sails.

"Uh, yeah," he answered, as it dawned on him that he had not mentioned this to me before. "That is the general idea." He searched my face for a response, but I only stared back in amazement.

He smiled as he understood my hesitation. "Oh, that's what you're worried about. I don't expect you to pay your own way. After all, you're my assistant."

I must have been holding my breath for a long time, because it came out in a sudden rush of relief and happiness. "Cool! We're going to India and Tibet? I don't know what to say."

"I'm afraid there might be some danger involved, so it will take some careful planning to minimize the risks." He took on his fatherly tone as he continued, "We certainly can't carry any materials which might prove, shall we say, compromising."

Excitement tingled through my body as I envisioned the trip before us. I yearned to exalt in the majesty of the Himalayas and breathe the cold, thin air of the high Tibetan plateau. I had researched the geography so thoroughly that I could already imagine being there.

Walt was saying something but I had ranged so far away that I didn't catch it. He called me out of my mountain fastness, "Kate!" I looked up at him, startled. Once more I found myself sitting at the table. Walt had risen to get some coffee.

He stood with the steaming carafe poised over my cup. "More coffee?" he asked, a quizzical expression giving his face an endearing, boyish look. "Where did you go just now, anyway?"

I laughed at my quick journey to the other side of the globe. " Tibet!"

"Well, it will be several months from now, so don't pack yet." He finished filling my cup and moved to refill his.

I changed the subject, asking him about his plans for Christmas. "Oh, I'll probably go visit my sister in West Virginia the week after. I like to stay in town for the holidays; it's so beautiful here at that time of year."

I told him about planning to get together with my mother and Caroline for Christmas. "Splendid idea!" he responded. "Will you be in town? Would I be able to finally meet your mother?"

When Mom had said she would be coming up to Fredericksburg I realized that I could finally introduce her to Walt. Having heard so much about him from me, she felt she already knew him. "He sounds like such a wonderful man, Kate. I'm glad I'll get to meet him at last!"

I nodded. "Yeah, Mom is coming up for a few days. I was thinking of maybe following her home with Caroline. She's never been to Blacksburg. Besides," I added practically, "I might be able to do some research at the library there. Your foray into science fiction has proved rather challenging to me."

That made him grin. Recently he had come up with a fascinating idea for a sci-fi novel. Of course, now I had to provide technical research to a man who hardly remembered his science classes. "It sounds like you have everything worked out, Kate." In this instance he wasn't playing the father figure. Instead, he was letting me take care of him; I rather enjoyed that.

November passed quickly. I had gone to Blacksburg to eat a vegetarian Thanksgiving with my mother. I returned to piles of research: Walt's and my own. My first novel was progressing at a fair rate. It was a period piece based on my Irish ancestors. I liked the story line, but I was not pleased with some of the characters. Walt was able to give me some tips on fleshing them out.

"Of course," he added. "You will get to know them better as you continue writing." As usual, I discovered he was right. In fact, I almost began to think of them as real people instead of my own creations.

In December I called Caroline at Samaritan House. We spoke pleasantly for a few minutes about what we had been doing during the fall. When I asked her if I could come up and bring her down for Christmas, she hesitated. "It's so nice of you, dear, but I think I'd better stay put."

I understood her discomfort. "Look, Mom knows you told me about Dad and your meeting with her..."

"She does?" Caroline's voice sounded heavy and flat.

"Yes, and we would still like to have you down."

"How can I? I feel partly responsible for what happened."

"You shouldn't. It wasn't your fault." I took a deep breath. "Why don't you let me pick you up?" I hoped my voice conveyed my sincere desire to have her as our guest.

"Are you sure your mother wants to see me?"

"Yes. She told me that more than once. I wish you would say 'yes'," I insisted.

I drove up to Arlington a few days before Christmas to pick her up. Caroline's face shone with delight when she saw me. I could feel her excitement and it reminded me of how I had felt about this holiday as a child.

We arrived back at the house around three in the afternoon. My housemates had already left for the holidays, leaving the house to us. Mom would be arriving that evening, so I busied myself with cleaning and last minute decorating. Caroline dusted the living room and helped put ornaments on the fresh-cut tree I had bought two days ago.

She beamed happily at each one as she picked them out of the cardboard Christmas box. "A harp! Ohh," she squealed, "it's beautiful!" She held the glass instrument up to the light. Its smooth curves contrasted with the knotted hand that held it so lovingly. "I love harp music!" She clasped it in both hands now, as if it held the key to another fond memory.

"Once, Kate, I was walking down a street looking in the windows of restaurants. It was Christmas time and I just wanted to see the decorations. Suddenly, there it was. The most beautiful instrument I'd ever seen: a harp. Someone was playing but I could barely hear it from the sidewalk. I stepped into the restaurant and walked up to it, standing in the shadows to listen. No one came up to me to ask why I was there. It was as though I was meant to be there, hearing music from heaven.

"The harpist was a young girl, a pretty, petite little thing with big brown eyes and long, black hair. When she finished playing she looked up and smiled at me. She must have known I wasn't a customer because of my ragged clothes. But it didn't seem to matter. The restaurant wasn't very busy at the time. The hostess came up to me and asked if I wanted a table. Of course, I had to say no, but she quickly offered me a cup of hot cider— on the house! She pointed to a nearby table, telling me I would be welcome to stay awhile if I liked."

Caroline looked wistfully at the ornament and moved to the tree. "I stayed until the girl had finished playing for the night. I sat sipping the delicious cider and listening to her beautiful harp. I thought I was in heaven, I felt so happy and at peace. More than that, I felt like a person, someone just like everyone else. Those two were very kind to me. They also treated me with dignity—something you don't get very often in my situation." She hung the harp on the tree and stood back to admire it. "Yes, I'll never forget that lovely evening of music."

I smiled up at my friend as I knelt beside the box of ornaments. "What a nice memory for you. It renews your faith in humanity to hear a story like that." I pulled out a wooden teddy bear and laughed. Holding it up for Caroline to see I said, "This one brings me back to my childhood. My mother put this on the outside of a very special present the year Dad died." A pained expression crossed my elderly friend's face. " I remember being so excited about the ornament that I almost forgot to open the box it came on. Mom had to remind me, 'Open your present, Kate!' It was that stuffed bear that you liked so much when you visited for the first time."

Caroline nodded, moisture blurring her usually clear eyes. "Oh, that must have been something when it was new!" Her enthusiasm covered the sudden emotion I knew she was trying to suppress. "It's still so cute now!"

My memory filled me with a child's joy, not sorrow. I had always treasured Gretchen Bear. It was our first Christmas without Dad. Mom had hunted everywhere just to find the kind of bear I told her I wanted. It was the softest stuffed animal I had ever felt. I remember holding it close every moment I could after opening its box. I don't think I put it down during Christmas vacation except to take my bath.

We took our time with the decorations. I think we both savored this special time away from our usual realities. After we had placed all the ornaments on the tree, we draped its branches with a gold garland. Stepping back to admire our work, we inhaled the spicy pine scent that filled the living room.

I put my arm over Caroline's shoulders and we gazed, almost mesmerized, at the tiny colored lights that glowed steadily, adding their own colors to the shining ornaments. "Now that's a tree!" I exclaimed softly.

"Yes, indeed it is, and the prettiest I've ever seen!"

Once the boxes were put away I brewed a pot of spiced tea. As I brought a mug of the fragrant liquid to Caroline the doorbell rang. I grinned expectantly. "I'll bet that's Mom!"

CHAPTER EIGHTEEN

Icy air rushed into the house when I opened the door. The cold only served to brighten the sparkle in her sea-green eyes and heighten the flush in her high, thin cheeks. Her joyous smile warmed my whole being despite the bitter cold, and warmth seemed to radiate through the heavy quilted jacket as she enfolded me in her arms. "Merry Christmas, Kate!" my mother cried with delight.

"Merry Christmas!" My answer rang in the foyer like welcoming chimes. I shut the door quickly against the cold and reached for her coat. I hung it on the stand by the door and we walked into the living room where Caroline stood, beaming happily, by the tree.

"Caroline," my mother exclaimed, hesitating as she gazed into the features that time and suffering had changed. She stepped quickly to the old woman and embraced her as if she were her own sister. She stood back and took both our hands in hers. They felt warm to the touch as if Mom had been sitting in the living room, too, instead of coming in out of the cold. "I have heard so much about you from Kate! She is so fond of you!" She looked at each of us in turn, her smile cascading love over us and throughout the room.

Caroline seemed too happy to speak for a moment, then found her voice. "Kate has told me so many good things about you, too. You've raised quite a fine young lady here," she added.

I could feel the flush rise to my face up to my eyebrows. I always felt uncomfortable when people talked like that about me, but part of me lapped it up with a surprising eagerness, which embarrassed me even further.

We settled down into the couch and old easy chairs, the threads of intense conversation weaving us closer throughout the evening. Caroline and I sipped more spiced tea while my mother nursed a hot chocolate. Mom told us about the long drive through the mountains. Apparently a tractor-trailer had slipped on a patch of black ice and overturned on the highway. It had lain on its side across all the lanes for a couple of hours before a tow truck could get through the traffic.

"I was pretty close when it happened. I jumped out to see if the driver needed medical assistance. When I climbed up to the side of the cab, he looked dazed."

"Oh, my! You were so brave to help out like that!" Caroline looked at my mother with a mixture of worry and admiration.

"Not really," Mom commented. "I was afraid he might have gotten seriously hurt or even killed. I'm not one to sit around on my hands when I can help someone."

"You're not one to sit on your hands in any circumstances," I added dryly.

Mom flashed a brief smile. "No, you're right. But when I told this guy I was in vet school he didn't seem to understand me at first. Then he finally said he'd never served in the military! Well, I wasn't sure if he was joking until he gave me sly wink. That's when I knew he was okay."

"Maybe he didn't appreciate having a future animal doctor come to his rescue." I interposed.

"Actually, he didn't mind at all. We spent the next two hours waiting for the tow truck. He told me all about his family and how his wife raised parrots and finches on their small farm. He said she made a little money at it but she had ended up with a lot of extra birds around the place. Of course, she loved them. He was happy she had them to keep her company while he was on the road."

Caroline shook her head. "Truck driving must be a difficult way to make a living. And to have to be away from your family so much... That must be very hard."

"He said as much, too," Mom added. "But he really enjoys driving his rig. And it was a beauty—teal-blue cab and lots of chrome. Good thing it was well insured!"

Toward midnight the congenial evening drew to a close. My mother was tired from the drive and Caroline seemed weary, too. I showed them each to a room, graciously offered by my housemates before they had left.

I sat up for a couple more hours, enjoying some homemade mulled wine and jotting down a few notes for my novel. For some reason the characters had started creating new situations, seemingly on their own, and I felt as though I were nothing more than a mere scribe obeying their wills. When that first happened I thought I must have been losing my mind. I had even hesitated to mention it to Walt. Of course, when I finally did tell him, he put my fears to rest, saying that the same thing often happened to other writers and actually would lend more depth to the story.

I recalled how he had tried not to laugh at the expression he saw on my face. I couldn't hide my worries about my own sanity. His amused smile was kind and lit up his features rather attractively. I stopped worrying then.

When I finally crawled into bed and settled down to sleep, I felt a rare contentment permeate my mind and body. It was Christmas Eve.

I awoke to the satisfying scent of fresh brewed coffee. I could hear my mother and Caroline chatting amiably downstairs in the kitchen. From time to time they giggled almost like little girls. I brushed my hair back with my hands and slipped into a thick, forest green bathrobe. Then I stepped sleepily into my old, fuzzy slippers and followed the tantalizing smell down the stairs.

My mother stood by the stove breaking eggs into a bowl. Her faded jeans fit snugly over her slender legs, while the oversized Virginia Tech sweatshirt hung like a thick cloud of warmth from her shoulders. She flashed a bright smile at me as I wandered into the kitchen. How anyone could be that wide-awake before breakfast, I didn't know. Even though I often ran early in the morning, that comfortable sleepy warmth usually clung to me for at least the first mile or so.

"Good morning, sleepy-head!" came Mom's mildly annoying greeting. I think I smiled in answer as I made straight for the coffee pot.

Caroline greeted me with her usual cheery grin. I realized why these two women had hit it off from the start—they were so much alike! I muttered my own greeting, remembering suddenly that it was Christmas Eve. Before I could say another word my mother quietly said, "Christmas Eve gift!" I laughed in mock exasperation.

"Really, Mom. That's not fair! I'm not even awake yet." We had continued another of my father's traditions. Whoever said "Christmas Eve gift" first on Christmas Eve got to open a present. We had even carried the tradition so far as to call each other early on that day just to say it over the phone, even when there was no gift ready for the winner. Sometimes we would laugh and get into mock arguments about who had actually said it first.

However, I had thought ahead yesterday and had already hidden a gift for Mom in a drawer. Opening it with a triumphant "aha!" I picked up the small package and presented it to her with a ceremonious bow.

"Talk about prepared," my mother said, blushing as she began to unwrap the present. "Oh, Kate, how thoughtful of you!" She took the teapot-shaped tea strainer out of the box and showed Caroline, who thought it was the most adorable thing she had ever seen.

The kitchen rang with our happy chatter as my mother cooked omelets with cheese, onions and green peppers. Mom and I were lacto-ovo vegetarians. We ate eggs and dairy products; we just didn't like eating creatures that had to be killed first.

After breakfast we decided to do a little window-shopping in the historic district just to see the shops with their lovely decorations and to join the Christmas throng that would be strolling gaily down the brick walks. Here and there we would step into a quaint store to get a closer look at some of their wares, miniatures, teddy bears, or maybe china.

A thin wallet caught my eye. It was cloth with a dogwood flower embroidered on the front. Inside were a few clear pages for holding photos. I bought it and presented it to Caroline, saying, "For your pictures." She smiled, uncomprehending for a moment, then looked a little uncomfortable.

"Uh, thank you, dear. How thoughtful!" she said, the instant of discomfort past. I hoped I hadn't done the wrong thing in giving it to her. Or perhaps she just didn't realize I had seen her photographs. We stepped back out onto the street and continued on our way.

Walt had invited us over for dinner that night and asked if we would like to accompany him to a local Episcopal church for Christmas Eve service. He loved going there every year at Christmas and wanted to share the experience with us. We gladly accepted.

Dinner was as delicious as it was fragrant. Walt had outdone himself with platters of vegetables, stuffing, and a vegetarian loaf shaped like a Christmas tree. "So you're a vegetarian?" my mother asked.

"I am tonight!" Walt replied suavely.

Admiring the tree-shaped loaf I commented, "I like the tree—so much better than a turkey."

"Well, I couldn't very well have you eating an animal shape, now could I?" and his eyes twinkled merrily as he grinned.

Mom loved Walt right away. He was about five years her junior. While he presented a very handsome exterior, she seemed more taken with his warmth and compassion. She had been sure to read some of his books before coming up, just to prepare for this meeting. I think she also appreciated the glimpse his writings had given her into the workings of my mentor's mind. After all, as my mom, she needed to know what kind of man was spending time with her daughter.

Walt was obviously quite taken with her calm and happy ways. Nothing seemed to disturb my mother. Her presence promoted harmony wherever she went. I had always admired her, even in my mildly rebellious teens. She had provided a love I could always count on when I needed it. Most importantly, I had always felt that I could trust her completely. No matter what problems I had, I knew that she would listen without judging me and would do all in her power to help me through them.

Our eyes lit up when Walt brought the cake to the table. It was his own creation: a cherry tart cake with real Devonshire cream.

"This is exquisite, Walt," Mom commented appreciatively.

He smiled, obviously pleased with himself. Bowing graciously he responded, "Why thank you, dear lady. Your enjoyment has made it worth the effort." And he had made quite an effort, almost as if he wanted to impress my mother for some reason I didn't want to think about or admit. In my mind I denied the possibility that either of us might want more than a friendly, professional relationship, but I blushed when he caught my eye for a moment across the cake. The moment passed and I gave myself to the scrumptious dessert, trying not to look too often at its creator.

Caroline had also thoroughly enjoyed the dinner, but I noticed she didn't eat very much. "Did you get enough to eat?" I asked.

"Why, goodness, yes, dear! I've eaten enough for a week."

I had never seen a merrier sight in Walt's dining room before. We laughed and talked in high spirits, enjoying the good food and fine companionship. Even families don't often enjoy such happy times. But that night would live in our memories for years to come, and offer comfort in the dark times ahead.

We arrived at historic St. George's Episcopal Church just before the preservice music. People filed quietly into the charming, nineteenth-century church on Princess Anne Street. The old wooden doors stood open in welcome. I brushed the golden-colored wood briefly with my fingers as I walked in behind Caroline and my mother. The wood glowed like honey in the light from the vestibule.

Walt was greeted by many of the parishioners, who often saw him there on Sundays. He smiled politely and wished them each a sober "Merry Christmas." I don't think he knew everyone who called to him, but he showed the same courtesy to all.

We walked with reverence into the nave, the worn wooden floor creaking and whispering in muttered prayer. I was immediately aware of a musty, yet not unpleasant, scent, like the smell of a venerable library. The scent of candle wax wound its way around us and up into the vaulted ceiling. Long brass candleholders, topped by glass chimneys, lined the two, wide rows of dark pews. The light of the candles warmed the air and filled it with a soft, golden glow. Walt stopped at one of the pews near the back of the church. Opening the tiny door, he gallantly gestured for us to file in.

I sat down on the heavy, well-worn bench with its high, unyielding back and tried to get comfortable. I must have squirmed for a few minutes because Walt glanced down at me with just a hint of a smile on his firm lips. I stopped instantly, returning his gaze with a sheepish grin.

Members of the choir began filing out into the sanctuary, taking their places in their own set of pews near the dark hulk of an old organ. That one was rarely used now. It was the rebuilt pipe organ above us that suddenly filled the church with the pure sounds of a Bach prelude. The vibrations of the music seemed to overtake my body and sweep through it, as though to purify any negativity left there by the dying year. By the time the choir had risen to sing, I had fallen into a deep meditation, only aware of my breathing and the lovely sounds pulsing around me.

Time lost its significance for a while. I had no idea how long I rested in this state, but the pre-service music was almost over when I became aware that Caroline was weeping silently on my mother's shoulder.

Alarmed at first, I looked helplessly at my mom. She held Caroline with one arm around her shaking shoulders and the other cradling a withered cheek glistening with tears. As she met my eyes I saw her serene face filled with compassion and love for my friend. I knew Caroline was sitting next to the right person. My mother had brought great comfort to so many people in her lifetime. Now she was there for Caroline, whose life held so little comfort and so much suffering.

My mother wiped the tears with tissues she had pulled from her pocket. Caroline smiled gratefully, taking Mom's hands in her own for a moment. By the time the choir had finished the performance, Caroline was back to her usual cheerful, almost childlike, manner.

I didn't remember much about the service itself, except that Walt took Caroline up to communion on his arm. My mother sat quietly praying, her face soft and glowing like the candle flames that illuminated her features.

Afterwards, Walt walked home, despite our offers of a ride. He said he wanted to "commune with the night". I understood. I drove Mom and Caroline back to the house. The sky sparkled overhead with stars, Orion standing tall and proud in the south. I was reminded that this day celebrated birth in the midst of the darkest time of winter. I wondered what new things would be born into our lives over the coming year. The world had become so promising that I began to cherish high hopes for all of us.

CHAPTER NINETEEN

Christmas morning dawned bitter cold. The dry smell of the electric heat soothed me as I lay silently in bed, my quilt pulled up around my ears. I thought contentedly of other Christmases, of my parents' warm smiles in the glowing lights of our tree. We each took turns, opening our gaily-wrapped presents one at a time. Each gift brought expressions of happiness and appreciation. My parents seemed especially delighted with the ones I had carefully made myself, with my own awkward hands.

Throwing the covers back I slid out of bed and grabbed my bathrobe. I skipped down the steps as eagerly as I did when I was a child. Mom had already started cooking breakfast. Caroline was just walking stiffly into the kitchen. "Merry Christmas!" she called happily. As she sat down at the table, I poured her a steaming cup of coffee. She inhaled its fragrance and sighed with contentment. I could not help feeling that Caroline belonged there, at my kitchen table.

The smell of baking cinnamon rolls filled the room with its pungent sweetness. As my mother opened the oven door, the scent seemed to roll out in a luscious cloud that enveloped the three of us. "Alright, Kate, you can put the frosting on these beauties," Mom said, after placing them on the counter. I rose to my task while Caroline set the table.

We ate with terrific appetite, probably sharpened by the cold weather. "It's supposed to be a very cold winter this year," Mom commented.

Caroline nodded, finishing her mouthful of scrambled eggs before responding, "Yes, I should probably go to Florida this winter. They say the whole East coast will have bad weather."

My mother and I exchanged a meaningful glance across the table. We had read each other's thoughts, apparently, because she started to nod agreement when I spoke. "Caroline, I was hoping you would stay with us this winter. Mom has a little house in Blacksburg and I'll be here...We would both be happy to have you stay in one of our homes."

Caroline swallowed the mouthful of cinnamon roll she had been chewing and looked down at her plate thoughtfully. When she raised her eyes to meet mine I knew she would refuse. "I love you both. You have been so kind and you've welcomed me like family. If I were not afraid of bringing danger to you..." She paused and shook her head resolutely. "No, I cannot allow anyone to be hurt by these people. I may have stayed too long already."

As I looked over at my mom I saw she still wore the same expression of serenity that usually adorned her features. Her eyes, however, glinted with suppressed tears. I turned to Caroline again. "I don't care about any danger. I care about you!"

A sad smile washed over her face. "I know you do. You're young and idealistic. I just want to make sure you get to be my age some day." She raised her hand to stop me from jumping in with a reply. "No, dear," she continued firmly. "My mind's made up. Besides," she added, brightening, "I have friends I haven't seen in a long time down there."

That was it. I knew that she would not have it any other way. At least I had tried, but Caroline was a strong-willed, street-wise woman. She had made her choice and would not waver from it. I admired her courage. Deep down, I felt a rising hatred of the men who had forced her to live this way. As a Buddhist I was supposed to hate the delusions, not the people caught in them, as these criminals were. But the hatred insinuated its way into my heart and I did not stop it.

After we finished breakfast we made our way into the living room where the tree glowed in its corner. The soft colored lights seemed to impart a message of peace to my soul. The angry spot dwindled in the love around me.

Beneath the outspread branches of the tree rested a handful of packages. Mom moved to the tree and bent to pick one of them up. She handed it to Caroline, who blushed happily and sputtered, "Oh, you didn't need to go to this trouble for me!"

She undid the paper carefully, as if it were going to be used again. Opening the box it concealed, her eyes lit up with surprise. "Oh, what a beautiful sweater!" she exclaimed. My mother had a sixth sense about gifts. She always seemed to give just the right thing. Caroline held up the sweater for us to see. It was a pale blue wool with delicately embroidered flowers around the neck.

"Real wool is so warm, you know. And it's hard to find these days.

Thank you, Melinda. This is wonderful!" Caroline held the sweater against her face to feel its softness on her skin.

Mom gave me a sweater, too. Only this one was cotton because I had an allergy to wool. She also presented me with a book written by the Dalai Lama, about anger, interestingly enough. Despite my Buddhist training, my Irish temper occasionally found expression, usually at the most inappropriate moments.

My mother seemed touched by my own gifts to her: a silk scarf covered with stars and a Tibetan prayer wheel of copper. Tibetans believed that every turn of a prayer wheel broadcasts the prayer inside and purifies the practitioner. "Lovely, Kate!" she said softly. "What a beautiful thought!"

Mom picked up a small package from under the tree. "Now those you must both open together," Caroline commanded mildly. Mom handed the gift to me and picked up its twin.

We glanced at each other and began to unwrap the paper. Inside we each found a silk pouch containing prayer beads. "One hundred and eight beads—I counted them," Caroline was saying. "I read that they represent the one hundred and eight Buddhist heavens."

My mother looked wonderingly at our guest and asked, "Did you make these?"

"Yes. A friend of mine helped though; I have a lot of trouble with my hands nowadays." Caroline blushed with pride.

"They're beautiful!" my mother exclaimed. "And so special since you made them!"

I felt touched by my elderly friend's efforts. "Thank you, Caroline. I'll think of you every time I hold them." I looked at the colorful beads strung together. A tassel of shiny red threads hung from the beaded circle that gleamed in the light from the tree. I looked into Caroline's shining eyes. "I'll treasure this always."

Mom picked up the last present and handed it to Caroline. As my friend took it into her gnarled hands she turned it over, mystified. It was flat, looking almost as if someone had just folded some wrapping paper over. Upon opening it she still seemed uncertain. "Why, what a nice picture of a bus," she said.

Mom and I both laughed. "Well," I began. "We weren't certain where you would be spending the winter. I remembered you mentioned going south like a bird, but we didn't know where." Caroline paused, open-mouthed.

My mother continued, "It's a bus because we wanted to give you your bus ticket to wherever you want to go."

"No," Caroline began. "This is too much. I cannot—"

Mom placed her hand gently on Caroline's knee. Looking steadily into her eyes she said simply, "Yes, you can."

After a long pause she nodded assent. "Well, I can't tell you how much I appreciate this. Thank you both!" Caroline embraced my mother and then me. "Thank you for one of the most beautiful Christmases I've ever had!"

Maybe life really was beginning to work out for Caroline. Obviously she had a lot of friends who seemed more than happy to help her out. If she would just relax and unbend a little bit, she might discover that the world was not such a bad place after all. Anyway, that's what I hoped would happen.

CHAPTER TWENTY

The week after Christmas passed quickly. I remembered wishing that the days would slow down for us. We had so little time left together. Of course we went out shopping a couple more times just to see all the decorations. An unexpected ice storm kept us in for the rest of the week. Caroline wrote a thoughtful holiday note to Aunt Maggie and a long letter to Franklin in Indiana. It needed two stamps. Walt had left on the twenty-sixth to visit his relatives in West Virgina so when New Years Eve arrived, it was just the three of us.

Mom stood in the kitchen stirring a kettle of non-alcoholic wassail, one of her specialties. The scents of cinnamon and apple filled the air. Caroline and I sat at the table happily munching the nachos that I had just pulled from the oven. "I love these," Caroline was saying with her customary enthusiasm. I always got the feeling that, to her, everything was new, even when it really wasn't.

"Wait 'til you try Mom's wassail. Your taste buds will feel as though they've reached full enlightenment!" I joked, in my idea of an Indian accent. I watched for my mom's reaction. It tickled me to see her blush; it happened so rarely.

My mother glanced at me as she shook her head. The slight blush that rose into her cheeks told of my success. "Really, Kate, you do exaggerate."

"Just calling it how I see it—or taste it, as the case may be," I answered, biting noisily into another chip. That one had a generous slice of jalapeno pepper and I relished its fire on my tongue, chewing deliberately.

Mom turned her gaze on Caroline, saying, "Do you have any special plans for the coming year?"

Caroline brushed some tortilla crumbs from her pale cheek. Nodding vigorously she responded, "Why, yes I do. After spending the winter down south I want to go back to Indiana to visit with Franklin. I might spend a few weeks there. He's always asking me to stay longer than I do. Besides, there might be some interesting celestial events to view at the observatory." She reached for another chip, pulling it from under a mound of cheese that stretched like taffy.

"How about you, Melinda?" she asked.

Mom paused with the wooden spoon poised in mid-air as she considered the year ahead. "I guess I just want to do my best in school," she answered, resuming her stirring. "I've still got two years left of vet school, so I'll have to keep my nose to the grindstone for awhile yet!"

"Just don't party too much, Mom," I teased. "I know how wild you really are!"

"Yeah, right, Kate." Mom grinned as she put down the spoon and took up the ladle. "Well, it's ready, let's see how it turned out." She pushed a baked apple into the bottom of each mug, and then ladled the fragrant liquid over them. Setting the first mug in front of Caroline, she turned back for the other two.

"Mmm," sighed Caroline, inhaling the rising steam. "This smells sensational!"

Mom sat down and sniffed approvingly. "It smells right, anyway."

We each sipped the hot wassail with care. It was certainly the best my mother had made yet, at least in my opinion. We savored it slowly. Caroline turned to me and asked, "What about you, Kate? What are your plans for the year?"

I gazed into the almost luminous brown liquid. I could just make out the shape of the baked apple at the bottom. What would my future hold this year, I wondered. Inhaling deeply of the spicy scent I dreamed aloud. "I think I'll finish my first novel in another month and start on the sequel. Meanwhile, I'll try to find an agent to help me sell them." I leaned back contentedly.

"Yeah. I'll sell the novels and some more short stories and then, when my books hit the Best Seller list, a big movie studio will decide to make movies of the books. Yeah," I murmured, closing my eyes as if I could see it all clearly in my mind, "that's what will happen. Then I'll buy an estate near Winchester, keep horses and write dozens of best selling novels. I might have to get into screenwriting, too, my books will be so popular..."

"Enough!" my mom cried, laughing. "All this in one year, Kate? What will you do in the next?"

Caroline smiled warmly. "Such nice dreams, dear. I hope you can make them come true."

We talked long into the night, almost forgetting to stop at midnight to greet the New Year. We hugged and wished each other Happy New Year while inside I wished fervently that all of our dreams could come true. I hoped that Caroline would find peace and stability somewhere, even if it was not with us. Though, as I formulated the wish, I had an uneasy feeling that it would never happen for her.

The next day I spent time catching up on housework; Mom helped out so I could get some writing time in. Later, she and Caroline sat in the living room watching television and talking while, at their insistence, I went upstairs to write. "You're not going to get 'The Great American Novel' written gabbing down here with us," Mom quipped. She gently took my shoulders and steered me toward the steps. "Get on with you, girl!" I grinned and obeyed meekly.

Settling down at my keyboard I slipped the disk into the computer and called up the file. As I reviewed what I had written in my last session, I began to lose myself in the story. My main character, the bold son of an Irish chieftain, was leading a raiding party against another clan. Little matter that it began over some stolen cows, there would be glory and enemy heads for all.

Soon my attention was riveted to my work and nothing else seemed to exist for me. I recalled hearing the phone ring a couple of times but my mother answered and must have taken the messages for me. She knew how absorbed I became in my writing. When I finally looked up at my clock radio I saw that four hours had passed. It certainly had not felt like that much time.

Night had already fallen outside. The air was clear and the moon shone brightly, turning the remaining patches of ice into mirrors reflecting its pure light.

After saving my work, plus a backup on disk, I turned off the computer and made my way downstairs. Mom was sitting close to Caroline with a hand on her knee speaking in low tones. She looked up at me as I entered the room and smiled, a tight little smile that told me something was not right. "Finally come up for air, huh?" she asked.

"Yeah," I answered. "Something going on?"

Caroline gave me a pained look. "A very dear friend of mine at Samaritan House is dying of AIDS. He's asked to see me. One of the directors just called to tell me. "

"I'm so sorry," I responded with sympathy.

She continued. "We knew he was not long for this world. Actually, the doctor was surprised that he made it through Christmas. He is slipping fast, so I need to leave as soon as possible. I'll call the bus station and see about a ticket."

I put up a hand, saying, "No, Caroline. Let me take you."

She nodded her head sadly. "Thank you, dear. I'm afraid I owe you so much for your kindness, I—"

I didn't let her finish the thought. "You don't owe me anything. I feel like you're a member of the family. Please, don't feel obligated to us."

We left early in the morning. There wasn't too much traffic, so we made good time. At Samaritan House I met her friend, Scott. He was hardly aware of what was happening around him. When Caroline took his hand, he recognized her and seemed to revive a little. He smiled wanly when she introduced me to him, but he could not speak.

He had decided he wanted to die at home, here with his friends. He was one of the founding members of The Samaritans. He never knew if he had contracted AIDS from dirty needles or unprotected intercourse. It really didn't matter. Either way, it was killing him, a man who had found his way off the streets and had devoted the rest of his life to helping others do the same.

Caroline spoke softly to her friend, bending down close to his face, one hand gently caressing his sallow cheek. I could not hear her words, but I could see that Scott took comfort in what she said. His eyes, bright with fever, seemed to soften and glow with an otherworldly light. He smiled serenely and relaxed his tense, frail body.

Gaige took me aside. We stood in the wide hallway on the old wood flooring that creaked whenever he shifted his weight from foot to foot, which, I noticed, he did quite frequently. I looked politely into his pitted face as he said, "Caroline has been a guardian angel to us, especially in the early days."

He must have seen the surprise on my face because he answered my question before I had a chance to ask. "Oh, yes. Didn't she tell you? That doesn't surprise me," he went on, speaking rapidly with lowered voice.

"Of course, she's never one to toot her own horn." His thin lips pursed into a rigid little smile. "No. But I'll tell you. She was with us from the first, encouraging us all the way. We all met in a shelter six years ago: Caroline, Scott, Sally, and me. We talked about what we needed to do to get off the streets and Caroline pushed us along, playing devil's advocate sometimes. She'd say things like, 'Ok, once you're off the booze, then what? What were you trying to treat with alcohol? Won't the depression come back? Where are you going to go from here to really get to the root of your trouble?'

"Man! She kept after us 'cause she knew we never wanted to live on the streets again. We resolved to help each other. We had to answer to Caroline, who kept asking if we'd gone to our treatment or our counseling or our AA meeting that week. She spent months keeping us on track. Finally, we realized that there was a terrible need for committed effort to keep street people from returning to their old ways. That's when Scott suggested Samaritan House.

"It started as a half-way house for reformed drug addicts and alcoholics. We lived together, made sure everyone got to their appointments with doctors, counselors and what have you. We also kept track of medications that any of the residents might need and made sure they got them and took them.

"It didn't take very long for us to start reaching out to the people in shelters, working in cooperation with a lot of the volunteer groups that help the homeless. Before we knew it, Caroline had helped us become a non-profit organization that could accept tax-deductible donations. Now we have three centers in Northern Virginia, one in North Carolina and we've got some people in Florida interested. Caroline will be going there this month to help them get started."

My eyes must have widened in surprise until they could not open any further, because Gaige looked straight at me and began to nearly choke with laughter. Trying unsuccessfully to suppress his mirth, he took my arm and led me out into the spacious living room. I could feel the heat in my face. I felt slightly annoyed at being the object of what must have been a great joke, but, more than that, I felt overwhelmed at the hard work Caroline had never even mentioned.

I looked around at the sparsely furnished room and noticed the smell of mildew from the donated furniture around me. In one corner three men were watching an old T.V. Gaige finally regained his composure and apologized, saying, "I'm sorry. I guess Caroline didn't tell you anything. It's okay. We respect her privacy, too. She's never told us anything about her past and that seems to be the way she wants it."

I understood that. Again I marveled in silence at the energy and dedication of this mysterious woman.

At this point she walked out to join us. Her face did not betray the sorrow I was sure she felt at the imminent death of her friend. "Well, you both must be having a good time getting to know each other. I heard a lot of laughter coming from this room," she commented wryly.

"I'm afraid this young lady has been sadly under informed of all the good things you've done," answered Gaige, a twinkle barely visible in his luminous brown eyes.

Caroline shook her head in mock exasperation. "You just can't keep quiet, dear," she said, as a blush rose to her cheeks. Turning to me she said firmly, "Now Kate, don't believe everything this rogue tells you. He is a bit of a storyteller around here." She winked at him as she took my arm and led me to the door.

"I know you need to get back to your work," she was saying. "I can't wait to read your novel when it's done."

I hugged her tightly as Gaige opened the door, letting in the frosty air. Caroline held me close for a long moment and whispered, "Now, you be careful out there, dear. I love you with all my heart."

"I love you, too," I answered, my voice catching in my throat.

As I stepped out the door, I turned and said, "Please—call me when you want to come back and I'll pick you up. And I'll be sure to have your ticket to Florida waiting for you."

Caroline smiled, "I will." She waved her frail hand in goodbye.

I tripped down the steps lightly and got into my car, pulling the door shut against the cold. I waved a gloved hand as I pulled away from the house and saw Caroline in the rearview mirror with her hand still raised in farewell.

CHAPTER TWENTY-ONE

Two days later I said goodbye to my mother when she left in her pickup to return to Blacksburg. It had been one of the happiest holidays of my life and I basked for days afterward in the warmth of its memory. When my housemates returned from their vacations I still felt warm and fuzzy inside.

Holly had gone skiing with her family in Vermont. They had a cabin near Stowe so they could ski without having to make reservations at an inn. She had come back bruised but happy, her usually fair face red with sun and wind burn. She had some special news for us. Her boyfriend, Bob, had proposed. She kept showing us her ring, a diamond surrounded by sapphires. We oohed and aahed over it, amused by the increased intensity of color in her already red cheeks as she blushed with happiness. Every time she said "Bob" her voice would take on a musical, dreamy tone. "Bob, Bob, Bob," sounded almost like a new song. We knew we'd grow tired of it, but it was funny and cute for a while.

Andy had spent her holiday with her grandparents in Charleston. Her grandmother was dying of cancer and wanted to spend some time with her favorite granddaughter. Andy seemed a little somber at first. She talked to us for hours about all the good memories she had of Grandma and all the vacations she had spent at her historic home in South Carolina.

I told them about my holiday with Mom and Caroline Rose and the revelations of her past at Samaritan House. I think they were as surprised as I had been to learn of all my friend had done to help other homeless people. "What a shame that she can't settle down and enjoy life herself," Holly said, still beaming from her engagement. She was so happy and in love that she wanted the whole world to share her joy. Maybe I would know that feeling someday.

We settled into our old routines quickly. I spent most of my time either at the library or in front of my computer. Walt had asked me to come by the next week with my research. I had fed him so many details of the cities of

Lhasa and Dharamsala that I thought we both would feel like we were at home there. However, I pushed the idea of a possible trip into the back of my mind. I didn't want to be disappointed if the dream didn't materialize.

On Friday we were greeted with freezing weather in the form of an "arctic express" that clutched us all in its icy grip. Temperatures dropped into the teens and the wind chill factor went below zero. Our heating unit just could not keep up with the cold, so we stayed wrapped up in blankets or winter coats to stay warm.

Sitting huddled in a quilt in front of my computer, I wondered how Caroline was doing, glad that she was safe among friends at Samaritan House. I was working diligently on the last chapters of my novel, eager to finish by the time I saw Walt again. In a way, I felt a little scared to show it to him. After all, it was my first effort in this genre. Maybe he would tell me to throw it out and stick to short stories and articles. I did take comfort in the memory that he seemed to like what he had read in November. Then again, maybe he would think I had taken it in the wrong direction, or he might hate the ending, or... These fears had to be typical for any beginning writer, I thought, and shrugged them off before once again losing myself in the work at hand.

We made it through the weekend, although I wondered if my fingers would ever feel warm again. The cold slowed my keystrokes a little, but we kept hot tea on the stove and hot coffee in the coffee maker. Frequently holding a hot mug of steaming liquid seemed to thaw my fingers enough to continue my writing.

On Tuesday morning we woke up to new problem- no water. My housemates and I searched the house but couldn't find a broken pipe anywhere. Down in the musty basement we stood looking at each other in a circle of dim light from the bare bulb overhead.

Andy shook her head, her tiny braids bouncing back and forth over her shoulders. She had hurriedly pulled a black, leather coat on as she ran up the stairs to awaken me. I thought the gray elephant slippers added an interesting fashion statement, but then my brain was too fuzzy to operate in a serious manner at six-thirty in the morning.

"Look," she was saying, pointing at the pipes we had just finished checking. "We'd better call Chad. He'll have to take care of it." Chad Hollins was our landlord, who lived, conveniently, just down the street.

Holly, in a teal ski jacket that seemed to match her eyes, agreed sleepily. "Okay, I'll call him."

We trooped up the narrow steps and into the kitchen. I looked hopefully into the pot for some leftover coffee. Not even half a cup remained. Andy laughed at the expression on my face. "It's okay, Kate," she comforted. "We've got plenty of bottled water, although I never thought I would make coffee with designer water."

"That'll probably taste pretty good," I answered, brightening.

Holly chattered cheerfully into the receiver. I wondered how she could sound that perky about our water problem. Listening to her end of the conversation, I gathered that Chad was not too happy to be called this early in the morning. Holly, however, in her engagement heaven, could very likely have soothed the most savage of beasts. Chad was a snap.

"Thanks a lot, Chad. See ya in five minutes," Holly gurgled happily into the phone. She hung up and turned to us, saying, "He's on his way!"

The three of us had always appreciated Chad's integrity and good nature. He repaired things when he said he would and never grumbled about his tenants. He owned two other houses in town and we had not heard one complaint about them. We thought he was a prince among landlords. He was probably one of the few who received Christmas presents and cookies from his tenants.

True to his word, Chad rang the bell five minutes later. Andy opened the door and quickly shut it after him to keep out the arctic blasts of wind that swept down the street. He was fully dressed in his typical work clothes, worn jeans and flannel shirt, and ready to go to work.

A middle-aged man of medium height, Chad had never married. He owned his own landscaping business, which he seemed to enjoy thoroughly. I think he also liked the break he had during the off-season. "Thanks for coming over so quickly, Chad," Andy was saying.

"Well," our landlord drawled in his Houston accent, "Ya gotta have water." He gestured with his flashlight. "You checked for leaking pipes?"

"Yeah," Holly answered. "We didn't find any leaks, and we looked everywhere we could think of." She indicated the entire house with outspread hands.

"Well, let me look around, but I think it may be a problem for waterworks." He sauntered into the bathroom and opened the cabinet door. First, he tried turning the faucet on but, of course, nothing happened. Squatting down on the floor, he switched on his flashlight and peered under the sink. After turning the valve and trying the faucet again, he nodded. "Well, you're right about that."

He checked the main valve in the basement, as a matter of course, and then asked for the telephone book. Apparently city waterworks was swamped with similar calls. As he hung up the phone Chad shook his head helplessly. "They say they can't come over 'til tomorrow, at the soonest. Damn."

I had never heard Chad swear before. This must have been a grim situation for him to use even one expletive. I watched him thinking to himself for a moment, absently turning his flashlight in his hands. He seemed to reach a decision because he nodded his head and began to speak in his drawly tones. "Do you ladies have a place to stay around here? 'Cause you won't have water for at least a day."

We looked at each other, hoping that one of us had the answer. I could probably stay with Walt, but I didn't feel I could ask him to take all of us. Holly was the first to speak. "I have friends on campus. I'm sure they'd let me stay with them, but what will you two do?"

I was about to open my mouth when Andy spoke up suddenly. "Jane and Mike live a couple of blocks over." She gestured toward me. "They have plenty of room. I bet they could take both of us."

"You better check and see if their pipes are okay," Chad said pointedly.

In fifteen minutes we had placed our calls and made our plans. Holly went to stay at Custis dorm on campus while Andy and I walked two blocks away to Jane's house. Chad had stayed with us until he was sure we had places to go. He seemed very protective, a trait engendered, no doubt, by the crisis at hand.

CHAPTER TWENTY-TWO

Jane Puckett had graduated with my class four years ago. We actually never met until Andy introduced us a year ago at a party. She seemed reserved, almost formal, so I found it hard to believe that she and her husband, Mike, were bikers. They belonged to a group of Harley-Davidson fanatics, who often traveled together to various motorcycle gatherings around the country. While they didn't participate in the less edifying activities, such as the annual polecat contest, they did enjoy riding and hanging out with fellow bikers.

I never asked, but I think Mike was in his mid-forties. He worked for a government contractor out in Dahlgren. His specialty was radar systems, but out of the office he spent most of his time riding or working on his Harley-Davidson hogs. His wife usually helped him with the bikes when she wasn't out assisting a local photographer. She hoped some day to have her own photography studio.

It was not difficult to feel welcome in their home. Both were very easy-going, Mike seemed fond of saying, "Live and let live, just share the road." He liked how it turned out to be a message to share the road with bikers and also to share the road of life. A simple philosophy, it suited him well.

Fortunately, Jane's computer had the same word processing software as mine. When I told her I was working on my first novel she became very interested, insisting that I use her computer. "Feel free to use it as long as you want. I don't even need it this week," she said, turning it on to show me how the system worked.

I spent most of the day at the keyboard. As I neared the end of my first draft the words seemed to flow even more quickly and smoothly from my mind. Andy had to remind me to stop for dinner.

We had brought some supplies from our own freezer. I slipped a frozen dinner into the microwave and fell immediately to thinking about the ending to my novel. I started when the timer beeped, having already forgotten the food.

"Hey, space cadet," Andy said, grinning. She stood at the stove cooking in the more conventional fashion. "I hope you finish that book soon." She tapped her head with an index finger. "It's affecting your mind!"

I laughed good-naturedly, reaching into the microwave to pull out my dinner. As I peeled back the plastic cover, the steam burned my fingers. "Ow!" I cried, popping them into my mouth to cool them.

Andy shook her head in mock disgust. "Like I said," and she lowered her voice to a stage whisper. "Better finish it soon!"

I slept on the couch in the den, curling up in three blankets. Andy grinned broadly and teased, "You just have to be near that precious computer, Kate!" But I knew she understood. Intensity was a trait we shared. She patted me on the shoulder. "You go, girl. I can't wait to read it! We'll be there, helping out at your book signing." I appreciated the encouragement. I couldn't wait to be finished. There was only one more chapter to write.

In the morning I rose eagerly from the couch and slid into the comfortable office chair at the desk. I inhaled the fragrance of the honey-colored oak as I flipped the power switch. My backup disk was seemingly sucked into its slot as the computer came to life under my gaze.

I gathered my thoughts for a moment, and then began typing with an almost regular rhythm as the story flowed out of my mind and onto the screen. I didn't even pause long enough to activate the screen-saver. I had become completely absorbed in the work.

Andy walked into the den at one point and stopped suddenly, probably startled to see me up so early without benefit of caffeine or breakfast. She knew that I was fond of both in the morning. She started to speak, must have thought better of it and left the room. I had hardly been aware of her presence except as a blur in my peripheral vision. Without responding I continued my train of thought.

A little while later Andy returned, set a cup of coffee on the desk and left. I think I murmured a soft, "Thanks, Andy." Like I said, she understood intensity.

In two hours I finally did take a break to eat and get dressed. Andy had left for the library and both Jane and Mike had gone to work. The weather couldn't keep the determined workaholics from their appointed tasks.

Though quiet, the house seemed to pulsate with energy. I imagined that it must be the energy of creativity, surrounding me and filling me with its own life-force. Whatever it was, it carried me to the end of my last chapter before anyone had returned home for the evening.

Andy walked in the front door just as I sat back in the chair to watch the laser printer spit out the last pages of my work. "Hi, honey, I'm home!" she shouted in her best Ward Cleaver imitation. I knew she didn't care if anyone else heard her besides me.

"How was your day, dear?" I answered, also in character.

She stepped into the den, pulling off her black leather gloves and stuffing them into the pockets of her coat. Her face lit up with a brilliant smile as she noticed the papers sliding out of the printer. "Are you done, Kate?"

A broad grin spread across my face, possibly in danger of slipping off and landing on the floor. I felt as proud as if I had produced a number one bestseller with promise of a movie contract. "Well, it's just the first draft." I could feel my face growing warmer by the moment. "Now I've got to start rewriting."

"How long will that take?" Andy asked with honest interest.

"Until Walt thinks it's ready. Who knows?" I shook my head, sighing with the joy of having gotten this far. "But it shouldn't be too hard now that the story itself is down on paper."

Andy gazed at the screen, beginning to read my closing chapter, when the telephone rang. "I'll get it," she said as she hurried into the kitchen to pick up the receiver.

I closed my file and slipped the disks into my canvas briefcase. It had become my novel's home away from home, and also contained the growing hard copy of my book and my research notes. My last chapter sat cradled on the printer. I added it to the rest of my manuscript. With a sigh I straightened the pile and held it in my lap, a feeling of satisfaction flowing through my body. It wouldn't last very long, but I enjoyed my moment. Whether the story proved to be good or bad didn't matter right now. I had done it. I had written my first novel.

As I placed the papers carefully into the briefcase, Andy walked into the den again. She had taken off her coat and stood in the doorway with hands in the pockets of her bib overalls. "That was Chad," she said flatly. "He says they haven't gotten to our house yet. They think they can do it tomorrow."

"I guess a lot of people are having the same trouble. It's in the newspaper." I got to my feet, picked up a copy of the paper and handed it to Andy. "On the front page."

"So you actually took time to read the paper?" she asked, incredulous.

"Yeah, I picked it up when I had lunch." I grabbed my coffee mug and started in the direction of the kitchen. At the doorway I paused. "Hey, have you checked our messages by any chance?"

Absorbed in the article she mumbled, "Yeah, I listened earlier. Walt called; that's it."

Still flushed with pride, I called my mother that evening. "I'm so proud of you, honey!" she said. I could hear the happy tones in her voice. They would have been there no matter what I told her, but it seemed especially nice to hear them that night.

"I'm really excited about getting this far, but I am a little scared to show it to Walt," I told her, once more expressing my doubts.

Mom's voice sounded practical and reassuring. "That's natural with anything we create because we reveal parts of ourselves in the work. You know what I'm going to say, Kate."

I smiled, realizing that I had already repeated this answer to myself hundreds of times. "Yeah, but I want you to say it anyway, Mom."

"Don't worry about what anyone else thinks. You've accomplished something very special. How many other people have written a complete novel? There are probably a lot of unfinished 'great American novels' out there stuffed in drawers and file cabinets." Mom always had a way of turning any situation into a victory.

"Thanks, Mom. I knew I could count on you to say the right thing."

She laughed softly into the phone. "That's my job!"

I asked her about the weather down in Blacksburg. Apparently they had experienced more snow than ice. My mother loved the snow. She and her friends had gone sledding on campus with some of the younger students. I could imagine her face pink and glowing with the cold and excitement. I thought her voice had taken on a younger tone as she spoke of the events of the past few days.

"Have you heard from Caroline?" she asked suddenly.

"No," I answered. "I imagine she won't budge until the weather clears."

We talked a little longer. Mom wished me luck in my meeting with Walt. "He's such a kind man," she added.

"Yeah, he is." I hoped Mom didn't catch the sudden emotion in my voice. Walt had become more to me than a kind teacher. I just didn't dare admit it to myself, much less to anyone else. My relationships with men had always seemed problematical at best. Keeping my distance felt safe but hardly satisfying.

We said our good-byes and I promised to call and let her know what Walt thought of the novel. Though she was eager to read her daughter's first book I insisted that I couldn't send her a copy until I had done at least one rewrite. She understood.

As I curled up on the couch for another night away from home I thought of what wonderful things the future might hold for an aspiring, young writer. My thoughts drifted away from my fantasy career to the people who couldn't make their dreams come true. I began to wonder how the homeless were managing to survive in the terrible weather this past week. Caroline had always found her way, but what about those who were not equipped with her kind of ingenuity? What were they doing on a cold night like this?

Despite my fleeting happiness, my dreams were restless and filled with disturbing images. I found myself walking through dark streets trying to find Caroline and her friends at Samaritan House. The house had been destroyed and all its residents were living in cardboard boxes in dirty alleys. I brought blankets to them, but the blankets turned to ashes as I gave them out.

I awoke in a cold sweat. Something felt wrong; I didn't know what. I got up from the couch and dressed quickly. The rest of the house would awaken soon. It was six AM. I downed a quick cup of coffee, hardly tasting it. Telling myself I was just nervous about my book, I decided that I would start editing it that morning.

Mike walked into the kitchen at that point, greeting me with a smile and a nod. "Up early this morning, I see."

"Yeah—couldn't sleep anymore," I answered in clipped tones. "Thought I could get some work done."

Mike poured himself a cup of coffee and sat down at the white-painted table. "You look jumpy," he commented. "What's up?"

I glanced up from my blueberry muffin, noticing that the hand that held it was shaking slightly. "I don't know why, but I guess I am."

"Worried about something?" he asked.

"No—maybe—I don't know!" I answered, a little confused. "Had a bad dream. Maybe I'll feel better once I get to the computer."

"Nothin' like work to ease the spirit. Go for it, Kate."

I stood up suddenly. "Yeah. Thanks, Mike." I wrapped the muffin in a napkin and set it on the counter. I could eat it later after I had calmed down. Still wondering why I felt this way, I walked out of the kitchen. I decided that the best thing to do was to go back to my house and pick up an extra package of paper before starting the editing process. Besides, I wanted to leave my hosts with a good supply of printer paper in exchange for monopolizing their computer. I hoped the water line would be fixed soon. I hated to impose any longer on Jane and Mike.

The sky was just lighting up with pinks and yellows as I made my way carefully over the ice-covered paths. In the dawn color the hard-packed snow and ice looked more like some giant had spread pink sherbet over this part of the world.

As the house came into view I quickened my steps and promptly lost my footing, landing painfully on my rear end. "Damn!" I muttered. I pounded the snow with a gloved fist and pulled myself to my feet. Finally I reached the door and fumbled with the lock, performing the proper combination of pushing on the door while turning the key and knob. Well, it was cold and the lock was worn.

Once inside I went straight up to my room and picked up the paper. When I came back down I strode into the living room, remembering the phone message waiting for me on the old answering machine. I jammed a finger into the button and heard the familiar sound of the tape rewinding. It took a little time. There must have been more than one message. Walt never spoke very long on the machine.

I smiled when I heard his rich baritone fill the room. "Hey, there, Kate, it's Walt." As if I needed him to identify himself, I thought with a chuckle. "Let's postpone our meeting until next week. The weather should be better. Call me and let me know how the book's coming along."

At first I didn't recognize the next voice. "I'm calling for Kate O'Brien. I thought you should know—Caroline took the bus down this morning to see you. She said she'd go to Florida from there. It's Wednesday and this is—well, I guess you remember me—Gaige from Samaritan House. Anyway, I told her to wait for me to drive her down or have you come up and get her but you know Caroline—strong willed lady. No one can tell her 'no.' Keep an eye out for her—" and there the machine had cut him off.

"Wednesday was yesterday..." I heard myself saying aloud. My heart began pounding against my ribs as though it were a bird intent on escaping from its prison. With the cold last night, where would Caroline have stayed? "Oh my God!" I whispered and ran from the house.

CHAPTER TWENTY-THREE

I raced to the car, slipping on the icy path. Desperation seemed the only thing that kept me on my feet. The door handle stuck with the ice. I yanked on it. The thick coating cracked, fell to the ground and shattered. I prayed the car would start. It hadn't run in two days. As if in answer to my urgency, the engine roared to life almost immediately. I silently blessed my mechanic and all of his progeny for generations to come. He had kept the car in top condition, perhaps just for this emergency. My stream of thoughts churned wildly as I wondered what could have befallen my friend. Despite her many strengths, I knew she was still quite vulnerable.

The icy streets had been sanded recently so I could drive almost up to speed. I made my way to the bus station just a few blocks away. Perhaps Caroline, after finding me not at home, had stayed there overnight. Homeless often took refuge in places like that.

The bus station looked deserted when I arrived. Getting out of the car, I slammed the door and hurried over to the small building to take a look inside. I slipped, not on the ice—that had been cleared from the parking lot—but on the sand and dirt coating the floor of the station.

"Are you okay, miss?" the attendant asked in a solicitous tone.

With my heart pounding in my chest I could barely speak. "Yeah, fine." The attendant, a middle-aged woman with a pronounced southern accent, immediately noticed my agitation.

"Something wrong? Can I help you?"

"I hope so." I described Caroline to the woman, who listened thoughtfully. "She came in yesterday. Did you see her by any chance?"

Shaking her head, she replied, "No. I haven't seen anyone of that description around. But I came in around three yesterday, so I could have missed her." She called across the room to a man sitting in the far corner.

"Otis! You see an older woman like that yesterday?"

Otis, an old man as creased and worn as the newspaper on which he sat, rose slowly to his feet. Deep in thought, he took his time answering the question.

"Otis stays here when it's really cold and he can't make it downtown," the woman explained in an aside.

"No, Linda. I don't s'pose I saw anyone like that." As he moved closer I could smell the foul odor that seemed to accompany many of the homeless people I had met. He shook his head, the gray locks swinging stiffly over his shoulders. I took an involuntary step back.

Fixing me with bloodshot eyes, possibly brown— I really couldn't tell— he continued. "If she didn't get down to the shelter she probably found another place to hole up. It was too damn cold last night to stay out, that's fer sure." He gestured to his head. "She's okay up here, ain't she?"

I nodded. "Yeah. Actually, she's a pretty smart lady."

"She'll be fine, then. Don't you worry none, little girl. She'll be jess fine." I didn't find his words reassuring.

Turning to the attendant I got an idea. "Do you have a phone book?"

She pointed behind me to a public telephone. On the shelf underneath sat a faded phone book. "You can use that one. Do you have some change?"

"Yeah. Thanks." I crossed the room and flipped the pages to find the number for the shelter downtown. Perhaps Caroline had gone there. I fumbled with the coins, finally getting them into the slot. My hands were shaking again.

"No, ma'am. I'm sorry," said the volunteer when I asked for Caroline. "No one by that name came in yesterday. In fact, we didn't get any transients last night. I guess it's too cold to travel."

With sinking heart I turned to the attendant once again. She shrugged helplessly. "I hope you find her. This is a bad time to be out."

The old man waved a hand at me and shuffled back to his corner, muttering, "Bad time ta be out in the cold. Bad time."

Thanking them both, I returned to the car. Maybe I shouldn't be looking for her. Maybe I should just put a note on my door and wait at Jane's. No, that didn't seem right either. But where could I look?

I sat motionless behind the wheel for a moment. I couldn't understand my nervous state. Caroline was a smart woman. She knew how to survive in any weather. "Think, Kate, think!" My voice felt strangled with a growing fear. Where would she be? My mind wandered back to the day I had first met her. Could she be out panhandling for bus money at her accustomed spot? I steered the nose of the big station wagon toward the highway and eased out into the sparse traffic.

Turning off onto Route 3, I headed to the mall, where I had first met my friend. In my mind's eye I could see her, out on this cold day holding her cardboard sign. It probably read, "Need money for bus to Florida." I glanced at the clock on the dashboard. It was around seven-thirty.

I passed over the interstate, watching both sides of the highway for any sign of Caroline. I created a picture in my mind of finding her at the intersection. She would be cold and maybe up for a hot meal somewhere. Her eyes would shine with delight when I drove up to her. I smiled. I could see it all so plainly.

I was still smiling at my fantasy when I noticed the birds. A group of big, black birds occupied a stretch of open land in front of the import shop. I'd never seen so many before in one place. My breath began to come in short gasps. My heart beat slowly and painfully in my chest. They were vultures. I pulled off the highway into a small parking lot.

Some of the birds just stood quietly, as though waiting their turn. The center of the group was active, obviously at work on some hapless, dead creature. No, I told myself. It couldn't be a person there. Someone would have seen and stopped them. But I noticed that the central group plied their grisly trade out of sight from the highway, on a downward-sloping piece of land.

Fear grappled with my mind, constricting my movements. The car door seemed to slam shut in slow motion. I was hardly aware of my body as I walked over to the birds. There must have been about twenty of them, big, black, with naked heads and wrinkled throats.

Suddenly, I began to run, tearing off my coat and shaking it. They moved away reluctantly, flapping their wings in almost half-hearted strokes. The great birds settled only about ten yards away, glaring sulkily at me for having interrupted their meal. Hesitating, fearful to look upon the sight that awaited me, I turned to the pile of rags and flesh left by the vultures.

The walking shoes I knew. How many miles of pavement they had tread for their owner, I could not have guessed. The purple coat, now torn and stained rust-red, had been her favorite color. Under the pink, knit cap, still tied tightly under her chin against the cold, a fringe of white hair fell, matted with frozen blood.

Anger welled up in my chest. I hated the vultures, which stood on the ice preening their shining feathers. They had torn the flesh from the face I had grown to love so well. They had scattered clumps of bloodied, white hair around the body. They had torn through the coat for the flesh beneath it.

I looked away from the horrible sight, away from the birds, and felt sick. The hollow feeling that began in my stomach seemed to expand, carving out my insides until I felt completely empty, like a cast-off shell. I took a step closer, then another, and draped my coat over her body—the body of Caroline Rose.

CHAPTER TWENTY-FOUR

I stood there, motionless. How long, I could not tell. I was alone, not even aware of the sound of passing cars. All that I could hear was the rustling of glossy feathers and the petulant mutters of the carrion birds. They waited, hoping I would leave so they could finish what was left.

Standing in the cold of that winter morning, in a timeless world of emptiness, I hung poised before the shockwave of grief. I did not even know what sights my eyes beheld in that moment. Their messages had no power to impress themselves onto my brain. I stood waiting, waiting for life to start up again, even if it only brought pain.

Then, behind me, I heard a car door slam and footsteps struggling hastily through the hard-packed ice and snow. "What is it?" came a voice in masculine tones. "It's not— oh, my God!" The last words came out in a choked yelp of shock and pity. I turned to face the newcomer.

He looked away from the grisly sight, only partly covered by my coat. His breathing came in short gasps. "Oh, my God," he whispered over and over again. I merely stood and watched, unmoved and unmovable.

Suddenly, I felt his touch on my arm. Our contact brought me to the agony of reality. I exhaled as though I had been holding my breath for a long time. The tidal wave of grief crashed into its intended target. I looked into his face, which reflected the sorrow that had finally struck my heart with its crushing blow. Hot tears stung in my eyes despite the cold around me.

"Are you okay?" the stranger asked.

I could not speak for a moment. I nodded my head, hoping that would relinquish any obligation for response.

"I'll call the police from my car phone," he said and hurried off. He probably felt relieved to do something and get away from the terrible reality that still lay at my feet.

"Oh, Caroline!" I heard myself whisper. "Caroline!" I dropped to my knees, only feeling the icy cold beneath them from what seemed a long distance away.

I marveled at the courage of the man, who returned to stand at my side. I felt his hand on my shoulder, assuring me that someone cared about this tragedy that had torn my friend from the sufferings and comforts of her troubled life. Strangely, I seemed most aware of the movements of the vultures, who still stood nearby. One at a time they began to flap off into the cloud-filled sky. They would circle and then fly west, toward the country, perhaps hoping to find other, more available, carcasses from which to feed.

I lost feeling in my knees and lower legs as the cold seeped into them and tried to claim them for its own. It did not concern me. My mind was with Caroline. We were traveling on the bus to Indiana, in my car to Newport. We were sitting on the stone bench watching the sea birds wheel and cry over the sound. My hand sought the prayer beads I wore around my neck, the ones she had made with her withered hands.

They felt warm with the heat of my own living body. My lips moved in silent prayer. I could feel her gentle presence and a greater Presence. In my mind they met and merged as one. Caroline had gone beyond, where I could not follow. I prayed that she went to a joy she had rarely known on this earth, in this life. But I did not know.

Distant sirens sounded in the brightening daylight. They neared and ceased their insistent whine. I heard the police cars park below where I knelt still on the ice, without feeling but filled with pain.

"Oh, my God!" the officer exclaimed under his breath when he saw the remains. I wondered why everyone kept saying the same thing when they arrived at this tragic scene. Perhaps I shouldn't have wondered. Who else should they call upon at a time like this?

Several officers arrived. The local medical examiner came soon after. A sensitive man, he usually spent his days caring for children as one of the city's leading pediatricians. Today his task was a grim one. Yet, as I watched him gently remove the coat from her face to look directly, courageously, into the reality of Caroline's death, I saw a compassion that convinced me he cared about my friend. To him she was not just some anonymous corpse. She was a human being with all the loves, joys and pathos that status implied.

I watched, horrified and gratified at the same time, as the good doctor made his cursory exam. When he finished he laid a gentle hand on her shoulder for a moment, as if in silent blessing. He looked over at me, meeting my eyes with his bright, blue ones. A wave of understanding passed between us. "You knew her?" he asked softly.

"Yes, she was my friend."

An officer walked over to us. "It's cold, Miss. Why don't you put this on?" he said quietly. He knelt by my side on the ice and held out a police jacket. Mechanically I slid my arms into the sleeves as he pulled it on. I hadn't noticed that I was shivering.

The officer turned to the doctor, saying, "Tire tracks over there," indicating the highway with his head. "And footprints her size by the side of the road. Looks like a pickup truck skidded on a patch of ice and plowed right into her."

The medical examiner nodded. "I'll be there in a moment. You've called Homicide, then."

"Right. He's on his way." The officer's gloved hand felt reassuring as he held my elbow to help me up. "We've got to get your statement, Miss." We walked to one of the squad cars and he opened the front door. As I slid into the seat he spoke across me to another detective.

"This is Kate O'Brien. She found the body. She knows her." He gave me an encouraging pat on the shoulder. "The detective will take an initial statement if you're ready." With that he closed the door and walked back to the scene, now outlined with yellow police tape.

"I'm Detective Brower," began the older man behind the wheel. His iron gray hair stood in short waves, which he occasionally brushed back with a thick hand. "I'm sorry you had to be the one to find the victim. It's terrible to see that." He pulled a pen from his flannel shirt pocket and clicked it open. After jotting something down on his notepad, he looked up at me.

"So, you knew her?" he began.

"Yes." I pushed the grief away. Somehow I had to get through this without losing control. I answered his questions tonelessly, empty of all feeling: of love, of tenderness, of pity, of anger. I felt none of these in that moment. I felt nothing.

I remembered feeling this void inside once before, at my father's funeral. I remembered the casket draped with lilies. All around me I saw the pitying looks for the poor, fatherless girl. Their faces bore the sorrow they felt for me and my mother, but what made me look away, even at such a young age, was the realization that the sight of us was painful to them. In a way, the widow and her child were no longer persons but human-shaped pain.

Maybe I judged the other mourners rather harshly. What I did learn was that grief carried with it a complex web of feelings, difficult to sort out. In fact, I had spent years trying to make sense of the conflicts they aroused in me. On this day, I held them at bay for as long as I could.

I had to think carefully when Brower asked me Caroline's name. At first I simply answered, "Caroline Rose. No, not just that; there's more," and I sat silently, trying to recall the name the retired detective had mentioned when we met him at the Newport Creamery.

"Just relax. You'll remember," he told me, leaning back into the seat. I noticed he had begun to doodle absently on the pad. I followed the graceful lines of his pen, mesmerized. A lotus flower began to take shape on the paper. He glanced at me and stopped suddenly, embarrassed. "I'm sorry. It helps me relax."

"It's beautiful," I commented. I could feel a hint of a smile curling the edges of my mouth. I bit my lip and the feeling vanished.

I thought back to that chance meeting in Newport. I remembered the strange look in Detective Burkette's eyes as he gazed at Caroline. It was the only time her face had hardened into an unrelenting mask. "Oh, yes, I do remember. Caroline Rose Spencer Dawes. That was her full name." I watched the thick hand write it down, not even hesitating over the spelling. "Her mother loved roses," I added, in explanation of her middle name. Caroline had told me that when I had brought her up to Samaritan House, the last time I ever saw her.

"A lovely name," the detective responded gently. He glanced out the windshield at the young policeman, who made his way toward the car carrying something in a large plastic bag. He opened the back door and slid his burden into the seat behind me, saying, "Your coat, Miss O'Brien. Uh...it's a little messy."

"A cold water wash should clean that up, if it's washable," Brower added helpfully.

It seemed strange to be so mundane about Caroline's blood on my jacket. Of course, I would have to wash it off. "Thanks, Officer," I mumbled.

The young man shut the car door again and walked over to a pick-up truck, speaking to the emerging driver. I watched, disinterested, as the officer pointed in our direction, and then walked off. The other man zipped his navy parka closed and hurried toward us.

Detective Brower opened his door and stepped stiffly out of the car. "Stacy!" he called. "Where the hell have you been?"

CHAPTER TWENTY-FIVE

The newcomer slapped Brower on the arm and shook his hand. "The doctor. My kid sprained his wrist falling on the ice." The man stooped, as tall men often do, as if to make himself shorter. I had slipped quickly out of the car during their interchange, glad to breathe the fresh air again.

Holding out a thin hand to me, the newcomer introduced himself. "I'm Detective Stacy. I'm going to have to ask you some more questions down at the station." He glanced at the other detective and added, "I hope this old bear has been polite to you."

I supposed he meant to lighten the situation with the comment. I just ignored it and waited to be told what to do. I really didn't care where I was or what I did at that point. Glancing up the hill at the scene, I noticed that Caroline's body had been taken away. "Where are they taking her?" I asked impassively.

"Richmond. The autopsy will be done there. Does she have any family?"

I shook my head. "Not that I know of." I slipped my hands into my pockets and shivered in the cold. Brower walked around the car to speak with his associate.

"Excuse us, please," Stacy said, and they both moved away from me, deep in conversation.

Detective Stacy took me to the police station in his truck. It still smelled new when I climbed in the cab. He drove cautiously down the highway. There seemed to be about half the traffic as usual at this time of day. Most people had obviously decided to stay off the still icy streets.

The detective tried to engage me in conversation, talking about how his two children spent every day outside sliding and scraping up snow and ice to form tiny snow people in the back yard. I nodded politely and turned to look out the window, not really seeing anything. My gaze focused inward.

If only I had been home for Caroline. If only I had paid more attention to the answering machine instead of focusing obsessively on my novel. Why hadn't my friend called before she had come down, to make sure I was there?

I recalled her words to me before our trip to Indiana. "You're not responsible for me," she had insisted. She was my friend. Of course I had a responsibility to help her, no matter what she might have said. Surely she had not wished to die like this. My mind whirled in tormented tangles of thought. Then, abruptly, reality broke into my inner world. We had arrived at the police station.

Detective Stacy led me into a small office and asked me to sit down by his desk. He hung my borrowed jacket over his parka on a nearby chair. I noticed the pictures of his family sitting on the desk in clear, plastic frames. Everything about him seemed spare, even the unadorned frames.

He looked older than he probably was, judging by the ages of his children and the pretty young wife, smiling with her arms flung round his neck, in the picture. I guessed him to be about forty-five, though his hair had turned completely gray. He looked into my face with a pair of piercing, slate-blue eyes and spoke softly. I could feel the compassion in his tones and in the kindly expression on his lined face.

"How long had you known Ms. Dawes?" he asked.

"I met her last April." I sat up a little straighter in my chair. "On the street," I added, for no particular reason.

"And, as far as you know, she has no family?"

"She never mentioned any living family members," I answered.

"Then they're dead?" His eyebrows arched up toward the straight hair that fell in careless strands across his forehead. I was fascinated by the man's eyes and the movement of the thick brows over them.

"Oh," I started, struggling to pay more attention to the questions. "Yeah. They were murdered, actually." As soon as I had offered the last information, I wished I could have called it back. There was no use in bringing up an old case, especially now that I knew it also involved my father. In fact, I began to feel I had made a dangerous admission. But the detective, whose eyebrows had risen even higher at my statement, pursued the new line of questioning.

I told him the whole story of Caroline, her husband and son. I talked about the murders and the embezzlement of all her wealth out from under her. He took copious notes with a black fountain pen, all the while nodding and moving his eyebrows up and down. I, of course, omitted any connection to my father's murder.

"So, she never told you any names?" he asked more than once.

"I don't remember any, if she did," I insisted. Perhaps Caroline had mentioned the name of her personal business manager but nothing came to mind. That was probably fortunate.

Detective Stacy had some carryout brought in from a nearby Chinese restaurant. I thanked him, but found I could eat no more than a few bites of the fragrant food. "It's okay," he assured me. "You've been through hell today."

"Was that what it was?" I murmured, almost to myself. He, on the other hand, had eaten heartily, and now he sat pulling a fortune cookie apart.

"'You will meet a beautiful young lady,'" he intoned in a prophetic voice, holding the thin strip of paper at arm's length. Middle-aged eyes, I thought to myself.

I shook my head and almost smiled, "It doesn't say that."

"Well, it should," he replied, his eyes twinkling for the first time since I had met him. "Let me take you home. You look tired."

He was right; I was tired. I needed some time alone to process the day's shocking events. Soon, I would lose the firm control that had gotten me through these hours without becoming a hysterical wreck. I knew I had to get away from the crowded station before that happened.

Detective Stacy dropped me off at the parking lot next to my car. "Are you sure you can drive home okay?" he asked.

"Yeah, I'll be fine." I looked into his deep-set eyes, recognizing the understanding there. "Thanks." He nodded.

I looked around the parking lot. Curious onlookers craned their necks for a glimpse of the crime scene before they walked into the store. Those leaving the shop glanced back over their shoulder at the police tape flapping in the cold wind. I thought it likely that none of them knew what had happened there. They had no idea of the tragic drama that had played itself out on that icy bit of land. I envied them.

CHAPTER TWENTY-SIX

Tossing the bag containing my bloodstained jacket into the back seat, I slipped behind the wheel, slamming the door behind me. My movements felt automatic, as if I were not really the one performing them. I was only an observer. Someone else drove down the highway, slipping now and then on the sand more than on the ice. Another person carried the bag up the steps to the house and unlocked the door.

The distant feeling had gotten me this far, but it disappeared as I dropped my burden on the carpet. Tears flowed down my cheeks, raw with cold. I felt my body begin to shake as my mind played, over and over again, the scene of Caroline's death. I thought I could hear the rustle of the vultures' wings and their low mutters. Why had this happened to my friend? Why did she have to die like that—alone, in the cold, with only carrion birds as witness?

Some time later, the front door opened and Holly walked in, a cheerful smile on her face, her cheeks rosy with the weather. I raised my head from the couch. I really didn't know how I ended up kneeling on the floor with head and arms sprawled on the sofa.

When our eyes met, her face reflected shock at my appearance. "What happened?" she cried in dismay. I wiped my sleeve across my wet face. "Are you okay? We were so worried about you. We expected you back this morning..." she trailed off, reaching for my arm to help me up.

"It's Caroline, Holly. She's...she's dead!" The tears started again and I let them fall. I no longer cared who saw me like this.

"Oh, my God! How? What happened? I'm so sorry!" Holly strove to comfort me, hugging me tightly as if to give me some of her own strength.

Haltingly, I told her what had happened. Holly's face mirrored mine as tears began to roll down her cheeks. She sat with me on the couch, holding my hand in hers, struggling to understand this terrible turn of events.

"How horrible!" she exclaimed when I told her about the vultures. "Oh, how awful for you to have found her like that!"

I raised my tear-stained face and whispered hoarsely, "I should have been here, Holly. I should have been here." Over and over that one thought rolled through my mind. I felt as though I had caused her death. I had killed her by not being at home when she stopped by. My shoulders sagged with the heavy burden of guilt.

Holly grabbed my arms firmly and shook me to add emphasis to her words. "It is not your fault, Kate." I watched her lips moving as if I could not understand by hearing alone. "You are not to blame. You didn't know. She didn't call before she came down. You can't blame yourself for her death."

I was not yet ready to believe her but she had sown the seeds of doubt in the fertile ground of my self-blame. I hoped that I could come to believe her words eventually, but it wouldn't happen today.

When Andy arrived home from work a few minutes later, I had calmed down enough to repeat the tragic story with Holly's help. "Oh, no!" Andy whispered, holding her hand to her mouth.

Holly rose from her station at my side and gestured toward the plastic bag on the floor. "The water's back on and your jacket needs to be washed before the stain sets in. Why don't you let me do it?"

I looked into her shining eyes and smiled slightly. "Thanks, Holly, but I'll do it. I'm okay now." Rising slowly, I picked up the bag and walked to the basement door. I turned to my friends. "You guys are great." Then I made my way down the creaking steps to the washing machine.

The musty air in the basement carried a sharp, icy odor. I shivered involuntarily as I passed over the cold cement, feeling a damp current flow through my sneakers and up into my feet and ankles. The bag rustled with a dry whisper, as I set it on the floor.

The jacket had stayed sealed in the bag for several hours. As I untied it and reached for the garment, the metallic scent of dried blood rushed into my face. I recoiled in revulsion, brushing my cheeks with my hands. I noticed they were shaking slightly. "Damn it!" I muttered to myself, annoyed that I had reacted like that. "Don't you have any guts, girl?" and I pulled the jacket out with a ferocious yank.

Spreading it out on top of the washing machine, I scanned it for stains. The inner lining bore two, large, rust-colored splotches, with smaller spots scattered around and between them. As I reached for the treatment spray,

I noticed a small tuft of gray down. It waved delicately in an invisible current of air. Slowly I plucked it from one of the large stains to examine it in the light.

The feather felt soft, as fragile as a spider's web. I rubbed it between my fingers and the dried blood that clung to it came off. I had never thought much about vultures before. It hadn't occurred to me that they might have the same kind of down feathers that protected other, more beautiful birds. They, too, were living creatures that needed food and warmth to survive.

My thoughts fled back to our bus ride to Indiana last April. We had talked about so many things. I remembered how Caroline had known a surprising amount about the Tibetan people, including their practice of sky burial. Yes, it seemed to make sense somehow. My friend had expressed her appreciation for this strange, seemingly gruesome custom. Perhaps it was fitting that this homeless woman had, at her death, experienced that tradition of giving to other living beings.

I placed the feather in my pocket and continued the task at hand, suddenly dismissing these thoughts from my mind. She was still dead. I didn't want to find comfort now in any philosophical flights of fancy.

The lid of the washer thumped shut with a peculiar sense of finality. I rested my hands on the machine, feeling the vibrations of the water as it poured in. I shut my eyes as if I could shut out reality with that gesture. Though I could wash Caroline's blood from my jacket, no cleansing could wash the sight of her torn body from my memory.

"Caroline!" I whispered, the tears starting again. I dropped my head onto my hands. "Why didn't you call me?" The washer continued filling. There was no answer.

CHAPTER TWENTY-SEVEN

I must have stayed in that position for some time because when I finally raised my head to stand up, my back and shoulders had grown stiff and sore. The washer dial indicated the end of the rinse cycle. For a few moments there was silence, then the basket began to spin.

I turned quickly and headed up the stairs. As I opened the basement door I heard the insistent ring of our telephone. Andy's voice answered in the living room. I could see her from where I stood in the hall. She raised her head to meet my gaze. Gesturing with the receiver she said, "It's Walt. Do you want to talk to him?"

"Yeah," I returned, walking slowly into the room. Taking the phone from Andy's hand, I tried to make my voice sound normal. I was not successful. "Hey, Walt. Sorry I haven't returned your call..."

"What's wrong, Kate? Your voice sounds strained, like you've been through an emotional wringer lately." Walt knew me frighteningly well.

"It's Caroline. Something terrible happened!" I blurted out the last sentence, suddenly fighting hysteria.

"I'll be right there," was all he said before he hung up the phone. I held the receiver to my ear for a few seconds as though I had forgotten it was there. Andy watched me from the couch, a questioning look on her face.

"He said he's on his way," I answered the look, replacing the receiver in its cradle. Within ten minutes, he rang the bell.

Almost as soon as I opened the door, I was enveloped in Walt's powerful arms. My cheek rested on the wide, shearling lapels of his heavy coat. The scent of leather became stronger as my tears dampened its soft surface. Walt's reassuring tones fell on my ears like a soothing balm. "I'm so sorry, Kate. I'm so sorry," he repeated over and over again.

Somehow I found myself on the couch, sitting with my hands enclosed in his. He had become my shelter in the storm, a port of safety and reason in a suddenly senseless world. I dried my eyes and blew my nose without embarrassment in his presence. It was safe to be human, even with a broken heart.

Holly made her own version of hot buttered rum and brought it into the living room for us. I sipped the rich liquid gratefully. It helped me relax, briefly creating a fuzzy distance between me and reality. A little anesthesia seemed appropriate at this point, I remembered thinking.

Walt listened carefully to every detail of the day's events. I could see compassion reflected in his eyes, which today, carried a sea-green hue in their depths. The warmth of his hands seeped into my body and sent waves of healing energy through me. I was glad that he had come over so quickly and I told him as much. "Of course," he answered simply.

After feeding us a supper of carryout from his favorite Italian restaurant, Walt reluctantly decided to go home. He offered to spend the night on the couch but I refused. "I'll be okay, Walt. I really will," I insisted.

"Are you sure?"

"Yes, Walt. Go home." It was sweet of him to offer, though. I hugged him goodbye. I still felt a little buzz from the alcohol. It seemed to help. I was removed enough from the pain to face the other tasks I had set for myself that night.

Holly gazed into my eyes a moment. I felt a responsibility, as the oldest housemate, to reassure her. "I'm gonna make it, Holly." Patting her on the shoulder, I took a deep breath. "Now, I guess I've got some phone calls to make." I did not want to make them; I dreaded making them, as a matter of fact. But I knew I could never sleep until I had called Franklin and the guys at Samaritan House.

"Phone's all yours," Andy called, as she strode down the hall to her room.

"Okay," I muttered aloud to myself, "you can do this calmly." But I wasn't convincing myself.

Going upstairs to get the numbers, I returned to an empty living room. The girls had made themselves scarce. I could hear Andy's television. Casting a glance down the hall, I noticed the flickering light coming from beneath her door. I envied them both at that moment. They could lose themselves in front of the magic box. With a sigh I turned to my own task.

"Hello, is Gaige there?" I asked an unfamiliar voice at Samaritan House.

"Yeah, I think so. Let me round him up for you."

I could hear the radio in the background and a heated discussion between a man and a woman, something about her boyfriend and a baby. I didn't catch very much of it before Gaige came on the line.

"Kate, hi! You got my message," he called into the phone.

"Yeah, Gaige," I spoke evenly. "Yeah, I got it..."

The voice on the other end quickly became guarded. "Uh, is everything okay down there?"

"No." I inhaled sharply, forcing back the emotion. "Gaige...Caroline's dead. I don't know what happened, hit-and-run or something, but she's dead."

There was a long silence. I heard a choking sound as he, apparently, struggled to retain his composure. "When?" he asked tightly.

"Early this morning they think. There's an investigation." I felt separate from all feeling again.

"I...uh...when's the funeral service?" His question startled me. Of course, someone would have to take care of the final arrangements. It hadn't occurred to me that I would be the one.

My hand gripped the receiver more tightly, as if by sheer strength I could exercise control over the situation. "I don't know yet. I'll call Franklin and see if she told him what she would want...in this situation." Franklin might know, I reasoned. They had been quite close.

"Alright, Kate. Let me know, please. And we'll try to plan something here, too." I could hear his heavy intake of breath. "And if you have any kind of service, I'd like to be there."

"You bet." I tried to sound casual and in control as I said it. "I'll talk to you soon."

"Thanks. I know this has got to be hard on you." He paused. "You know, she thought the world of you." The receiver clicked as he hung up. I clutched the phone. Its smooth reality seemed to anchor me in the world that must always continue.

Well, one call was finished, now for the other, more difficult call. How do you tell someone that the person they love most in the world has died? How could I break his heart with my words? I punched the numbers almost angrily and listened to the phone ring on the other end.

When Franklin's voice answered, unsuspecting, I almost hung up. "Hello?" he had to repeat.

"Uh, hi, Franklin. This is Kate, Kate O'Brien."

"Yes!" he cried happily. "How nice to hear your voice!"

"Well," I said, pausing momentarily. "You won't be happy to hear what I've got to tell you."

"Caroline..." he whispered, as if he already knew the rest of the message.

I told him gently about the accident. I spared him any knowledge of the scene where I found her body. If he never filled his mind with the horrible image of the carrion birds feasting on her remains, he might simply see her lying still, as if in peaceful sleep.

In our Western culture, being eaten by vultures is viewed as an ignoble end, a fate for an unloved and forgotten person. As much as I respected the Tibetans and their unique culture, my American sensibilities prevailed.

I felt removed by more than physical distance from the choked sobs I heard over the line. I had wept all I could weep. I was wrung dry, like an over-used dishcloth. The soothing tones of my voice came automatically, as if from someone else. The empty feeling that had begun that morning took over completely, shutting off any remaining emotion. It was probably for the best. There are limits to the amount of emotional stress a person can tolerate.

Practical concerns made their way to the forefront. "Franklin," I began carefully. "Do you know what Caroline might have wanted...uh," I paused delicately to find the proper term. "For her final arrangements," I concluded. Those words seemed polite and correct, removed from reality.

Franklin hesitated, changing his own mental gears to match my practical train of thought. "Yes, actually, she told me once, a few years ago, that she wanted to be cremated and her ashes..." he trailed off into a pause that suggested thinking rather than sorrow. "Yes, she wanted her ashes scattered at a beautiful, natural spot, preferably a river or stream."

"Then, shall I carry out her wishes here?" I asked.

"Well, I'll send you money for the cremation. She did not want a service, as such."

"I think Samaritan House will hold a memorial for her," I added.

"Yes, of course, she meant a great deal to them." He paused before starting in again, as if remembering another detail. "Oh, Kate. Please wait awhile before disposing of the ashes."

I thought that a peculiar request, but I was prepared to comply to the best of my understanding. "Okay," I began, drawing out the last syllable to communicate my need for more details.

"I'll be able to give you further instructions later." When I did not respond he continued. "I know it sounds kind of strange, but I can't tell you what needs to be done with them yet. I assure you I'll know soon, but until that time I can only ask you to be patient and keep them."

I shook my head, wondering what meaning might lie behind his words. However, I had grown used to the sense of mystery surrounding Caroline Rose. This seemed exactly in character. For the second time that day I smiled, feeling nothing more than deep affection for my friend. She had helped me expand my tolerance and appreciation of the human family. I never knew what new insights would crop up in her regard. Now I had another puzzle that future events might or might not solve.

Franklin's voice brought me back to the conversation with a suddenness that startled me. "When will the coroner return the remains?"

"I don't know," I answered. "The detective was not sure himself. It had to go down to Richmond for autopsy."

"Oh. Well, please call me when they give you more information. I'd like to know. In the meantime, I'm sorry I can't come and help you deal with the funeral home. I'll send the money as soon as you can tell me what it will cost." He, too, had taken on a business-like tone. Practical matters require dispassionate words.

We finished our conversation with promises to stay in touch. When I replaced the receiver, I felt an incredible sense of relief that I had discharged my duties for the day. Slowly, moving almost as in a dream, I made my way upstairs to take a shower and finally, crawl into bed.

As I lay gazing up into the darkness, I thought of my father and the stories he would tell me. I brought his image to my mind, taking comfort in the remembered sound of his voice. I could hear him telling me one of my favorites, about an undersized dragon.

I remembered almost all of his fantastic tales. I used to tell them to myself every night after he died. Why hadn't he written them down? It occurred to me that maybe I should do that for him, but after what had happened...I just didn't know if I could do it.

The tears fell from my eyes, making my pillow wet. I sat up and dried my face with my sleeve. Turning the pillow over, I pounded it with my fist. How could I have ignored my friend on that fateful night? How would I ever come to peace with what had happened to her—and to my dad? I lay down again and, after turning a few times in a vain attempt to get comfortable, fell into an exhausted sleep.

CHAPTER TWENTY-EIGHT

Surprisingly, I slept soundly that night. My dreams were filled with images of Caroline: in Indiana, in Newport, and at home in Fredericksburg. We walked the streets in those cities and did simple things like eating, talking and sometimes just sitting. We watched the waters of Rhode Island Sound. In the dream I didn't think it strange that the Rappahannock ran into it. When I awoke, my mind seemed preoccupied with that peculiar uniting of two, far-away bodies of water.

Suddenly, I felt, as though a hand had gripped my stomach as I remembered that Caroline was dead. I struggled to breathe, fighting the tears that threatened to fill my eyes again. No, I wasn't going to start this again. I reached for a book of Tennyson's poems. Escaping the memory of yesterday's events, as well as my dreams, was foremost in my mind. The world of Tennyson was so far away from this one. I knew I could lose myself for a while in the musical imagery that poured itself over my aching brain in soothing waves, like some sort of literary opiate.

I don't know how long I read. Reality finally edged its way into my consciousness. I sighed, set the book back on the nightstand and got out of bed. I dressed for the day—jeans and a ratty old sweater. What would I be doing today, anyway? Maybe coffee could offer some comfort, I thought, as I headed downstairs.

Walt was waiting for me in the living room. Good thing I had dressed before leaving my room. "I wondered when you would wake up. It's ten-thirty already." He greeted me with a warm smile.

"Walt, hi. What...how long have you been here?" I stammered in astonishment.

"I called about an hour ago. Holly told me to come on over."

I glanced across the room at my housemate. "Thanks for telling me," I said in a tone of mock exasperation.

"Any time!" she replied, rising quickly from her chair. She cast a knowing glance at each of us and hurried out of the room.

I watched her leave, puzzled at her look. "Well, guess she had some pressing business," I mumbled, mostly to myself. Glancing down at my sweater, I wished I had put on something a bit newer than that old thing.

"Actually," Walt began. "I came to take you to breakfast. I thought you might not think about eating and…maybe you wouldn't mind the company."

I forgot the sweater. Walt always seemed to know the right thing to do. I wondered if he had any idea of how much I would not mind his company. "Sure. I'll get my coat..." I hesitated on the stairs. I couldn't bring myself to wear the one I wore yesterday, even though the stains were gone.

Walt must have sensed my thoughts. "It's not that cold out today. You don't need a heavy coat, since you're wearing a sweater."

I brightened at the suggestion and hurried up the stairs. I had a thick denim jacket hanging in my closet. I grabbed it hastily from its hanger.

He took me to a nearby restaurant that served, in Walt's considered opinion, the best omelets in the city. Apparently, the man had a good appetite that morning, too. He ate a huge western omelet with toast and extra ham on the side, while I picked politely at my plate. I remembered his food better than mine.

"You've got to keep your strength up," he admonished between mouthfuls.

"Yes, Dad!" I teased, halfheartedly. The coffee smelled good to me. I focused on that for a while.

Gently he tried to divert my attention from yesterday's events. "How's the novel coming?" he asked.

I paused, then pressed my lips together as if to shut off the answer to Walt's question. When I glanced at him he was watching me closely. "Yeah, it's done," I answered bitterly. "It probably cost Caroline her life, but it's done."

"What's that supposed to mean?"

I looked him squarely in the eye and told him the whole story of the past two days. I told him how proud I had felt when I had finished my first draft and how my achievement turned to ashes in my mind when I found Caroline's remains.

He nodded and said nothing for a moment. "So, that's where you're going with this." Taking a deep breath, he seemed about to launch into a lengthy discourse but stopped. "No. It won't help to hear me tell you all the reasons why what you just said makes no rational sense. Reason has no part in your interpretation of events right now." He placed his hand over mine. His eyes spoke volumes. I clung to their message of love and hope as I clung to Walt's powerful hand.

"You're in a lot of pain right now, but you are familiar with loss, with this kind of grief. Did you blame yourself when the police came to your door to tell your mother that your dad was dead?" Walt looked steadily into my eyes. I nodded slowly, a dry chuckle shuddering in my chest.

A trickle of understanding edged into my mind as I remembered the seven-year-old girl standing behind her mother, while the officer explained my father's untimely death. "My dad had gone out to a convenience store for a couple of things. I begged him to bring me back some chocolate ice cream." I stopped and shook my head.

"I thought you were allergic to chocolate—"

My look stopped him in mid-sentence. "They found him by the freezer case, shot right through the heart."

I shook my head, fighting back the tears from that day. "You know what a little girl will think for the rest of her life: if she hadn't teased Daddy for ice cream, he might have left the store before the hold-up. He might have come home alive that night." I started to laugh, a mirthless laugh that shook my shoulders and the hand that still held on to Walt's. "I don't have any allergies. I just can't..." I shook my head in a helpless gesture.

Concern showed plainly on his face, along with the pain he must have felt at seeing my grief. I relaxed my grip on his hand and straightened up in the booth. "It's all right," I said softly. "I finally came to understand that I had used guilt to keep out the greater pain of loss. Maybe that's what I'm doing now. I'm not torturing myself; I'm trying to protect myself. If I focus on guilt, I won't feel her loss so much." A small, rueful smile curled at the corners of my lips. The movement of the muscles felt almost painful, like an involuntary cramp rather than a willing act of smiling.

"If you understand that, then you have gained an important insight—one that most people never see." Walt's features relaxed as he gently pulled his hand away to reach for his wallet. He eyed me with a look that suggested analysis rather than kindness. "Then you really don't require any of my rational reassurance." He smiled. "Actually, I'm relieved."

When we returned to the house I found a message from Detective Stacy on the answering machine. He wanted me to come down and claim Caroline's handful of belongings. Walt gallantly offered to take me to the station.

I enjoyed riding in his Suburban. Higher than most of the surrounding cars, we seemed removed from the masses of vehicles that lumbered down Route 3 through the sand and slush.

The detective came over to help me retrieve my friend's personal items. "I don't think you want this," he said, as he showed me a cardboard sign with Caroline's elegant handwriting almost crying out in denial of what was written: "Need money for trip to Florida."

I stared at the sign. Caroline had refused to let us buy the ticket for her before I took her to Samaritan House. She had insisted that she wasn't sure when she was going and didn't want us to go to the expense. She wouldn't even accept the money for a future ticket. When she was sure she was going, Caroline had said, she would come down to Fredericksburg for our gift. I wasn't about to argue with her. She always had a clear idea of how she wanted things done. I didn't find it at all surprising that, seeing I was not home, she had gone out to find the money herself.

"Yes, I do want it," I told the detective, taking it slowly from his hand. "I'd like to keep it." I signed for her other possessions, which included the wallet I had given her for her pictures, fifty dollars and Franklin's gift, *Great Expectations*. Stacy took us back to his desk.

"So far, we've pieced together her last several hours but we still can't identify the vehicle. We know it was a full-sized pickup, but that's all." The detective gestured for us to sit down. He remained standing, his hands gripping the edge of the desk.

Apparently, Caroline had been seen at the entrance to the shopping mall with her sign the afternoon before her death. A local fast-food restaurant manager had given her something to eat when he saw her trudging by that evening. He was struck by her bright smile and her gracious manner. "He almost couldn't believe she was homeless when she spoke with him," the detective added.

"That night, a stock boy in a nearby grocery store saw her sleeping in a corner behind some boxes. He didn't have the heart to disturb her." Stacy straightened and stroked his chin thoughtfully with a nervous hand. "The young man said she smiled at him as she walked out of the store before dawn. He wondered if she had known that he'd seen her in the stock room."

The detective shifted from one foot to the other, dark eyebrows moving up and down with his thoughts. He finally sat down in his chair, musing, "She was a pretty resourceful lady—knew how to take care of herself. The piece of cardboard came from a gas station on Route 3. She'd borrowed the pen there, too. Everyone we talked to, who came into contact with her, thought she was very friendly. They didn't mind helping her out." His voice expressed a deep admiration for Caroline and her ability to survive on the street.

Walt smiled at her memory, adding, "She was a charming woman, Detective."

"So I hear. I would like to have met her myself. After all this investigation, I almost feel as if I had!" He chuckled softly under his moustache. "Well, she would have been just fine if the truck hadn't skidded on a patch of ice. She was headed east on three when she was hit. Speed must have been a factor, too. She was thrown pretty far from the road."

He fixed his gaze on me. "The coroner is certain that she died instantly. I thought you might find some small comfort in that."

I did. At least Caroline hadn't spent her last moments on earth bleeding her life out on the icy ground, while the vultures gathered for the inevitable feast. I wondered if she had been on her way to see me. The fifty dollars in cash had probably come from her day of panhandling outside the mall. That wouldn't have been quite enough for the bus.

"They'll have the body ready in a couple of days," the detective continued in measured tones. "We'll need the name of the funeral home so we can arrange to have it brought back up from Richmond."

I nodded slowly. "Yes, of course. I'll let you know this afternoon."

"That'll be fine, Miss O'Brien." Detective Stacy rose and offered me his hand. "Good luck. It's not a pleasant task ahead of you." He shook my hand firmly with a crisp efficiency that did not exclude kindness. Then he reached for Walt's outstretched hand, "Nice to meet you, Mr. Cleary."

As we walked out of the building I felt a sense of relief that this part of the ordeal was over. At least I thought it was. I received another call from the officer at eight the next morning.

"Miss O'Brien." I recognized the efficient tones in his voice. "We need you to come down to the station this afternoon. There seems to be a new development in the hit-and-run case."

CHAPTER TWENTY-NINE

"Did you find the driver?" I asked, surprised at hearing from Detective Stacy this early.

"No, not yet. The Newport Police Department is sending someone down who specifically asked to speak to you." He spoke in a professional manner but I thought I could hear a hint of curiosity in his voice.

"Do you know what this might be about?" I asked.

"They've re-opened the Dawes double murder case."

I stiffened instinctively. For a moment I almost forgot the man on the other end of the phone. How much did they know about the murders? "Uh, when do you want me to come in?" I asked, remembering that I was still in the middle of a conversation.

"Their man should arrive by three this afternoon. We would like you to come down then."

"Okay," I agreed reluctantly. I really did not want to become embroiled in this old case. I feared that it might lead to questions about my father's murder. "I'll be there."

I decided to take a short jog to help calm my nerves for the afternoon. I hadn't been out running for weeks; I had been too busy with my writing. It was cold, but I didn't notice. As I ran, the events and worries of the past two days seemed to slip into a new perspective. There was really no reason for the Newport police to suspect any connection between the two murder cases. I pushed it out of my mind, denying the possibility.

I began to relax, enjoying the movement of my muscles and the warmth that seemed to radiate from my legs through my whole body. The air felt clean as I inhaled it deep into my lungs, expelling my breath in steamy puffs that I imagined hung in the air after my passing.

I took my time showering, perhaps to cleanse my spirit as well as my body. The water fell on my skin in a satisfying hot spray of warmth and purity.

By the time I walked out the door and down the short, stone pathway to my car, I felt renewed, ready for any challenge that I might have to face. At least I thought I was. As I opened the car door, I noticed a forest green minivan parked in front of the next house. I pulled away from the curb and thought nothing of it. Someone just visiting the neighbors, I supposed.

The path to Detective Stacy's office had become all too familiar. The door stood open expectantly. Pausing on the threshold, I peered into the corner where his desk sat under its weight of paperwork. The detective leaned on the nearby file cabinet, talking earnestly with a stout, older man, sitting in the same chair where I had endured most of the questioning about the case. I knew, before the man turned around to greet me, that the Newport police must have pulled him out of retirement just for this assignment.

Better to take the bull by the horns, I thought. "Detective Burkette," I called with more confidence than I actually felt. "I thought you were retired." As he rose from the chair I moved closer and held out my hand. He clasped it with a firm shake. He nodded, but did not smile.

"Well, young lady," he started in his deep, sonorous bass. I wondered if he had a singing voice to match those tones. "I didn't think I would see you again."

I smiled thinly, "Believe me, I find our meeting...equally unexpected."

Detective Stacy indicated the other chair. "Please sit down, Miss O'Brien. Since you've already met Detective Burkette, I can skip the introductions." He settled into his own chair, glancing at the open folder in front of him.

He glanced at Burkette, then turned to me and began, "Apparently, as I've been told, you are familiar with the unsolved murder of your friend's family. Mrs. Dawes refused to cooperate with police once she entered rehab. When her husband died, she was the only one who could have identified the murderers."

Detective Burkette took over the interview at this point. "Your friend's husband had come to one of my associates just before his death. He showed him documents that proved these people were using his business to launder drug money." He fixed me with a stern gaze. "His wife denied any knowledge of these documents after his death. She disappeared and we never found them among Mr. Dawes' papers. Did she tell you anything about this case?"

My eyes were drawn to the open file on the desk. I could make out Caroline's name on the top sheet of paper. Shifting my gaze, first to the tall detective, then to Burkette, I drew a deep breath. "Yes," I answered, almost guiltily. "She told me a little bit about what happened." I remembered the fear and pain in her old eyes as she had revealed this tragic episode of her life.

Burkette's gaze did not waver. I felt trapped by his look. "Well?" he intoned relentlessly. "What did she say?"

Dropping my eyes to the cluttered desk I told him everything that Caroline had shared with me that windy day when we had sat on the rocks overlooking Narragansett Bay. Detective Burkette remained expressionless during the whole story. I fought to control my emotions, speaking in almost a monotone. Looking into the old man's eyes, I felt as though I were defending my friend's honor. As I finished the tale, I explained how frightened Caroline had been, not only for herself, but also for her friends.

Burkette leaned back thoughtfully in his chair. His bulk seemed to settle like a ship come to rest on a sandbar. Cradling his chin in a large hand, he turned his eyes to Stacy. "So, that's the story," he commented quietly. The two exchanged a meaningful glance.

"That's all I know," I said, spreading my hands to emphasize my words.

"She gave you no papers to keep for her?" Burkette asked, but without hope for a positive answer.

"No. No papers, nothing to keep for her." I returned his look with an expression that, I hoped, conveyed my lack of further knowledge.

The detective persisted. "Did she have any other friends with whom she might have left any personal papers?"

I felt the tension in my forehead as my eyebrows knit together. I hadn't thought of that. "Um...maybe. She has, I mean, had, an old friend in Indiana. Franklin—yeah, she might have left something with him."

"Do you have his phone number?" I could hear the renewed hope in his voice.

"Yes," I replied, fumbling in my pack for the slip of paper with Franklin's number. I had left it there even after I had recorded it in my address book back home. I handed it over to Burkette, "Here it is, Detective. He's known Caroline a long time, much longer than I have." I felt relieved to shift the focus of his questions away from me. Let Franklin deal with this man.

He squinted at the writing for a moment and nodded his head. "Well, thank you Miss O'Brien. You've been, uh, helpful."

I rose quickly, eager to leave. I was just turning toward the door when Burkette's look stopped me. He raised his eyebrows. "Actually, I have just one more question."

My heart seemed to drop like a lead weight in my chest.

"Just one more thing, Miss O'Brien. Do you know of any connection between your father's death and the murder of this woman's family?"

CHAPTER THIRTY

I stopped. It seemed to take an eternity just to draw the next breath. His eyes glittered with a cold light. He knew. Indicating the chair with his hand, he settled back into his own. I sat down heavily, trapped, wondering where this line of questioning would lead.

"I knew there had to be something we had overlooked. Going back over the records, I noticed that a business card had been found on the body."

I shifted nervously in the chair. The old man inhaled deeply, like a smoker taking a long drag on a cigarette. "We still had Dawes' appointment calendar. Flipping through it, I discovered several meetings with the accountant named on the card." He fixed me with a stern look. "He was Sean O'Brien, your father, I believe."

I nodded. My mouth had gone dry.

"When I got the report from the Providence police, I noticed something odd about your father's murder. Very strange, in fact." He rubbed his chin with his hand. "It was described as a convenience store robbery gone bad, and that seemed to fit—except for one thing."

He leaned forward, grasping the arm of my chair. I felt my body shift away from him. I could smell garlic on his breath, and a scent that I often associated with old men.

"They forgot the money. Or they never intended to take it in the first place." He pulled back. I relaxed slightly.

"Now, I had to think about this one. The two men came in, handed a bag to the cashier and ordered him to fill it. According to the cashier's report, one of them walked straight up to your father, looked him over, raised his gun and fired point blank into his chest. Not once, but three times." I winced at the picture his words conjured up for me. I had never heard these details before.

Burkette went on, relentless. "Three shots. Then he went over and kicked him with his boot to make sure he was dead." I pressed my hands to my forehead as if to shut out the sound of his words. "Three shots" rang in my brain over and over again. I almost thought the detective was still saying it to torture me. But he had stopped talking and sat quietly, watching me with his cold, impenetrable gaze fixed on my face.

Then someone broke the silence. Someone far away choked on the sob that racked my chest. I realized I was struggling to speak. "I never knew..." I sucked in my breath and held it a moment to calm my quivering nerves. "I never knew that."

Burkette's gaze softened slightly. "I thought you did."

"Caroline told me once that he was killed by the same people who killed her family." I looked squarely into his eyes. "That was all I knew until now. My mother spared me most of the details. I suppose she meant well."

The detective ran his fingers through his sparse hair. "Apparently she also spared the police. She didn't mention anything about it to them, either."

"Maybe she felt they should do their own detective work," I returned, with a hint of bitterness creeping into my voice. His eyebrows shot up at my words, but he did not answer.

"I'll need her number so I can question her as well."

I nodded and wrote it out on a slip of paper. Handing it to the old man, I stood up. My legs felt weak. "May I go now?"

Burkette nodded. "I've had very few unsolved homicides in my career. This is one I don't mind coming out of retirement to finish, if I can."

He shook my hand and walked me to the door. Patting me on the back, he said good-bye. "You know," and he paused, his bear paw of a hand resting on my back. "I knew it was her that day at the restaurant. If I hadn't had my grandson with me I would have followed you." He pursed his lips thoughtfully. "Now I wish I had."

I gave him a polite nod, feeling an incredible sense of relief when he withdrew his hand. I walked out of the building and got into my car. I sat quietly behind the wheel, breathing slowly to calm myself before driving off. As I pulled away from the curb I glanced in the rearview mirror, noticing a green minivan parked on the opposite side of the street. I tried to put the interview out of my mind. There was research I had to do at the library.

One of the things I liked most about writing was that it gave me an opportunity to learn about subjects that interested me. Walking into the library, with its smell of books, always brought a spring to my step in eager anticipation for new research. That day I had to find more details on international law regarding treatment of prisoners of conscience. Walt wanted to include several chapters about Tibetan political prisoners in his book.

I soon became engrossed in my studies. Several hours passed without my notice. The work took my mind off recent events so much that I actually dreaded the return to reality when the library finally closed for the night.

Carrying a tall stack of books in addition to my backpack, I made my way carefully to the car. My muscles relaxed in relief as I dumped the stack in the back seat and swung my pack to the floor. I slammed the door shut and turned to open the front door when I heard a step behind me.

As I glanced back I saw, in a flash of movement, two men leaping toward me. I felt a damp cloth cover my face and glimpsed a green van pulling up. My body slumped and I knew no more.

CHAPTER THIRTY-ONE

The first sensation that eased into my awareness was the cold, smooth feeling of leather on my cheek. I felt removed from my body for a few moments while the effects of whatever drug had been used wore off. My head ached as I raised it slowly. A powerful light was directed into my eyes.

"She's awake," I heard a voice nearby. It sounded more like a growl than an actual human voice. Shaking my head to clear it, I squinted beyond the light.

All I could make out were three figures, just shadows against the opposite wall. They appeared to be seated. Beside me the growl sounded again. "Sit up!" and I was roughly jerked upright. The light was too bright for me to see my surly captor. I sat rigidly on what I perceived to be a leather couch.

From across the room one of the figures, the tallest shadow, spoke quietly to me. "I must apologize for the roughness of my associate. He takes his work very seriously." His voice was business-like, but pleasant. "I have a few questions to ask you. Answer them truthfully and you will have nothing to fear from him."

"Of course," I commented dryly, struggling to stifle the terror that made my breath come in short gasps. Slowly I gained control, forcing myself to breathe deeply to relax my body. If my suspicions were correct, I would most likely be killed by these men no matter what I did. Better to die calmly than in a panic, I thought.

"I understand you were a friend of Mrs. Carol Dawes," the tall shadow began. I still had trouble relating that foreign name to the woman I knew as Caroline Rose. "She fell into some rather...tragic circumstances. I had no idea she had become homeless."

I couldn't hold my tongue back from almost certain destruction. "Weren't you the ones who put her on the street in the first place?" I asked, almost spitting the words across the room. These had to be the men who also ordered my father's murder. I bit back the next accusation that rose in my throat.

"I can understand that you are upset, but you have no reason to accuse me of any wrongdoing. I had nothing to do with her...difficulties." The voice almost sounded wounded by my rash words. "That was a long time ago. My only concern is that she might have told you something that could compromise your safety, Miss O'Brien."

"How do you know my name?"

"I know a great many things about you: your address, your phone number and even that you are a struggling writer. I know which credit cards you have and that you have, I might add, a sterling credit record." Useful information, I supposed. But no credit record could help me now. This debt was not payable upon receipt.

I shaded my eyes with a hand but still could not make out the faces of the men across from me. Suddenly my hand was struck away from my face. "Don't try to see them!" the growl warned. I looked up at the huge, dark figure standing beside me. My wrist throbbed with the pain of his sharp blow. I shook my hand and the throbbing subsided to a bruised ache.

"If I were you," the tall shadow said in a stage whisper. "I would cooperate. That large gentleman by your side has a tendency toward violence. I think it's his upbringing—tough neighborhood, you know." He inhaled sharply and continued his pleasant tones as if he were speaking in a business meeting. "Now, then, you must tell me all you know about Mrs. Carol Spencer Dawes, the woman known to you as Caroline Rose."

I shut my eyes against the light for a moment, and then opened them enough to look down at the carpeted floor. That seemed to be the best thing to do in the almost unbearable brightness. Since they obviously had the means to drag the truth out of me one way or another, I decided to be frank and tell them the whole story of our meeting and what she had revealed to me about her past. I made no mention of her friends or acquaintances. Though I could probably not lie undetected, omission came more easily to my quiet nature.

The truth seemed to work rather well. My surly companion remained silent as I spoke. I glanced at his feet from time to time. He stood quite still. I noticed he wore expensive dress shoes and the cuff of his pants broke in just the right place. When I stopped speaking, I leaned back on the couch, hoping that I had not jeopardized anyone with my words.

I glanced briefly across the room. The three shadow figures sat in silence. The tall one was obviously the leader. The shorter shadows faced him as if waiting for his command. My gaze fell to the couch. Its smooth, black surface seemed unmarred by use. I ran my fingers over the leather absently, listening attentively for any movement or words from my captors.

"I'm glad that you have chosen to be open with us, Miss O'Brien." The tall man spoke in his most courteous tones. I wondered why he bothered. Maybe they didn't plan to kill me after all. I tried not to think about any future beyond the moment at hand. I had experienced few times in my life when I felt so alive, alert to every nuance of the present moment.

"Did Mrs. Dawes give you any names of the men involved in her story?" he asked quietly. The room seemed poised for some action that would depend on my answer to this question. I knew, with a cold certainty, that my life hung on my next words. If I had learned any incriminating names I would be nothing more than a liability to these people, a liability that they likely would not tolerate.

I took a deep breath and let it out slowly, allowing the action to relax my body and center my mind. "Yes," I responded in a firm voice. "She told me one name." The room became quite still as I paused. "The name of the business manager was Simmons, Brad Simmons." I couldn't worry about what would happen to me. At least I had not compromised anyone else in my admission.

Silence greeted my words. I squinted across the room at the tall figure. It seemed that he was staring at me when, suddenly, he threw his head back and laughed. I watched in amazement as his whole frame shook with laughter at some, obviously, hidden joke.

When he regained control of his voice he spoke, punctuating his words with throaty chuckles that seemed to express admiration for the originator of the joke. "Simmons!" he chortled. "That woman just saved your life!" I saw him reach into his breast pocket and pull out what I guessed to be a handkerchief. He began to mop his face with it.

I didn't realize that I had been holding my breath as I waited for his response. Now I released it in a rush of relief and slumped back into the couch.

"Simmons!" The man almost choked on the name. "It was before your time. He was a state senator who promised to rid his state of organized crime. The people were not impressed with his platform. He never held public office again. Funny how easy it is to lose favor with the voters." I guessed that they had had some influence with the voting public, but I kept that thought to myself.

The tall shadow stood up to continue. "The man she called Simmons made a lot of enemies with his methods. He turned out to be a rather careless fellow—died in a boating accident just last summer. Such a shame." I detected no regret in the voice, only a hidden tone of warning.

I grew bold, the question burning in my throat. "Don't you feel any regret about what you people did to Caroline? Her family was murdered; her life was ruined! Think of the lives you destroyed for the sake of money!" Whether or not he felt regret I quickly felt it for my words. No need to anger these people, I reminded myself. Besides, I couldn't help Caroline or my father by getting killed.

However, the man answered very calmly, without a hint of offense. "It was tragic, what happened to her family. Bad business practice, that whole incident. Like I said, Simmons made some poor choices. As for your friend, she had such destructive tendencies. Between the alcohol and the drugs, I think it's amazing she lived as long as she did."

I could hardly control the angry words that rose in response. Coughing seemed to stifle them. I took a deep breath, congratulating myself on my quick recovery.

"Did she have any other friends, this Caroline Rose?"

"How could she?" I evaded calmly. "She never stayed in one place for very long. She was afraid Simmons would hunt her down and kill her."

"Her ploy worked. Simmons lost track of her completely. In fact, we didn't even know she was still around until we heard about her passing. Imagine our surprise when Detective Burkette was called out of retirement to investigate her death in Virginia."

"How'd you hear?" I asked, and then wished I hadn't.

The man chuckled softly. "If I tell you, I'll have to kill you." He sounded as if he was joking, but I knew he meant it. The other two men rose next to him, as if in response to a silent signal.

"That's okay. I really don't need to know," I replied quickly.

"No, you don't. One more thing, Miss O'Brien," came the cool voice. "It is not my habit to apologize for anyone else, but," and he paused. His voice took on a warmth that almost frightened me in its stark contrast to his business-like politeness.

"I, too, lost my father when I was young; a hit just like Mr. O'Brien."

The revelation astounded me. For a moment I could not speak.

"Yes, does that surprise you?"

"Not if he was a criminal like..." I stopped myself.

He laughed. "Like me?"

I nodded. "Yeah. Doesn't my father's innocence make it a little different?"

"It would, if my father had been 'in the business' so to speak. But he was not."

"Oh, sorry." I could feel the blush rise in my cheeks but the intensity of the situation stopped it quickly.

"It may satisfy your sense of justice to know that all of the men responsible for your father's murder are dead. Turnover is hell in this business."

"I guess so."

"I will leave you with a warning. As long as you do nothing to further this case—and there really is no point now—our paths will never cross again. Your life will be in no danger." He cleared his throat. "But," he continued, "if you go to the police with information about us, I assure you that an unfortunate accident will be unavoidable. Do you understand?"

"Yes," I answered, my mouth almost too dry to speak. I felt a new tension in the air.

"Let me now impress upon you the seriousness of my warning."

He turned to the other two shadows and whispered something inaudible. I could see his arm rise in a gesture toward me as he spoke across the room to the brute beside me. "She can be returned now. Take care of it."

The man turned to me and grabbed my wrist, pulling me roughly to my feet. "Hey!" I protested. "You don't have to..." Suddenly I saw his huge hand swinging at my face from out of the darkness. I warded it off with my free hand. He only clipped the top of my head.

Angry now, he grabbed my other wrist and, in one swift motion, turned and threw me over his shoulder to the floor. I landed with the breath knocked out of me. I felt a suffocating pain in my chest. I gasped but could barely pull any air into my lungs. He grasped the collar of my shirt with a powerful hand and pulled me up off the floor. I hung from his fist like a trapped animal.

From across the room I heard the calm voice saying in disgust, "Such a brute. He has no finesse."

In his black ski mask and dark glasses, my attacker seemed a mechanical being, not human at all. Still out of breath, I could not respond when I saw his other hand out of the corner of my eye. It struck across my face with a powerful impact that ripped through my head and sent me hurtling into darkness.

CHAPTER THIRTY-TWO

Cold. I felt very cold. The sharp points of gravel dug into my face as I opened my eyes. At first I couldn't tell if I had been blinded by the blow to my head or if it was just dark. I struggled to rise, the icy stones biting my hands and knees as I did so. The wind cut through my open jacket and the sweater underneath. I pulled the jacket close and huddled on my knees. Holding my head in my hands, I waited for my mind to clear.

The familiar murmur of the river filled my ears and, in the distance, the insistent pounding of wheels on steel track heralded the approaching, southbound train. The noise grew closer. I shielded my ears with my hands as the sound became too loud for my aching head. My ears felt as though they were full of water, adding a shrill scream to the lower tones.

Once the train had passed, its light streaming over the trestle and pouring past the station, I raised my head again. My eyes had cleared. I could see the river nearby, flowing in a dark mass of deadly water. I wondered if my close proximity to the river was part of the warning not to tell the police what had happened to me. Certainly I had no intention of disclosing the events of the past I-didn't-know-how-many hours to any authorities.

As I looked around I recognized the backs of the beautiful homes lining the lower part of Caroline Street. I tried to get up but fell back to my knees as waves of dizziness pushed me down. Breathing deeply of the cold air, I tried to think of what I should do. I remembered, dimly, that Walt's house was on that street. All I had to do was recover enough to walk over there.

Shivering almost uncontrollably, I decided I had better get up no matter how dizzy I felt, or I wouldn't live to recover from the concussion. The desire for life gave new strength to my body as I rose unsteadily to my feet and began the painful walk up the road. Slowly I fought my way up the steep hill, finally stopping to rest at the corner. I dropped to one knee and cradled my head in my hands for a few moments. Just two more blocks, I told myself. A dog barked menacingly from a nearby yard. I hoped that he couldn't jump the fence. I was in no condition to escape the snarling jaws that flashed suddenly in the streetlight.

Grasping a low tree branch, I hauled myself to a standing position and leaned against the cold bark. My head felt heavy and clouded with pain. I moved along the sidewalk, steadying myself now and then with the thick branches of the old trees.

Just ahead now, a little further down the street, stood Walt's house. I could see the glow of light radiating from the study. Just one more block and I would be there. I saw his Suburban gleaming dully in the driveway, reflecting the street light on the corner. The light outside his door blurred into a yellow globe as I kept it in my gaze, like a ship relying on a lighthouse to lead it safely home.

By the time I had reached the driveway, my feet had become steadier and the globe of light had grown clear. The weight in my head seemed to lift as I touched the shining vehicle. It served as a touch stone for my return to reality. The metal felt cold and smooth beneath my fingers. I let my hand slide carelessly along its length as I made my way up the driveway and to the front door. Ringing the bell, I leaned back on the outer wall. Relief flooded my mind when I heard Walt's familiar step.

As the door swung open, I turned to face him in the lamplight. "My God! What happened to you!" he cried. I must have looked rather the worse for the wear, judging by the expression on his face. Walt helped me into the house and brought me to the overstuffed couch in the living room.

I sank gratefully into its cushions while warmth began to seep back into my body. My mentor seemed at a loss as to what to do next. I had never seen him this way before. For a fleeting moment he appeared confused, even helpless. In that instant I felt as though I were watching from a distance, detached as much from him as from my own body.

"What happened to you, Kate?" Walt's anxious voice broke into the haze that had again surrounded my mind.

"Walt," I began, feeling that my voice came from somewhere outside myself. "Boy, am I glad to see you!"

"What the hell happened? Who did this to you? Were you in an accident?"

I put up my hand. "Whoa! Too many questions." I chuckled despite the pain in my head. The reaction of this man, who never seemed to lose his cool no matter what, amused me in some distant manner. "Yes, you could call it an accident—a collision with a huge fist."

"Let me take you to the emergency room. Come on," Walt ordered.

"No!"

"What are you talking about? You're badly hurt. You've got to see a doctor..."

"No, Walt. If I go to the hospital they'll have to fill out a report. I'm not going!" I lay back on the couch. Tears ran slowly down my cheeks. I felt overwhelmed with a jumble of emotions: grief, anger, fear. The physical pain kept me grounded to reality.

Walt knelt by my side. Covering my eyes with a hand I mumbled, "Please, just get me some ice."

He rose silently and crossed the room. I could hear him in the kitchen. The ice clattered noisily out of the icemaker. He returned, placing the ice pack carefully against the side of my head. I reached up to hold it myself. Our hands touched briefly and an electric current of warmth passed between us.

Walt sat on the floor, one elbow resting on the coffee table. His eyes glowed with love and deep concern. For a moment I drank his expression in through my own tear-filled eyes. Quietly I told him what had happened. As my story unfolded, his eyes took on a completely different expression.

I had never seen him angry before. I was familiar with Tibetan depictions of wrathful deities. That night, Walt could have been one of their models. His usually clear features clouded into an expression that I had never imagined could mold his handsome face. "We've got to report this," he said urgently, his voice as tight as the clenched fist that shook the table.

"No," I answered steadily. "No. We're not going to report this. My life won't be worth a damn if I meet those bastards again. They mean business. Next time, I won't survive the meeting." I sat up, feeling stronger and more clear-headed now.

"Walt, I never believed in true evil before, but after hearing the cold unconcern in that man's voice...I think I've met its human incarnation. I understand why Caroline was afraid of them. They care nothing for human life; people are to be manipulated for profit, and killed if they get in the way. I don't even know why they let me live. I suppose it would be too obvious if I had an 'accident' at this point."

Walt nodded. "You're right. I think it only served their own dark purposes to let you go free. But what happens if they decide that you really are in their way? What then? They can find you so easily."

"Then I won't give them a reason to make the effort," I answered, trying to sound confident. "I didn't see their faces. I have no way to identify them for sure. They're certainly not in any danger from me." I set the ice pack on the table and slowly rose to my feet. I felt a little dizzy at first, but the feeling passed. Taking a deep breath, I made my way across the room and down the hall to the bathroom. "Be back in a minute," I called to Walt, who had risen to help me if I needed it.

"You sure you'll be all right?"

I turned, wincing as I tried to grin. "I'll be fine. I think I can do this by myself."

Walt fixed some supper for me. He had already eaten. Apparently I had been with my captors for almost two hours. It was eleven o'clock by the time I had arrived at his house.

I called Holly and told her I would be spending the night at Walt's. He was loath to let me out of his sight until he felt certain that the concussion was not serious. I rather enjoyed his mother hen routine—yet another facet of the man to explore. Holly's response amused me. "Uh, okay, Kate. I understand. He seems like a great guy and lots of girls like older men."

"It's...it's not like that, Holly," I stammered, blushing mostly because Walt was standing nearby. He paused, holding a dish over the dishwasher, then continued to fill the machine, trying not to hear my end of the conversation.

"I had an...accident, Holly. I hit my head and Walt wants to make sure I'm alright before he sends me on my way." I hoped that she would accept my explanation without further questions. I hated to lie but the truth might put her in danger, too.

"Are you okay? There are still a lot of patches of ice out there. Did you slip?"

"Something like that. I should be back tomorrow. I've just got a headache now, so I'm sure I'll be okay," I reassured her. There was another mother hen in my life, but I didn't mind.

"Well, I hope so. Oh...You got some calls today. Some guy from Samaritan House wanted to invite you to a memorial service for your friend tomorrow night, and the police called to tell you that they were releasing the...the body to the funeral home next Friday. I thought you should know..." Holly trailed off, obviously uncomfortable.

"Thanks, Holly. You're a real friend. Don't worry about me, now. I'll see ya tomorrow."

"Yeah. Watch out for those older men, Kate. You know they only want just one thing!" she teased.

"Oh, I know," and I looked meaningfully at Walt drying his hands. "They want me to get my research done!" I watched his eyes widen at the last remark. I grinned at him innocently. When I hung up the phone I told him, "Holly just wanted to warn me about older men."

He chuckled, tossing the dishtowel on the counter. "That's right, better be careful." Glancing at my face, he frowned momentarily. "You're going to have a shiner on that eye. Holly will think I'm beating you, too," he added in a mischievous tone.

After showing me the spare room upstairs, he handed me a pair of flannel pajamas. "They're a bit big but they'll keep you warm."

"Thanks."

"Why don't you let me wash your clothes so you can have them fresh for tomorrow? You could just leave them in the bathroom. I'll take care of them later," he offered.

I was grateful for his kindness. I took a long shower and slipped into pajamas and robe, giggling at how big they were on my small frame. By midnight I had finally climbed into bed and wearily pulled the blankets up around my chin. Walt looked in on me to say goodnight. "You sure you feel okay? I'm not certain if I should let you sleep if you have a concussion."

"Yeah, I'm fine, just tired. As for sleeping, I don't think you can stop me," I replied, drifting hazily into semi-consciousness.

I slept well and woke to a sunny day. Glancing around the room, I noticed Walt slumped in the rocking chair at the foot of the bed. I smiled sleepily. I could hear a slight snore now and then. When I sat up in bed and turned to slide on a pair of borrowed slippers, he awoke suddenly, startled.

Grinning sheepishly, he admitted, "I just wanted to make sure that you kept breathing all night."

I was touched by his concern. "That's so sweet of you." Vaguely uncomfortable, I joked, "Hope I didn't snore."

"Not much," he returned with a sly wink.

After breakfast I felt well enough to drive home. Walt took me to the library, where my car still sat waiting for me. I waved as I pulled away from the curb. The side of my face looked puffy and bruised, but I felt pretty good. At least my head no longer ached.

Back home, Holly and Andy seemed impressed by my injury. When I tried to explain it as a fall, Andy shook her head. "You should know better than that. I used to work in a hospital. I know the difference between bruises from a fall and a fist."

She pointed to a spot near my hairline. "I can even see the imprint of his knuckles there."

Yeah, I should have known better than to try to fool her, but it had been worth a try. I decided to tell them the whole story. Holly seemed a little frightened, but Andy took it in stride. She was always the fearless one.

"So, now what?" she asked.

"I guess I'll watch out for green minivans," I replied lightly.

"And so will we!" Holly added, her face wrinkled with concern.

I spent the day trying to rest, using the time to return telephone calls. When I spoke to Gaige at Samaritan House, he repeated his invitation to the memorial service.

"I really don't feel up to it." I told him the acceptable story about hitting my head.

"Gee, I'm sorry. You've got to watch out for those patches of ice. They're really dangerous."

"Yeah, that's for sure."

"Man! I can't believe Caroline's gone! I expect her to come up and tap me on the shoulder and say something about cleaning the bathrooms or changing Scott's IV...." He paused for a moment. "Scott and Caroline in the same month. It just blows my mind!"

"I miss her, too." Her death still did not seem real to me. I wondered if it ever would. Gaige invited me to come up any time. Soon they would be opening their sixth community home. This one would house people needing long term care for mental illness, those who can't live on their own but not ill enough to be committed to an institution.

"You know, Gaige, you guys are the best. You're doing great things up there. I hope other groups follow your lead."

"Well, it seems to work here. I think it's worth trying in other cities, too. We'll see what happens. I'll be going down to Florida to talk to some interested volunteers down there. That's where Caroline was going when she left. If she had taken the money I offered her for the trip..."

"But she didn't. You can't blame yourself anymore than...than I can. I've been feeling guilty for not being home, for not insisting she take the money with her. We couldn't force her to do anything, even if it was for her own good. She was a strong, stubborn woman." I paused. "Maybe that's one of the things we liked best about her."

"Yeah, I suppose you're right."

When I hung up I wondered if I would ever understand Caroline Rose and what had moved her to live as she did. My intuition hinted that I still had not heard the whole story. Perhaps I never would.

CHAPTER THIRTY-THREE

My face looked better in the morning. I had resolved the night before to try to find Caroline's friends and tell them what happened to her. They had a right to know, I reasoned, although I wasn't sure where they might be.

I walked down Caroline Street, passing under the railroad tracks where some of the homeless often took shelter. Then I made my way along Sophia Street, peering into alleys and around a handful of abandoned buildings. I kept looking over my shoulder, expecting to see the green minivan. My stomach felt tight with an anxiety I could not shake.

Finally, I headed for the river. It seemed a cold day to be down there, but that's where I found them. They were fishing off the dock.

"Jonas!" I called, raising my hand in greeting. The old man squinted at me for a moment, then grinned a yellow-toothed smile of recognition.

"Why, here's Caroline's writer-friend, Charlie!" Jonas pointed me out to his sullen companion, who simply nodded at me without smiling. "How ya doin'? I forgit your name, honey, but it's nice ta see ya." He looked at my face for a moment, but made no comment about the bruises or the fading black eye.

"Jonas, I've been looking for you." I extended my hand and gripped his, dry and gnarled from age and neglect. The cold air carried the stale smell of unwashed flesh quickly to my nose. I tried to ignore the unpleasant odors from the two men. I supposed they were used to it by now.

"I'm glad I found you both," I said, glancing from one to the other. "I've got some bad news. Caroline...Caroline Rose died last week."

"Lord!" Jonas exclaimed with a low whistle. "I'm sorry ta hear that, Miss. She was sich a kind-hearted woman. I was real fond of her, yes indeed!"

Charlie nodded curtly. "What happened to her?" he asked, with an almost disinterested tone.

"Hit-and-run on Route 3. Someone skidded on the ice and ran right into her."

"People die," was all he said, before quickly turning his head away. He wiped his eyes with a gloved hand.

"Well, like I say, I'm terrible sorry ta hear that," Jonas continued. "I liked her a whole lot, I did."

Now that I had discharged my duty, I felt anxious to leave. I noticed the distressing smell again. The wind must have picked up. I took a step back. "Well," I began. "I just thought you both would want to know. She liked you very much. I know you shared some good times together." I took another step back.

"Yes, we did, indeed. I am so sorry. And I'm sorry for ya to hafta come tell us that sad news." He took a step forward. "I think ya were a good friend ta her."

I nodded. "Yeah. We were friends."

"Thanks for comin' down here, miss. Sure do appreciate it." Jonas smiled at me and stepped closer to shake my hand again. He glanced again at the injured side of my face. "Ya take good care o' yaself, now."

"Thanks, Jonas," I said with feeling. "You, too. Take care, both of you." With a nod to Charlie, I turned and walked off the dock and up the street.

When I got home I found a letter and a check from Franklin. He had sent enough to cover Caroline's last expenses. I deposited the money in my account that afternoon. The note simply repeated his request that I wait for further instructions before dispersing the ashes. Well, I would just have to be patient with this rather odd circumstance concerning Caroline's final wishes.

I stayed close to home for the next few days. I had no desire to appear in public again until my face had returned to normal. Though I usually didn't wear make-up, I was using foundation just to cover the bruises.

Walt insisted that I rest and put the research on hold for a couple of weeks. Once I was healed and had completed my duties regarding Caroline, he would have plenty for me to do again. Instead of working, I spent much of my time reading: Dickens, Steinbeck, Rand. Why had I thought I could be a writer, anyway? I just didn't have the heart for it anymore. How could I tell that to Walt?

I couldn't even bring myself to look at the manuscript. There it sat, in its gray box on a shelf in my closet. It almost seemed to taunt me whenever I opened the closet door. Finally I threw an old sweatshirt over it so I didn't have to see it. But somehow, a bit of the box managed to peek through despite my best efforts to cover it up.

Caroline's remains arrived at the funeral home on schedule. I had made arrangements to have them cremated without a ceremony. She had not wanted one and very few people in Fredericksburg actually knew her anyway. The next day I drove down to pick up her ashes.

The funeral home was properly appointed, beautiful in the way an arrangement of wax-flowers would appear. Though it did not smell strongly of formalin like the place where my father was brought many years ago, a mild chemical scent pervaded the air. The director strode out of his office to greet me with a studied sort of sorrowful smile. His line of work must be difficult, I thought to myself. What does he do to lighten his day?

"Miss O'Brien, how do you do?" he asked in courteous but hushed tones.

"Fine, thanks"

"Please, come to my office." He gently took my arm and guided me down the hall with its thick red carpet that seemed to muffle the sounds of life so they would not disturb the dead.

Since I had already paid for their services, I had only to receive a receipt for my payment and, of course, Caroline's ashes. Franklin had told me that there would be no need for an urn in which to keep them. The funeral director gave them to me in a sturdy cardboard box with an elegant logo imprinted in gold foil. It felt odd to hold the box, knowing that it contained the last physical remains of my friend.

Looking into the polite face of the director, I recognized the compassion in his large, sad eyes. I wondered what made someone choose this line of work, dealing constantly with the final tragedy of life. "I'm truly sorry about your friend," the gentleman continued with a sincerity I knew he felt. He had dropped the formal tone.

"Thanks," I replied. "I appreciate your kindness."

He must have sensed my eagerness to leave. "Let me walk you out to your car." He gestured for me to step out the door in front of him, and then he walked quickly beside me down the hall, gallantly opening the outer door for me.

"What is your line of work, if you don't mind my asking?"

"I'm a writer," came the swift reply. I had spoken without even thinking. I made no allowances for whether or not I would ever write again. I made no apology for my right to that title. Maybe that meant I really was one. Could it be that I actually had no choice but to be what destiny seemed to have made me?

"Oh, how nice," the gentleman responded. The polite veil had returned to his voice. I imagined it was the only way he could maintain his sanity from day to day. He would have made the same response if I had said I was a secretary, a house painter or a scientist. But my words had meant something to me.

He opened the car door for me and I slid into the driver's seat, placing the box beside me. We exchanged courteous good-byes and I drove off quickly.

Once home I went straight to my room and looked around for a place to keep the ashes. I couldn't very well store them under the bed. Where do you keep the ashes of a dead friend, anyway?

Finally, I decided the closet would be appropriate, as respectful a storage place as I could manage at the time. Clearing a space on the top shelf, I set Caroline's box carefully in place. My manuscript, which had formerly occupied that spot, was relegated to the floor of the closet. Glancing from one box to the other, I began to think that I would not be able to bring myself to work on the second until I had dealt with the other, more precious burden.

The guilt I felt at not being there for Caroline had subsided somewhat, but deep down, I wondered if my writing could ever carry the joy and significance it once had, before her death. With the ashes in my closet, I felt that I could not move on until there was some feeling of closure. What was I supposed to do with them?

"Kate," came Franklin's business-like voice over the phone, "I'm so sorry that I can't give you an answer now."

"Well, I just wanted to let you know that I've done what you—she—requested." I hesitated. I couldn't let Frank know that I was having trouble handling these last details. "It just...uh...feels kind of strange to have them in my closet while I wait for some unknown instructions."

"I know. If it would make you feel better, you could send them to me for safekeeping," came the helpful reply.

I couldn't stop myself from giggling at the thought. "Yeah, I could send them UPS...that's okay. I'll live with it."

"That's a girl. I know she would be proud of you." Suddenly his voice took on a serious tone. "Caroline told me you were a wonderful friend to her. You still are."

The phone call did nothing to satisfy my quandary over what to do next. I had no heart to write. This crisis had stopped me in my tracks and I felt almost helpless in the face of conflicting thoughts and emotions. Should I even be a writer? Could I make it at what I really loved to do or was I just fooling myself? Or did I even love it anymore?

Maybe I should dedicate my life to helping the homeless instead. Wouldn't that represent a nobler endeavor? When I made that point to Walt over the phone, he insisted that I had to do what I enjoyed in life. "Writing has the potential to make a terrific impact on society, if that's what you really want to do."

I clung to the telephone receiver as if to life itself and poured out my greatest fear. "Maybe I don't have a purpose, Walt. Maybe my stuff won't be worth reading." It was a good thing Walt couldn't see me as the tears started in my eyes.

His voice sounded strained but patient. "Why don't you let your mentor tell you those things? Let me see what you've got."

"I don't think I'm ready for you to see it. I don't think I'm even ready to look at it right now."

"Well, when you are, bring it over." He paused a moment and took a deep breath. "I wonder if taking a break is such a good idea for you now. It seems that work might help put you in a better frame of mind."

"Yeah, but we've got a lot of material now. Isn't it time to put it all together?" I asked a question I had wanted to ask for weeks.

"To be perfectly honest, I want to see my contacts in Tibet and India before I do much more on it. They have promised me some...shall I say, unique material."

I did not speak. I felt the next move should be his. It was not my place to remind him of our promised trip.

"Maybe we should start planning our trip east," came the expected response. Already I began to feel a renewed sense of purpose. Walt was right. A break was not what I needed. Work would provide the necessary balm for my soul. Perhaps it would bring me the sense of personal worth that I had somehow lost in the past three weeks of turmoil.

"Yes. I would like that. Of course, I'm not sure when I'll be finished with...well, this whole issue of what to do with Caroline's ashes is still unresolved," I admitted.

"What do you mean?" he asked. I explained that Franklin had not yet told me what to do with them. "How odd," he commented. "What do you suppose he's waiting for?"

"I have absolutely no idea. I think it's peculiar myself, but all I can do now is wait, as he asked."

"Well, then, that's what you've got to do. We can put off our trip until you're ready." I could always count on Walt to be flexible.

"Thanks." I brightened. "Now you've given me something to look forward to when I'm done with this whole business."

Over the next two days Walt and I planned our itinerary at his kitchen table. We wanted to go straight to Lhasa, the capital of Tibet. Walt had contacts there who had offered to show us the city and take us to places that were not usually on the Chinese-approved tours. He figured we would need to spend at least two weeks there before moving on to Dharamsala, the headquarters of the Tibetan Government in Exile in India.

"If all goes smoothly, we could be home in three weeks time." Walt fixed me with a concerned gaze. "Although, maybe we should stay out of the country a little longer, given your situation..." He trailed off without continuing the thought.

I shook my head. "I can't stay away forever. If I were in danger from our criminal friends I would already be dead." I managed a grim smile but I knew Walt would still fear for my safety for a long time to come.

"I suppose you're right."

When I decided to return home, he watched me gather my things with a look that, to my mind, seemed regretful. "Well, do we meet tomorrow?" I asked.

"Yes. Let's do lunch. There's a new restaurant I want to try downtown," he added, rubbing his hands together. He enjoyed fine food. The prospect of another good restaurant pleased him.

As I drove home, I smiled at the thought of going out to lunch with Walt the next day. I tried not to think of where this relationship might be going. I didn't dare see him as more than a friend, the father figure that I had come to rely on so heavily, especially in the past few weeks. It couldn't be possible to want more. Surely he saw me as no more than a kid, a nice kid, maybe, but a kid nonetheless. Thinking of him made me feel warm, despite the cold outside. For the first time in a long while, I felt a fleeting sense of contentment.

I had just settled down to read when the phone rang with an odd insistence. The answering machine must have been switched off because it did not pick up as usual.

My housemates were out and I just didn't feel like moving. The ringing finally stopped. When it started again I jumped up with a muttered curse and ran downstairs. "Hello," I answered, irritation straining my voice.

"Hello," came the reply in strangely familiar French accents. "This is Therese DuVal, from the department of astronomy at Indiana University."

"Dr. DuVal?" I exclaimed in confusion.

"Yes. You remember me, then?"

"Of course," I replied, still stunned at hearing her voice. Why would she call me? Perhaps she was, very thoughtfully, expressing her condolences. After all, she had known Caroline for a number of years. They may have enjoyed a closer relationship than I had previously understood.

"This is Kate, no?"

"Yes. It's so nice of you to call..."

"I really don't know how I should say this. I cannot believe it myself. Franklin came over to visit after Ms. Rose died to tell me—if it wasn't for the proof he brought me I would have thought he was completely crazy."

"What are you talking about? What proof?"

The voice sounded distressed. "Ms. Rose, our Caroline Rose—she was my mother!"

CHAPTER THIRTY-FOUR

The receiver dropped from my grasp. Quickly I picked it up, fumbling with the now tangled cord. Raising it to my ear again, I whispered urgently, "She's your mother? I...I'm so sorry—not that she's your mother, but that you lost her..."

"I didn't know what to think but Franklin had the birth certificate and pictures of my father and her—and one of me when I was christened."

The christening picture! It wasn't Kenny; it was Therese! Now I understood why it was in black and white. It was older than the others. "But how?" Caroline had never told me anything about a daughter.

"She was very young. They weren't married. Apparently they met in Paris and lived together for a few years. They were very happy until after I was born. Then Ms. Rose— my mother—started to have problems with depression and alcohol. Her parents came to France and took her home for treatment. Perhaps I should let you read it in her own words. She wrote me a letter to explain."

"Letter?" I murmured, dazed by this revelation.

"Yes. Franklin had been keeping a letter from her. She told him to give it to me after her death. You were her friend. I would like to send you a copy. I think she would have wanted you to know these things about her."

For a moment I did not answer. My mind reeled at the new pieces now added to Caroline's puzzle. Then, returning to the present, I said, "Yes, I'd like that, Dr. DuVal."

"Please—Therese, call me Therese. Franklin told me you took care of her final arrangements. I cannot find words to thank you for your kindness. I know it must have been hard for you. He said you are waiting for instructions on what to do with her ashes. I am not sure yet. This has all happened so fast. I cannot ask my father because he died several years ago, when I was still in school."

I began to regain my composure. "It's okay. Take your time."

"I would like to come see you in the next few months."

Suddenly, it dawned on me why Caroline had never told me about her daughter. She must have feared that Therese might be discovered by her old nemeses.

"Could I come to Fredericksburg to see you?" she was asking.

"No!" I blurted out. "No. Don't come here. It might be...uh...dangerous."

"Ah, I understand. My mother explained in her letter. Perhaps we could meet somewhere else." She paused. "I know. I am coming to Virginia in April. There are some conferences at three of your universities. I could meet you at U.V.A., Old Dominion, or Virginia Tech. I can only afford one."

"You know, Virginia Tech would be a good meeting place, if you want to go to that one. My mother goes to school there. I'm sure she would be happy to have you as her guest. That way you could save money on hotels..." An idea began to form in the back of my mind. "There is a lovely spot in the mountains that I think you might like to see."

"I would enjoy the conference at Virginia Tech. Yes, that sounds wonderful. Are you sure your mother won't mind?"

"Of course not. She'll be very happy to meet you. She and your mother hit it off really well at Christmas." I began to feel a sense of resolution about Caroline's life and death. Things were starting to make more sense in the light of this new revelation.

I told Therese about our Christmas with her mother. She seemed delighted to know more about this mysterious woman who had visited her with such regularity over the years. Although a little overwhelmed, she was taking it all in with a positive attitude.

She told me she would be in touch with me again soon to finalize our arrangements for April. I hung up thoughtfully. How could my friend have had a daughter that never knew her? I looked forward to receiving the letter. Perhaps I would finally have the whole picture of Caroline Rose.

For the next few days I spent my time doing research, either surfing the net or taking notes in the library. Walt was sketching out his science fiction novel and was having difficulty with the futuristic technical aspects At least that's what he told me. I didn't ask if he just wanted to keep me busy. It felt good to immerse myself in the work. I noticed that I looked over my shoulder less often, although I still scanned the streets every time I went anywhere, just to make sure there were no strange vehicles hanging around. Once I saw a man in a dark suit standing near my car. I ducked back into the library and waited until he had left. That, I told myself, was just common sense, even for someone who wasn't paranoid about being abducted again.

Still, I avoided writing. Sometimes I told myself that I was just taking a break from it. At other times I reasoned that I shouldn't write anymore—that research was my real calling anyway.

One evening, after a long day at the library, I arrived home to find a letter from Indiana on the kitchen table. Holly was just washing up her dishes after a light dinner. "Hey, this came for you. Is that the letter you were expecting?"

"Yeah, I think so." Absently I grabbed a soda from the refrigerator and hurried upstairs, clutching the envelope. Tossing my pack on the floor, I sat on my bed and tore the letter open.

Therese had jotted a few lines to me, thanking me for my friendship with her mysterious mother. I scanned her elegant writing quickly before dropping the note beside me on the bed. The letter from Caroline to her daughter was a clear photocopy. I noticed the neat and deliberate script that I remembered so well. She had written with a strong hand, the same strength, no doubt, that had helped her survive so many years on the streets. I wondered how difficult this letter had been to write.

My Dearest Therese,

If you receive this letter, then I have passed on from this life to whatever rest or reward I may merit. Though I have suffered much, I do not feel that I can ever make up for the suffering I have inflicted on you. You grew up without a mother to love and care for you. I never revealed myself to you for many reasons. I hope that you will understand them and, if your heart can bear it, forgive me.

Many years ago, before you were born, I dropped out of college and ran away to France against my parents' wishes. I wanted to "really live," I told them. I thought Paris would offer me the excitement I could not find as a student. I even got a job, which surprised my parents. It may even have pleased them, though they never told me.

A year later I met your father, Georges. Oh! Was he handsome! And so romantic! He was my ideal French gentleman. We fell in love, but since it was the sixties—the age of "free love"—we lived together instead of marrying. Marriage was for conventional people, not us. Three years later, our darling Therese was born. I loved you so much! I held you almost all the time! For the first month I thought I was in heaven, with my beautiful, happy family.

My joy did not last. The doctor told me I just had the "baby blues." He thought I was exaggerating when I described how terribly depressed I had suddenly become. It felt as though a black cloud had descended on me and was suffocating all my happiness. He said not to worry. I should just go home and enjoy my baby and stop thinking about it.

Not much was known about post-partum depression then. In fact, depression itself was not well understood. I had suffered from it since childhood. The depression would come in bouts that lasted anywhere from a day to a month. Several doctors had told me it was all in my head and that I could work it out for myself.

But now, tragically, my attempts to "work it out" involved heavy drinking. Soon, by the time Georges would arrive home at night, I would be drunk. I tried to hide it, but he knew. Your father had grown up with alcoholic parents. He had resented the suffering their lifestyle inflicted on him. So, he had no tolerance for my addiction. More than once he told me to stop or he would take you and leave for good.

I didn't know what to do. His anger frightened me. I drank more, just to forget my fear of losing you both. One night he came home to find me passed out in the kitchen with a pot of food burning on the stove and the baby screaming in the bedroom. That was it. He had reached his limit. He put me in the hospital and called my parents to come take me home. He saw no hope of saving me from alcoholism. Now he had to think of your welfare first.

I don't blame him. I was unfit as a mother. He had told me that time and time again. I finally believed it was true. How could such a troubled woman take care of a baby? He said I would do you more harm than good.

It was the lowest point of my life. Even with all I have gone through, I have never suffered as much as I did then, knowing I could have hurt or even killed you that night. What if your father had been late? I try not to think about it.

We did what we thought was best. I told Georges that it would be better if you never knew I had lived. I begged him to tell you your mother had died after the birth. In a way, it was true. I felt I had died the day I kissed you goodbye and left Paris with my father.

It took years of treatment to battle my alcoholism and depression, but my father never gave up on me. I wished you had known him. He would have been a loving grandfather. You missed out on so many wonderful relationships because of my inability to cope with my own problems.

To Georges' credit, he did keep in sporadic touch with me over the years. While I was still at the treatment center he sent a lovely picture of you in your christening gown. I carry it to this day.

I want you to know that I did get better. Several years later I was sober and no longer needed medication for my depression. That was when I met Neal. He made my life a true joy, and I am so grateful for every minute I had with him. I even became a good mother to our son, Kenny. He was your half-brother. You would have loved him, I know!

They were both murdered. I won't tell you who did it. Once they died I had nothing left in the world but you, and you didn't even know I existed. The man who stole my wealth and had my family killed threatened everyone related to me. I had to hide.

I called your father and told him a little of what had happened. You could have been in terrible danger if these evil men discovered you were my daughter. I told Georges to burn everything he had kept that might link me to you, including our love letters and any photographs with me in them. I felt they would only endanger our precious daughter.

For a long while I avoided calling, but I couldn't bear not knowing how you were doing. You were all that was left to me in the world.

When your father answered the phone, I could tell from the weakness in his voice that something was wrong. Georges told me, ever so gently, that he was dying of cancer. He wanted to make amends for what had happened. His fear and anger at his parents' alcoholism had gotten the best of him those many years ago. How he wished that he had been more open to helping me with my problems. Maybe we could have worked things out and stayed together.

We both wept during that call. His greatest hope was that you would eventually be able to forgive us both, once you learned the truth. He urged me to reveal myself to you, but I felt it would still be too dangerous. Better to wait until it was safer, I insisted.

The next time I called, two months later, you answered the phone. I almost hung up, I was so afraid I would tell you who I was. Instead, I simply asked for Georges. You told me that he had just died. It did not surprise me. I hid my emotion from you, but I even felt a physical pain in my heart at our loss.

After that, I began to travel to your university, where you eventually became a professor. I was so proud of you! How I longed to reveal myself, but I still didn't dare.

When Franklin became settled in his business, he offered to keep an eye on you for me. It was through him I learned of your marriage and the birth of your son, my grandson!

Still, I could never forget the cruel man who robbed me of my family and fortune. I devoted my life to protecting you from his evil threats. Now, you had a family. How could I risk exposing any of you to danger?

Please, let me assure you, that though my life was hard, knowing you and your precious family were safe made it seem that much easier. Besides, I became quite adept at meeting my needs during my wanderings. There were many kind people willing to help a poor, homeless woman. Whenever I felt sad, I had only to think of you and I would feel so much better.

I suppose I also took solace in the possibility that my suffering could redeem my many sins. After all, through my mental illness and addictions I had brought tremendous suffering to the people that I had loved the most: my parents, Georges, and, most especially, you.

Growing up without a mother must have caused you so much pain. I hope and pray that someday you will be able to forgive me. And if you can forgive me, do not grieve for me now that I am gone. Remember that I loved you through all the lonely nights of your life. A day never passed when I did not kiss your sweet picture and pray for your happiness and safety.

This same picture that I have carried all these years has given me the strength I needed to live and, yes, even to die. My love for you has brought me through difficulties and joys. Yes, dearest Therese, there were also joys in this homeless life of mine. I want you to know that, too. The simple joys of nature's beauty, the kindness of strangers, and the love of friends were available even to me as they are to you. I have treasured them throughout my life.

May you treasure your life and its many joys. Your life is a gift, given you by your Creator and your parents. Remember that it has been protected vigilantly at great cost. Use it wisely and well. Above all, be happy.

My dear one, please remember me kindly if you can. I don't know what happens after death. I do know that I have done what I could to salvage the twisted wreckage of my life. I will be at peace when I die, of that I am sure. Perhaps that is all that matters.

All my love and prayers go with you as you continue down life's unsure pathway. Love your family with all your heart. Pray with fervor and live in happiness and peace. These are my last words to you until we meet again, my dear.

With love now and always,
Your adoring mother,
Caroline

The paper fluttered unnoticed to the floor.

CHAPTER THIRTY-FIVE

I knew that I had to get out of the house. Grabbing my jacket and keys, I hurried down the steps. As my hand closed on the doorknob, Holly whisked around the corner.

"Where ya goin'?" she asked cheerily, a bit too cheerily, it seemed.

"Uh...walk—yeah—I need a walk."

My brusque manner stopped her short. She nodded solemnly, her red curls bobbing up and down in merry contrast to the concern that showed suddenly in her face.

"Don't worry, mother hen," I reassured her with a lighter tone.

"Me, worry? You know I never worry about you. Especially after your brush with the mob or whatever they were."

"Who knows," I threw back glibly. "Walt's cousin Paulie thinks they're an independent group."

"Very funny."

"Okay, he doesn't have a cousin Paulie. But maybe there really is honor among thieves. Some just have more finesse than others," I added, remembering the words of the tall shadow. "See ya later."

Shivering in the chilly air, I zipped my jacket all the way up over my chin. Hands in my pockets, I walked rapidly down the street. My mind whirled with conflicting reactions to the letter. How? How could these terrible things have happened to Caroline? And why?

My first intuition—that she suffered from psychological problems—had evidently been true. I felt disappointed, in a way. My picture of Caroline Rose had grown into what I now saw as an illusion. The wise, clever, old woman had turned out to be, in reality, no more than an alcoholic with serious depression. Or maybe that, too, was an illusion. Who was she? How could I come to terms with the person I had come to love so dearly and the mother who had abandoned her daughter in guilty torment?

Could it be that Caroline was just a frail human driven by fear and guilt into a life of suffering? It was a course most of us would shun, yet she had embraced it as the logical expression of a life gone terribly wrong.

The cold air bit into my cheeks, grounding me in its own frosty reality. My breath puffed out in visible clouds before me as I continued, not even paying attention to where my steps took me. As long as they carried me quickly, the torrent of thoughts whirling in my brain seemed less chaotic.

What kind of man would abandon the mother of his only child? Why had he done nothing to help her? Had she seemed so past help then? Did memories of his own tortured past rise up to haunt him as he witnessed the decline of the woman he loved?

Perhaps now they were both at peace. At least death seemed a peaceful conclusion to their painful lives. I could do no more than speculate about their motives and the possibilities they had ignored.

I lost track of time. Suddenly I was standing at the gate of the Confederate cemetery. The headstones stood out sharp and clear in the starlight. Here and there the light caught the tiny quartz crystals in the older stones and shone like diamonds offered to the spirits of the dead. I grasped the icy bars of the gate and clung to them a moment, trying to calm my breathing and, in turn, slow my racing mind.

Life exists in countless possibilities of thought and action. Those possibilities seem to narrow as we continue to make choices. With every word, every decision, large or small, we carve our path deeper and deeper into the future. For Caroline and Georges the path had deepened so much that they could neither change nor climb out of it to escape into happier times. Or so my thoughts ran as I let go the bars and headed home.

My steps no longer felt urgent. My thoughts had come to an uneasy peace with life as it is lived and life as we often dream it. Now I had choices to make. How would I carve my own future?

Walt looked extremely pleased with himself as he led me into his living room the next morning. "I've got a great surprise for us." He rubbed his hands together and pressed the button on the tape recorder.

"Welcome to the 'Easy Language' course in conversational Tibetan," the tape began.

"Alright!" I dropped my pack under the table and sat down, eager to learn. We didn't have much time to acquire a good familiarity with the language. We would be leaving in mid-May, just a month after my planned meeting with Therese.

Walt seemed thrilled to learn as well. He did have a distinct advantage over me. He was fluent in Mandarin and a few other Chinese dialects. I would have to settle for the scant knowledge I could glean from my traveler's book of Chinese. At least one of us knew it, just in case we ran into trouble with government officials.

After a few hours of study together, Walt decided we needed to go out for lunch. I didn't mind. Actually, I felt hungrier than I had in days. A returning appetite is a good sign of healing, I told myself, looking forward to the meal.

We walked down to the nearby Chinese restaurant, of course. Walt ordered in Mandarin, which impressed our waitress, who giggled and sighed whenever she looked at my dinner companion. So, Walt was charming in more than one language. Hardly surprising.

They carried on a lengthy conversation, the young woman blushing and answering in soft, but animated, tones. I only hoped that their discussion would bring me the Hunan-style bean curd that my stomach seemed to crave. I pushed away a vague feeling of jealousy by studying the artwork that brightened the dark walls.

When the waitress finally left to place our orders, I remembered the letter and began to tell Walt about it. His reaction surprised me and gave me new food for thought. He seemed completely sympathetic toward both Caroline and Georges.

"How tragic. They had to make such terrible decisions when they were both so young," he commented.

I suppose that I expected things to make sense in black and white. Though I often thought in shades of gray as well, Walt seemed much more aware of the mixed nature of reality. "Things are not what they seem," Franklin had told me. I realized that I had always wanted a concrete shape to events and situations. Life, as I was learning, seemed to offer only shadows at which to grasp.

So I listened to Walt as he talked about the painful choices of youth, hardly aware that our meals had arrived. I had thought I understood people fairly well, but I did not comprehend them, either fairly or well.

"I had to make some hard choices when I was young," he said wistfully. "I sure made some blunders myself."

"You, Walt? They couldn't have been that bad."

He smiled, stirring his food with an idle fork. "Yes, they were. I had to help raise three younger sisters after Dad walked out on us. At twelve I had a hell of a lot of responsibility on my shoulders. Mom had trouble coping. She looked to me for strength. There were times when I felt like the only parent in the house."

A new realization dawned in my mind. "That's why you've played the father role so well."

"And why I always played the protector in any relationship with a woman, even my ex-wife."

My jaw dropped open. I shut it quickly, hoping he didn't notice my reaction. "Ex-wife?" I asked delicately.

Nodding his head, he stabbed his fork into a piece of chicken. "It was as much my fault as it was hers. She needed protection, I thought. That's what I gave her. What she really needed was a lot of counseling and..." He did not finish.

"And what?"

"I wanted to say the toe of my shoe...but that wouldn't be very sympathetic, now would it?"

"I suppose that depends on if she really needed it," I suggested lightly, and then regretted it.

I had never seen this pain in his eyes before. For some reason it made my chest hurt and my jaw tighten.

He closed his eyes and took a deep breath. Letting it out slowly, he looked into my face with a searching gaze. He smiled suddenly and reached for my hand. His touch felt warm and comforting.

"I guess I needed your protection," I said, my voice growing hoarse for a moment.

Walt squeezed my hand with a surprising gentleness. "If that is what you need, then it's yours." He continued to peer into my eyes, but looked away just before I began to feel uncomfortable.

"You see?" I pointed out. "Just then. You…you always seem to know the right thing to do."

He let go of my hand and picked up the teapot. "More tea?"

CHAPTER THIRTY-SIX

The weeks hurried by while Walt and I worked hard at our Tibetan. He seemed to learn so much faster than I did. I had always believed that young people could learn new languages more quickly than older people. Listening to Walt zip through the lessons while I seemed to plod behind became a humbling experience. Of course, secretly I felt proud of him, just another reason to admire him, I admitted to myself.

Together we pored over maps of Tibet, its capital city of Lhasa, and the adjoining portions of India and Nepal. My excitement over the trip grew with each passing day.

I tried not to think about my upcoming meeting with Therese, but I was reminded every time I opened my closet door. I often purposely averted my gaze from the box of Caroline's ashes. It seemed pretty bizarre to keep them there.

I also tried not to look at the other box that still sat on the floor. My novel continued to gather dust. I had no desire to touch it and certainly not to read it.

Walt told me that was just fine. Novelists often left their first draft alone for months at a time. I just nodded my head and pursed my lips. I couldn't possibly be a novelist I kept telling myself. I should just stick to research. I knew I was good at that.

It was after one of our lessons that I expressed my growing frustration at the injustice of my father's murder. "I mean, where is the resolution in all this? The men who killed my father and ruined Caroline's life, they just got rich. They were never arrested, much less tried, for what they did."

"But didn't you say that they're all dead now?" Walt said. "Haven't they paid with their lives?"

I shook my head. "It still doesn't seem right."

"Or are you really looking for revenge?" He had a point. Maybe that's what I wanted.

"If I am...I guess that's not very Buddhist of me, is it?" Suddenly I felt embarrassed that I had shown myself to be vengeful in front of Walt. I wondered what he would think of me.

"No, but it is human." He opened the door and stepped outside with me. "It's understandable. Karma may have caught up with them, but the law never did."

I tossed my pack into the back seat of my car and turned back to face him. "I guess I'm learning a lot about how the world really works these days and I don't care much for it sometimes."

Walt noticed the bitter tone that had crept into my voice. "The world is what you make it, Kate." He gave me a stern look. "As a writer you should know that better than anyone else."

I gave in to my frustration. "I don't think I know anything anymore!" The weeks of doubt and guilt ignited my anger. "And what good is it to write fiction, anyway? So I can live in my own fantasy world? So I don't have to deal with things as they are?"

Walt's look of surprise lasted only a moment. Well, now he'd glimpsed my Irish temper, but at the moment I no longer cared what he thought of me. A half-smile lit his features. "No," he began patiently. "You write fiction so you don't have to accept things as they are. Sometimes you can tell more truth that way than you can with facts."

The anger passed. Now I just felt confused. "Huh? What do you mean by that?"

"Think about it. You don't have to have all the answers right away." He waved and turned back toward the house.

Finally the day came when I had to pack the car and head for Blacksburg. I usually loved going there but today I felt nervous, no, afraid of facing Caroline's daughter. I didn't know why. It was almost as if I bore some responsibility for what had happened to Therese. I wondered if I would have to defend her mother's hurtful actions.

April had arrived in a glory of green leaves and fragrant blossoms. The tender growth danced in the soft breezes as I traveled down the highway. I had the windows open so I could smell the fresh, sweet scents of spring. The mountains glowed with new life and, as I drove deeper into the Blue Ridge, I even began to feel a sense of renewal.

The trip to Blacksburg usually relaxed me. I had wondered if it could work its magic this time. Surprisingly, it did. The stress of the past three months seemed to melt away. Perhaps I had simply left it behind in Fredericksburg. It didn't matter. The majesty of the green mountains around me made the details of my existence seem small in comparison.

I stopped at the Afton Mountain overlook and stepped out of the car. The breeze stirred my hair around my shoulders as I walked to the stone wall at the edge of the cliff to gaze down into the valley below. The view extended for miles. I felt like I was standing at the end of the universe itself while all of its beauty and grand possibilities stretched out below my feet.

In the chaos of change lies opportunity. My own life seemed to have gotten out of control. Since losing Caroline, I had lived in grief for her loss, guilt for my supposed inadequacies and fear for my own safety. I had allowed these crippling emotions to rob me of my desire—my life-long passion—to be a writer, just as my friend had let guilt and depression rob her of the happiness of motherhood.

I breathed the heady scents of mountain flowers. It felt as though I could inhale the power of life, bringing it into my body to give it strength to live as I ought. I knew that I stood on the brink of an important discovery about myself, about what potential still lay hidden in my being. Its fulfillment would require great courage, perhaps more than I possessed at that moment in time. I turned to go.

As I reached out, my hand paused on the door. A hawk cried overhead. I watched it circle a few times, in ever-widening arcs, before it flew out of sight among the distant mountains. It had its destiny, its purpose. The hawk never had to ask what it was. What was mine? And why did I even have to ask?

The car seemed to make its own way through downtown Blacksburg without my guidance. How many times had I driven these streets? I pulled up to my mother's small, two-story house. She had fallen in love with it the moment she saw the lovely stone facings fringed with ivy. She even trimmed the windows in a blue-gray to highlight the darker stones. Daffodils bloomed alongside the petunias and impatiens my mother had just planted. Mom was still in class so I let myself in and settled into the room she always kept ready for me.

Just after I graduated from college, I had come here often. As time passed, I had visited less frequently. Still, my mother never pressured me to come down. She knew I was busy building my own life in Fredericksburg. That made her happy, she would tell me. If she missed me, she didn't let me know. Maybe she did miss me. Maybe the time had come to make my family—what little I had left—a greater priority in my life. I had actually begun to think along those lines after Caroline died. Her death continued to remind me of the fragile nature of this existence.

By the time my mother arrived home I had made tea for us both and had put fresh croissants on the table to tempt her. She could afford the extra calories, anyway. She was as thin as I, maybe thinner since I saw her last. "Willowy" was the word she liked to use, but Aunt Maggie preferred to use "rail-thin," as she eyed us with a certain envy.

I sat at the table while my mom bustled around the kitchen.

"When did you have time to get these?" Mom exclaimed, kissing me more than once on the top of my head.

"I stopped in town. How are classes going this semester?"

"Great, except I'm having a few Buddhist qualms about working with the experimental cows. Other than that, the professors are good, working us to the bone as usual." She took a delicate bite of the pastry. I wondered why I had never learned to eat as politely as she did. Too much trouble, I thought, as I bit into an apple cinnamon croissant.

Fixing me with a motherly gaze she asked, "How are you doing now?"

"Just fine." To avoid talking about how the grieving process was going—her real question—I hurried into a list of my preparations for the trip to Tibet.

"That's all very exciting, but you haven't answered me."

I could never pull anything over on my mom. "I'm okay, taking it one day at a time. You know how it is."

She nodded, patting my arm with a sympathetic hand. "Yes. And your novel?"

I laughed. "My novel? I haven't touched it since."

"Look, Kate. You can't fool me. I know how hard you worked on that first draft and how proud you were to finish it. I felt so happy to hear about it when you called that night."

"Well, lots of wannabes have a novel or two hidden away in a drawer or closet. It doesn't mean anything. It was probably just some juvenile attempt to find meaning in life, the same old same old."

"No, from what you told me, it was a little more than that." Grasping my hand firmly she looked directly into my eyes to add emphasis to her words. "Don't give up now. You've had this dream since childhood. Don't you think I remember reading your stories, listening to you talk about writing as if nothing else in the world mattered?"

"That was a long time ago, Mom."

She gave me a wry smile. "Not as long as you'd like to believe. Anyway, my point is, you've wanted this all your life. Hasn't Walt told you that you've got talent?"

"It takes more than that." I stared sullenly into the bottom of my cup.

"And you have that, too."

"You have to say stuff like that 'cause you're my mom. All moms talk like that to their kids."

"Maybe, maybe not. How do you know? Just don't make any rash decisions and throw away something important."

"Like my manuscript?"

"Yeah, or maybe your future."

Her words reflected my thoughts during the trip down. Despite the fact that she was my mother, I really did take her seriously. I always had.

"When does Therese arrive?" Mom asked, changing the subject. She had made her point already.

"She was supposed to arrive in Roanoke today sometime. She said she wanted to stay overnight with a friend. She'll be here in the morning."

"Good. Let me take you out to a great veggie restaurant tonight. You'll love this place." She glanced out the window at her gardens. "But first, I've got some gardening to do. Want to help?"

I expected that.

Outside in the bright sunlight, Mom looked weary after her long day of classes and lab work. She smiled when I told her to put down the bag of mulch she had carried from the garage.

"The back garden can't wait," she protested. "The weeds look poised for a hostile take-over."

"I'll do it, Mom. You should rest."

"I'll let you carry the bag for me, but I don't need to rest. I've still got a lot of life left in me, you know."

"Yeah," and I winked, hefting the load. "Age is supposed to be an illusion, anyway."

She gave me a sidelong glance. "Well, then, when you've brought that bag around back, get the wheelbarrow out for this mirage." She walked in front of me carrying her gardening tools and an empty bucket. She shook her gray locks back from her face and strode across the grass in her earth-colored sandals. Definitely a Flower Child, I chuckled to myself.

I thought her an attractive woman, unafraid to show the gray that she told me came from wisdom. I supposed the deepening lines must have come from the same place, of course.

The back garden grew in partial shade from a pair of tall black oak trees. Mom had set the beds in front of an unused wooded area that adjoined her property. This was my favorite spot. Against a dramatic backdrop of wild rhododendrons with their long, shiny leaves and tightly wrapped pink buds, flowers and foliage glowed in healthy brilliance.

Mounds of hostas bore delicate blue flowers, surrounding a tall tree stump covered with purple clematis. I recognized the leaves of the later-blooming asters, daisies and mums. Mom had already planted a lovely border of impatiens, petunias and sweet William.

I dropped the bag and inhaled the scents of woods and garden. My mom figured that the work would calm my troubled spirit. She was right, as usual.

We filled in areas where mulch had turned to soil over the long winter. Side by side we pulled the vigorous weeds that had crept into forbidden territory. From the end of a particularly extensive root system, a tiny snake wriggled free and dove back into the soil.

"Oh!" my mother cried in surprise. "A worm snake! They are such wonderful creatures. I didn't know I had one back here."

That was my mom. She had a terrific respect for all living beings, including a humble snake. I glanced at her face, radiant with appreciation for a simple reptile.

"Pretty, thing, too," I commented. The snake's pinkish skin had flashed an iridescent glow in the sunlight just before it disappeared back into the earth.

Mom continued working. "Do you remember the snake your dad caught in our back yard when you were six?"

I nodded. "It was a big rat snake. We kept it in a tank for a couple of days to study it."

"Your father didn't want you to be afraid of snakes like his sister." She pulled another handful of weeds. "You wrote a story about it, remember?"

I yanked harder on some wiry crabgrass.

"Don't you remember, Kate?"

I let out a breath in annoyance. "Of course I remember. Some silly story about a snake that didn't like killing mice."

"Your father was so proud. You gave it to him for his birthday. You even drew illustrations. You said you wanted it to look just like a real book."

"I know what you're trying to say, Mom."

"Do you?"

"Yeah. You're going to tell me what Dad said." I stabbed the ground with the trowel.

"What did he say?"

I dug viciously into the soil. "He said I would make a great writer. For cryin' out loud, Mom, I was only six years old! No one knows what they want to do when they're six!"

"You did."

CHAPTER THIRTY-SEVEN

The vegetarian chili was the best I had ever tasted at Tofu Magic, our favorite restaurant in Blacksburg. It came in a sourdough bread bowl, steaming hot, with red onion and a rainbow of diced, fresh peppers. "If you need any help with that..." Mom began, eyeing the dish with envy. Just then her quesadillas arrived dripping with Monterey Jack cheese, broccoli and jalapenos. Her eyes lit up with delight. She glanced at me with a mischievous twinkle. "Extra hot. You want to try it?"

I knew that Mom loved spicy-hot food. I had even witnessed her devour what most people would consider inedible peppers, and not suffer at all. I had watched to see if her eyes teared, but they stayed dry, as though she had eaten nothing more than a sweet, bell pepper. "It's gotta be that cut you got on your tongue as a kid," I had told her. She had just grinned, as she was doing now.

"No thanks," I responded. "I'll let you enjoy it all to yourself." I sniffed the steam rising from my chili and stirred it around in its doughy bowl.

"Suit yourself," Mom answered, cutting a piece of quesadilla with her fork and tipping it toward me in salute. "Cheers."

I couldn't finish my chili so I asked for a box to take it home. The waitress smiled as she handed me the Styrofoam container. "It is a lot of food," she commented.

Mom paid the bill despite my offer to treat her. "Oh, no. You did all that gardening. I want to treat you."

"Thanks."

"Oh, by the way...I want to show you something when we get back home."

"What is it?" I asked, intrigued by the tone of mystery in her voice.

"You'll see." She rose and slung her patchwork bag over a shoulder. We walked out into the spring evening. Breathing the fragrant air, I anticipated a lovely walk back to my mother's house. I knew there would be no point in asking Mom what she wanted to show me. I even tried not to guess as we wound our way through the quaint neighborhood, with bright blossoms shining in almost every yard we passed.

All of the flowers in Blacksburg seemed brighter than any back home. I wondered if it was from some concerted effort on the part of the townspeople to be particularly attentive to their flowers, or if, maybe, it was from the elevation and the fresh mountain air. I knew I felt better, too. But I don't think I was any brighter.

The house welcomed us with its homespun charm. Mom went straight into the living room and indicated the easy chair. "Now, sit down and close your eyes."

I relaxed into the chair. "Okay, if it makes you happy, Mom," I answered and obliged her by lightly shutting my eyes.

"No peeking!" She walked out of the living room. I heard her steps fade as she went to the study. I leaned back in the easy chair and tried to clear my mind of its multiple thoughts. What a relief it was to have some quiet between the busy stream of images and words that usually flowed in a constant stream. I savored the peace in that space of time until I heard my mother's returning footsteps.

She stopped at my knee and laid something in my lap. My hands dropped to the object and quickly felt the outlines of three notebooks bundled together with string. "Okay," Mom said. "You can open them."

I gazed at the notebooks, curious. The covers were faded shades of black and gray. I looked up at my mother. Her face had taken on a solemn expression. "Go ahead. Read them." She turned and sat in the rocker by the stone hearth.

My hand trembled slightly as I opened one of the books. I felt vaguely apprehensive as my eyes fell to the first page. The handwriting was bold and barely familiar. Yes, I had loved how he used to make those strong, square letters. They trooped fearlessly across the page in one of my favorite stories, one I would often ask him to tell me before I closed my eyes for sleep.

A tear dropped on the page. I dabbed it quickly with my sleeve before it made a splotch on his writing, his words. Putting the sleeve to my eyes, I dried the tears that threatened to ruin what my father had written so many years ago.

"I packed them away... just after he died," my mother said quietly. I looked up, as if only now realizing she was still there. She shook her head and wiped an eye with her fingers. "I couldn't read them without crying, so I put them away. Then things got so busy. I never took them out of the box again until last week."

"I didn't know he'd written them down." How many nights had I lain awake in bed remembering his stories, almost afraid to commit them to a page? No, I had to remember them as he told me—with the inflections he had used and all the wonderful animal sounds he had made.

But here they were in his own hand, in the blue felt-tip ink he had liked so much. I leafed through the pages with care. Had I discovered a lost scroll that survived the fire in the great library of Alexandria, I could not have treated it more carefully. Every story was here, just as I had remembered them. In the margins Dad had even sketched a few of the main characters. His pen brought them to life with its bold strokes, as his words had done so well.

"They're all here," I murmured in wonder.

"Yes. He once thought he would publish them." At these words I glanced up. Mom must have sensed my thought. She nodded, smiling. "Yes, Kate. I think we should publish them for him. In fact," she continued, smiling even more broadly, "I've already started entering them on my computer."

"I didn't know Dad wanted to be a published writer."

"It was something he wanted to do when—" but her voice caught in her throat. She swallowed and finished the sentence, "when he retired."

I nodded. "Then we can do this for him."

"Yes, but more than that—he had hoped..." She fixed me with her bright eyes. "He used to tell me that he thought his Katy would be published first."

I looked down at the handwritten pages and studied them, not knowing what to say. Was writing only my father's dream, or was it my dream too?

CHAPTER THIRTY-EIGHT

Therese looked more beautiful than I remembered. Her hair hung down to the middle of her back in lustrous waves of shimmering black. She stood watching us for a moment, then, dropping her bags, she enfolded us each in a warm embrace.

Though much taller than Caroline, her face carried the unmistakable, delicate features of her mother. I wondered why I didn't realize the resemblance before. Of course, I had met her in a dark observatory.

We sat in the kitchen and exchanged pleasantries for a little while. Therese even showed us pictures of her children. She seemed a happy person. I guessed I was looking for signs of her mother's depression. Maybe she didn't inherit that.

Yet, as the afternoon wore on, a cloud seemed to come over her features and settle in her heart. Something was eating at her, I knew. Finally, Therese could hold it in no longer.

"I do wish that I had known her. I am envious that you both got to know her better than I did." Sitting rigidly at the kitchen table, she tried to continue as calmly as possible. I knew it was beginning to take more effort on her part. I could see the tightness in her jaw and the bloodless skin stretched over her knuckles.

"I know she wanted to protect me from...those men, but..." The struggle grew within her and she gave in to it. "I wanted a mother so much! Why didn't she tell me who she was?"

Mom reached out and gently took her hand. "She feared for your life, Therese."

"I don't care about that! Do you know how I dreamed of having a mother? Do you know how much a little girl thinks about what her dead mother must have been like?" Tears filled her dark eyes and spilled unheeded onto the table.

My mouth tightened to hold back the emotion that threatened to show itself. After years of dreaming about my father—yes, I knew something of what she had gone through.

Therese fixed her gaze on my mother's face, serene yet filled with compassion. "You're a mother. You love your daughter."

"Yes," Mom answered evenly. "I love her more than anything in this world."

Therese turned her eyes on me. "You have your mother. You are so lucky to have grown up with her constant presence in your life. How would you have felt to be without her?"

I shook my head. No words came to my aid. No wisdom rose from the depths of my experience. Only the hollowness of my own early loss grasped at my throat. I shut my lips tight against it.

The black curls shook violently as emotion exploded in an agony of raw pain. "I hate her! I hate her for what she did! I never got a chance to love her, to know her." The shoulders slumped, finally dropping their burden. Her head fell on extended arms. Therese sobbed in heartbroken anguish, her body shaking and heaving with every breath.

Mom moved to kneel by her side and held her as she wept. I could hear her murmur comfort into the distraught woman's ear. I sat quietly, not knowing what to do. Here was my friend's daughter and I felt unable to help.

"If your mother hadn't left to get treatment, she might never have overcome her problems," I heard my mother saying. "She and your father spared you that pain. They thought they were doing the right thing." Therese raised her head and wiped her eyes with a handful of tissues.

Finally she nodded. "I suppose you are right."

"You're a mother, too," Mom continued. "You know how difficult it can be to make the right decisions for your child. Your parents were in a terribly difficult situation. They were so young."

Therese relaxed into the chair and blew her nose. Her eyes shone in the light that streamed through the kitchen window. Suddenly I reached into my pocket and brought out the black-and-white picture that Caroline had treasured. "Therese," I began, hesitating. "I think that this is the picture she mentioned."

As she reached out to grasp it slowly with her graceful fingers, I could see the hint of a smile beginning to play on her features. "Yes, that is the one. My father had a larger one in a frame on the mantle." Looking deeply into my eyes she said a quiet, "Thank you."

My mother had risen to bring a pot of tea to the table. We remained silent as she poured out the golden-brown liquid. Therese picked up her cup and held it, gazing into its liquid depths. How like her mother she seemed in this action. I almost felt that Caroline sat with us, drinking tea in delicate sips.

"It will take a long while for you to heal, Therese," Mom said softly. "Give yourself plenty of time. Don't expect to come to terms with this quickly. It could be years before you can understand why your mother did what she did. Just remember, she loved you very much."

"I suppose she did, Melinda. It's just hard to see right now."

"Caroline gave everything for you," my mother added. "What greater love is there than that?"

In the morning we packed a picnic lunch and headed up into the mountains to the Cascades. The road twisted steeply. At times we felt we were clinging to the sides of the mountain. Mom's minivan climbed valiantly up the steep grades, giving me a new respect for the "little engine that could," her pet name for the vehicle.

Arriving at the park, we got out and prepared to hike up the trail to the waterfall. The morning felt cool and brisk. Our breath turned to a light vapor that trailed over our heads. Mom walked ahead of us, her feet never faltering even over the rocky parts of the path.

We had taken the fire road up the mountain. The lower trail was closed. It had become flooded in some areas because of the spring rains. Today, however, the sky shimmered in pale blue with wisps of high clouds overhead.

Mom pointed out the spring flowers now and then. Wild geraniums raised their pink heads over patches of wood anemone. Blue periwinkle flourished in abundance, often hiding the tiny asters at their feet. Therese followed, admiring the forest with its lush, green growth. Though she was not a hiker, she kept the pace very well. "Do you come here a lot?" she asked, still awed by the beauty around her.

"As often as I can," Mom responded with a sigh.

"I think we come up here every time I visit," I added. If I had to choose my favorite wild place in Virginia, this probably would have been it.

We saw no other humans on our hike. The woods reverberated with the sounds of life: warbling birds, insects humming, and squirrels dashing along their tree-branch highways. I could almost feel the pulse of life surrounding us in its many forms. In the underbrush I heard the rustles and crackles of hidden creatures going about their daily business. The loudest and most constant sound, the rushing waters running just out of sight beyond the trail, served as backdrop and bass to the living song.

After climbing for about a mile and a half, the trail leveled out. Now we trod across large, flat rocks along the riverbank. Upon closer inspection the rocks yielded an ancient secret. Many of them looked pitted, imprinted with the shapes of fossils from a prehistoric sea. My mother and I had occasionally collected a few of the smaller stones. One from this very spot sat proudly on my desk back home, to remind me of the ancient beauty here.

"Oh!" Therese exclaimed, stooping to examine an expanse of fossil-covered rock. "Have you seen these before?"

"Every time we come up here," I answered.

"I loved fossil hunting when I was a girl. My father and I collected them in France, too."

Mom stood on a rock overhanging the river. She seemed the quintessential woodswoman in her down vest, gray felt crusher and hiking boots. She smiled at Therese and the childlike excitement that sent the younger woman from rock to rock, peering at the amazing number of fossils.

We continued on our way, climbing over rocks, sometimes slipping on the wet ones. The sound of falling water grew louder as we approached the end of the trail. My mother gasped in awe as she clambered over the last rise and saw the falls in full view.

I hurried after Therese and came to stand beside them both. Caroline's daughter stood in silence, drinking in the glorious sight. From the top of a cliff, about a hundred feet above the river, the water cascaded down, sparkling in the sunlight. It fell in front of a sheer wall of stone and churned in a wide but shallow pool at the bottom. Every time I saw it I felt struck with wonder at its beauty and raw power.

"Melinda! What are you doing?" cried Therese, as my mother tossed her boots aside, pulled off her socks, rolled up her pants legs and waded straight into the water. When our guest turned to me I had already followed suit, grinning at her open-mouthed stare.

"Come on in," I called as I waded out to join my mom. "The water's fine!"

Therese put her hand in the river and jerked it out, shaking off the water. "It's cold as ice!"

"Your feet will get so cold you won't notice it. Where's your sense of adventure?" I teased, grinning happily.

"Sense of adventure? Who says icy water is an adventure? I think you're both crazy!" So saying, Therese pulled her socks and shoes off and followed us to the middle of the pool.

Long ago the strata here had been thrust up and turned on its side. The various layers of sedimentary rock were plainly visible. The softer sediments had been worn deeper by the water, creating long grooves in the rocky floor. I felt them with my toes.

Around us the ground rose steeply so that we felt we were in a tall, natural amphitheater of rock, trees and water. Looking up, I saw that the few clouds had dispersed, leaving a fresh, spring sky. I raised my arms as though to embrace the sun just overhead. Its warmth poured into my body in contrast to the freezing water that lapped around my shins.

Mom had walked over to the falls. She stood in front of the white sheets of water, extending her hands into the sparkling wall. "Cold enough for you, Mom?" She smiled and nodded. She looked like she was communing with the spirit of the water. Therese gingerly made her way over the slippery bottom to join her.

"I see why you both love this place so much." She had to shout to be heard this close to the falling water. My mother only nodded again. Therese put her hand in the white spray and pulled it back, shivering slightly. "It's cold, but very beautiful."

I left them contemplating the wall of water and wandered along the edge of the pool. Further down, away from the main falls, the rock glistened with a thousand rivulets that seeped along its face. I touched the wet stones with my hands. I imagined the power of the cold rock itself flowing into my palms and through my body.

Following one layer of strata down the shelf, I climbed out onto a boulder and sat for a while, warming myself in the sun. Over our heads birds flitted from tree to tree, occasionally stopping to bathe in shallow pools formed by the rocks. The world seemed at peace, here in this refuge along the river, its noises replaced by the sounds of the falling water, its sights blotted out by the wild beauty that stretched for miles around us.

After a while—I supposed Mom's feet were getting cold—the two women made their way back to the trail. As they began putting their shoes back on their wet feet, I reluctantly returned to do the same.

"This is perfect," Therese was saying. "I know she would have loved it."

We trudged up the steep trail to the top of the falls. From here we had an exquisite view of the water dropping into the pool below. "Is this the place?" I asked quietly.

"Yes. This is just right. I feel it," Therese answered, looking out over the treetops below.

Slinging my pack to the stony ground, I nodded in agreement. I knelt down to unbuckle the flap and reached inside. The birds called and sang for their mates. New life budded and blossomed everywhere we looked. Spring pulsed with its many and fertile forms. Yes, this was the right place, I thought, as I drew the large bag of ashes from the pack. They had sat in their box in my closet for a little over two months. Now we could finally fulfill Caroline's last wishes.

We stood above the cascading water, my mother, Caroline's daughter, and I. All three of us touched the bag as the white ashes fell in their own small cascade, into the white sheets of pounding water. Silent tears accompanied them on their downward journey. I watched the sunlight glimmer on the light specks, realizing that just a year ago I had met the person whose substance they were.

I shook the last particles out over the falls and folded the bag to return it to my pack. "Be at peace," I murmured, pausing to look down into the river. The falling torrent seemed to snatch my words and carry them away with the ashes, down into the woods, into the valley below and on to ever-larger rivers, finally to the sea.

I remembered the words of the Spanish poet, Jorge Manrique. He said that our lives are rivers that flow into the sea, which is death. But new life follows death, I added to myself, as though hearing the message of the newborn forest all around me. Life flows into death and returns to flow again.

We made our way carefully down to the pool. Mom wanted to make sure the ashes had not collected in one of the areas where the current did not reach. Walking out into the water we could not find any trace of them. The river was doing its part for Caroline.

Therese remained thoughtful for the first mile of our hike back to the car. Suddenly, she saw something. Bringing her finger to her lips, she gestured up along the small stream where a deer stood with a tiny fawn at its side. We watched the two animals, enchanted with the sight.

The mother looked around, her ears moving to catch the slightest sound. We remained very still, watching as the doe finally bent to drink. Then her head came up in a startled motion. She must have sensed our presence. Perhaps the wind had changed. Turning quickly, she and her fawn leaped off into the underbrush.

"How lovely!" Therese exclaimed softly. She began to talk animatedly about the deer and other wildlife she had loved to watch when her father took her on hikes near their home long ago. Hearing her words seemed to lighten the burden of sorrow I had carried up the mountain. Having fulfilled my last duty toward my friend, I could carry the lighter, happier burden of her memory.

CHAPTER THIRTY-NINE

When we arrived back at my mother's house, Therese excused herself for a few minutes. Mom stood at the stove heating water for tea. I sat at the table. We said nothing. There seemed no need for words at that moment.

The kettle whistled happily, as if in harmony with our contented mood. Mom plucked it from the burner and poured the steaming water into a flowered teapot. The fragrance of orange and spices filled the room.

"I brought something to show you both," Therese said, as she walked into the kitchen carrying a gray firebox. Placing it on the table, she unlocked it and carefully opened the lid. It was stuffed full of papers.

Therese handed one to each of us. "Franklin gave these to me. They were my mother's old papers."

Mom gasped. I glanced over to see her holding a hand over her mouth. I looked down at the paper in my hand. It was a ledger. At the bottom I noticed a familiar handwriting. I remembered seeing it the night before when Mom showed me my father's old journals. The writing was identical.

"How did she..." My mother reached toward the box. "May I?" she asked, glancing at Therese.

"Of course. I...I don't know what I should do with these. By rights they really belong to you now." Therese shook her head in bewilderment. "Franklin warned me that a homicide detective in Rhode Island wanted these, but he did not want to tell him about them, or me, for that matter."

As Mom looked through the other papers in the box she caught my eye. "These are what Burkette was looking for when he called me."

I nodded slowly. "But if he gets them now, what then?"

"Then Caroline's sacrifice," she dropped the stack of papers to the table, "will have been for nothing." She sat down heavily and laid her head in her hands.

"No, no!" Therese exclaimed. "Who will be brought to justice?" She looked to me for support. "Kate said the killers are dead. What point is there in solving the case now?"

"It'll sure make Detective Burkette feel good," I commented wryly.

Mom raised her head. Gazing at each of us in turn she spoke quietly. "Kate has already been threatened. Her life, all our lives, will be in danger if this evidence gets out. Caroline gave up a life of comfort to see that we would be safe." She turned to Therese. "But she left them to you, to do with them as you feel best."

Tears sprang into her eyes, the eyes that looked so like her mother's. "No! If it were up to me I would destroy them! I don't even know why my mother kept them!"

"Insurance, probably." My mother rose from the table, one hand resting on the pile of papers. "If we get rid of these we will be guilty of destroying evidence."

"And if we don't, we run the risk of being killed." I stood and shrugged my shoulders. "Solve a puzzle for a Newport detective or live...tough choice, huh?"

Mom nodded, giving us each one last searching glance. "We are agreed, then?"

Therese walked over to the living room and picked up a box of matches from the mantle. She held them up for her answer. We followed her lead and stood silently by the hearth for a moment.

Mom took the matches and stooped to her task. Balling up some of the pages she placed them on the grate. The match flared when she struck it on the side of the box, the pungent smell of burned sulfur filling the air. Lighting the crumpled paper, she began feeding the flames with page after page from the stack.

The fire burned brightly, the flames dancing over the numbers and words in the familiar handwriting. I almost stopped my mom for one last look at my father's work, but my hesitation faded with the writing.

The last page went into the flames, which licked hungrily for more. The papers darkened into ash, consumed completely by the fire. Finally, they crumbled into pieces and fell between the grating. They were gone. For a few moments we stared at the ashes in silent relief mixed with sorrow.

"There is no justice," I murmured.

My mother smiled up at me. "Perhaps not, but there is life." Standing up she took our hands in hers. "After so many years it's finally over. For all of us."

Therese insisted on cooking a special dinner for us that evening in celebration. She had devised a French-style tofu dish. My mother and I both proclaimed it the best we had ever tasted. "I didn't know you could do that with tofu," I commented, after stuffing myself to the brim with three courses that included various vegetables and portabella mushrooms.

"You'll have to give me your recipes," Mom said, rising to clear the dishes from the table.

"Of course. It's actually rather easy." Therese blushed and turned to open a cupboard. Bringing out three bowls she set them on the shelf. "Now, for dessert," she announced, pulling a carton of gourmet ice cream from the freezer. "I couldn't resist buying this when I saw it in the grocery store. It's my favorite!"

Seeing the label, my mother shot a glance at me. "Do you like Double Chocolate Fudge?" Therese was asking.

I blinked and returned my mother's gaze. "It's been a while since I've had any," I began, hesitating.

"Maybe it's about time," Mom commented in a quiet voice. Mom was never pushy but she possessed the ability to gently steer her daughter in positive directions.

I smiled, chuckling softly at the last burden of grief lifting from my heart. "Yes. It is about time." Chocolate ice cream never tasted as good as it did that night.

We said a tearful goodbye to Therese when she left in the morning for her conference. She had politely declined my mother's offer to stay at the house during the week. Mom understood. Instead, we exchanged addresses and promised to keep in touch.

I spent one more day with Mom, working all morning and most of the afternoon in her gardens while she went to classes. She took me out to dinner in the evening. I talked excitedly about the trip Walt and I were planning. She listened with pleasure showing plainly in her eyes. "I suppose I can trust Walt with my only daughter," she teased.

"Better than anyone else, I guess. But, sometimes I wish..."

"What?" Mom leaned forward on her elbows.

My cheeks flushed suddenly. "I...I don't know. It's just that," I looked into her loving face. "Sometimes I wish I could have what you and Dad had."

Mom nodded slowly in understanding. "You can. But you have to decide that you want it."

In the morning I tossed my pack and suitcase into the back of my old station wagon. Turning to my mother, I hugged her, holding on for an extra moment. She kissed my cheek. "Will I see you before you fly off on your Tibetan adventure?"

"I don't know. I've got a lot to do before we leave."

"Like what?"

"Well, for one thing, we're still learning the language. Besides, I think I have an idea for a new novel." At those words my mother grabbed me and gave me a powerful hug.

"I'm so glad!" she whispered. Her eyes brightened with moisture. So did mine.

I don't know if it was possible, but the mountains seemed even greener and more majestic on my trip back to Fredericksburg. I stopped again at Afton Mountain. The day was startling in its clarity. The sun poured warmth and life into the valley below. Over a distant mountain a group of vultures circled, patient for the death of another creature. Life and death intertwined in its endless, circling dance. Endings and beginnings—all happened at the same time. Perhaps there really was no distinction between the two.

My old station wagon rumbled along, humming its own song of life. I didn't push it, especially up the long grades. I felt content with the sounds and scents of the trip. There seemed no sense in rushing home.

When I finally reached the end of Route 20, the afternoon sun had hidden behind heaps of dark clouds. The storm came on suddenly, rain pelting the windshield faster than the old wipers could sweep it aside. I pulled the light switch on and the headlights shone in the streams of water that poured from the sky.

Arriving home, I left my pack in the car and ran up the steps to the door. It opened as soon as I reached out with my keys. "There you are," Andy greeted me, pulling the door wide so I could hurry into the house. "Your mom just called. She wanted to know if you made it home okay. She said you usually make the trip a bit faster than she does. Some comment about a lead foot." She grinned.

"Light feet today, Andy. Actually, I just took my time." I shook my head and drops of rain flew out of my dripping hair.

"Thanks a lot. We don't need the weather in here, girl!" My housemate, who often did the same thing to us, wiped a few drops from her face, flicking them good-naturedly back at me. "By the way, that detective called. Wanted to know when you'd be leaving town. Are they running you out on a rail, or something?"

"Very funny," I replied with a rueful smile. "Did they have any leads on the driver?"

Andy knew exactly what I meant. "I asked that same question. Nothing, Kate. He sounded pretty frustrated."

The news did not surprise me. They had so little to go on, anyway. I could imagine the good detective's high forehead creased by that familiar look of concern, the bushy brows arching over his eyes.

"Holly and I are going out tonight. My brother's band is playing downtown. You want to go?"

"The Six-Armed Monkey Boys?" I made a face.

"I know how much you like rockabilly!" Andy's tawny eyes gleamed mischievously.

"Actually, I'd like to go. It's not rockabilly that bothers me." I shook my head.

"I know. John is such a loser. If I'd known then what I know now...Anyway, it's all in the past. We'll leave at eight-thirty."

"Cool," I responded carelessly. Andy had once set me up with one of the band members. He seemed nice at first but he turned out to have a Jekyll-and-Hyde personality. I had ended the evening recommending he get therapy. He was mistake-date number one on my list.

CHAPTER FORTY

The Ready Musket boasted a dark dining room on the main floor. The walls were lined with signed pictures of Republican congressmen and a few presidents. We never ate there. Walking gingerly up the narrow staircase, we arrived at the smoke-filled bar upstairs. I flashed my I.D. and paid the four-dollar cover charge. I wasn't sure the Six-Armed Monkey Boys were worth four bucks but a night out with my housemates was. Holly seemed to like the Monkey Boys. I never understood why, especially after my fiasco of a blind date.

The music crashed in our ears. I couldn't hear what Holly started to say to me, something about a call. I figured she would tell me later when we could both hear again.

We took a table along the outside wall, not too close to any of the speakers. We wanted to be able to hear each other talk. Gillian, one of Andy's friends, came over to wait on us.

"Reds for you two," she shouted gaily, repeating my housemates' order. Looking at me she laughed and pointed a long nail, painted black with yellow stars, in my direction. "And you'll have the Stout, right?"

I nodded. I never ordered anything except the stout on draft. It tasted like beer and a meal in one, and it was very good here.

We talked and laughed louder with each round of drinks until the band finally took a break. Andy nudged Holly. "Here they come," she said, indicating the band members threading their way through the crowd to our table. Andy stood up to give her brother, Dean, a quick hug. Actually, Dean was her half-brother, from her mother's first marriage. His complexion was much lighter, like his dad's.

"Hey, little sister! Still churning out term papers in one night?" Dean smiled fondly at her. He gave Holly a light peck on the cheek. "And congrats on your engagement."

"Thanks," Holly replied, showing him the ring.

"Ooh, aah," he mouthed, looking at the ring from different angles. "Nice rock," he finally declared.

Dean turned to me and gave me a tight squeeze. We shared a sense of kinship, having both lost our fathers while quite young. We had commiserated over glasses of stout on more than one occasion. "How're things going, Kate?" He asked, taking on a solicitous tone.

"Fine."

"You sure?"

I nodded.

The three men pulled some chairs up to the table and sat down. I said a courteous "hello" to John and Terry. I avoided John's gaze, though I could feel it. Rejection hurts for a long time, I guess.

Dean and Terry ordered beer but John, surprisingly, only wanted a soda. "Not your usual brew," Andy commented.

John grinned, a little embarrassed. I had never seen him blush before. "I can't now, you know, drink alcohol."

Andy's eyebrows shot up for a moment, and then relaxed as Dean quietly told her, "It doesn't mix with his new meds."

"Oh, sorry," Andy added, then asked John, "How are you feeling these days?"

His lips tightened as he nodded slightly. "Better, much better." He turned to me as if to see my reaction. I felt surprised at the revelation. Whatever medication he was taking certainly had a calming effect on this guy who I had seen turn wild man at the drop of a hat. My gaze softened as I began to look at him with new eyes.

John leaned closer to me as the others went off into their own conversations. "You weren't the only one who told me that. I—I feel like a new person." He paused, embarrassed again.

For the first time since our date I smiled at him. He had changed. "I'm glad that you're...doing what you need to do." I fumbled for words that would not offend him.

"Yeah, thanks. How 'bout you? Still married to your computer?" His teasing tones held a hint of kindness and, perhaps, hope for a second chance.

I looked at his chiseled face. Though pitted with scars, it still looked handsome. Before I could answer, a familiar voice fell on my ear. With more eagerness than I wanted to show, I glanced across the bar. There he was, talking to the bouncer in the doorway. My eyes seemed to have a mind of their own. I could not pull them away from the tall, lean figure of Walt entering the bar.

He looked around the room and our eyes met. He smiled and waved, making his way, unhurried, to our table. In my peripheral vision I saw John lean back in his chair and sigh. "Guess not," he muttered to himself.

Holly grabbed my arm. "That's what I was trying to tell you." I looked into her earnest green eyes, startled. She pointed at Walt. "He called and I invited him to meet us here." Oh, thank the heavens for forward housemates! A feeling of pure joy filled my being. I did not want to admit why. I must have been relieved to have John's unwelcome attentions diverted, I told myself, knowing that wasn't it at all.

I tried not to smile too widely as Walt came up to the table. As I introduced him, not without a little pride in my mentor, I could feel my face flush. It was not just from the stout.

"Happy to meet you." Dean extended his hand with his customary enthusiasm. I avoided looking at John during the introductions. I could not help noticing how quiet he had suddenly become. From the corner of my eye I could see him slide back into his chair, as far as possible from Walt.

Holly started chattering immediately, filling him in on the band's music and plans for the future. I don't think I heard a word that she said. I felt alone with Walt. He responded politely to Holly's patter, but I could tell he wasn't paying close attention, either. Occasionally he glanced over at me and smiled, his eyes searching mine for a reaction to his presence.

"Well, I'd better go take a leak before the next set," John muttered as he scraped the chair back along the wood floor and stood up.

"Thanks for telling us," Andy commented dryly. "Why don't you just raise your fingers and let us know, like kindergarten."

He raised a finger, but not the one he might have used in school. "Catch ya later." With a last, disdainful glance in my direction, he stalked off toward the men's room.

"Pleasant guy," Walt interposed.

Dean laughed. "Well, he's pretty disappointed you showed up. He had plans to hit on her—again." He jerked his thumb in my direction. I blushed, the heat rising to the roots of my hair.

"Oh," Walt breathed, surprised. "I hope I didn't..." He looked at me with those penetrating blue eyes.

"No—no!" I stammered. "You didn't. Actually you saved me from another, uh, unpleasant rejection."

Walt looked puzzled.

"It started with a bad blind date," Andy explained.

"Oh, sorry." I could tell from Walt's tone that he really wasn't sorry. But he had to be polite. It was his way.

I smiled. "Don't be. I'm really glad you came."

The rest of the band got up and sauntered over to the stage to prepare for the next set. I glanced at Andy. She was beaming at us, nodding her head. Holly wanted to hear about our planned trip to Tibet.

Walt filled them in on where our research would take us. "Oh, how exciting!" Holly exclaimed. "Will you be in any danger?"

My mentor grinned and shook his head. "No. The Chinese permit tourists—and that's what we'll be."

"Do they know you're doing research?" Andy asked, leaning forward with interest.

"There's really no reason to tell them that. We're there to see the sights in and around Lhasa. We'll talk to some of the residents, Tibetans and Chinese. It's really no big deal."

A sudden splattering of percussion told us the music was starting up again. Walt's shoulders hunched against the sound, then he tried to relax and get used to the high volume. Rockabilly was not his cup of tea, nor was it mine. I leaned over and spoke into his ear.

"What?" he shouted back.

I raised my voice. "Do you feel like staying or going?"

He nodded. "Yes!" He stood up, motioning to my housemates that we were leaving.

"Have fun!" Holly shouted, winking at me. Andy smiled and waved us away, as if implying that we had stayed longer than she expected.

I felt relieved to get out of the smoky bar and into the fresh air. A few people were strolling along the brick walks and enjoying the warm evening. Walt strode by my side. I savored his presence as I savored the fragrant air scented with blossoms.

Glancing up into the sky, I noticed Leo standing high and bright over the world. In the east, Jupiter shone just above Libra, as if that planet held the starry scales itself. I shoved my hands in the pockets of my soft denim jacket and sighed inwardly.

We walked in silence for a while. Though Walt often engaged in animated discussions about a variety of topics, he also felt comfortable with periods of quiet. I did not feel an urgency to speak during those long silences. I simply relaxed and enjoyed being with him.

Just before crossing the street, a van just like the one used by my abductors, sped by in front of us. I turned my head to follow its progress, but without the slight ripple of fear that usually crept up my spine at the sight of green minivans. I stepped across, feeling a renewed sense of purpose. My feet felt lighter, reflecting what was in my heart. As we continued walking— now in Walt's quaint neighborhood—I wished the night would never end.

"Hey, what's going on with you, Kate?"

I turned my head to look up into his face. I liked how the starlight reflected in his deep-set eyes. "What do you mean?"

"That van. You didn't react like you have been. In fact, you almost seemed happy to see it."

"Well, I guess I'm not worried about that anymore." I breathed deeply of the heady garden scents that permeated this neighborhood in particular. Almost everyone on this street had a garden. "I feel happy and I'm not really sure why. Maybe I'm just excited about our trip."

We walked on a little further before Walt spoke again. "It's just, well, you seem different tonight."

"Maybe I am." I looked up into his eyes, before turning my gaze forward again. "That whole incident changed my perspective. I thought about it a long time afterwards and I realized something, something that I've never admitted to myself before."

"What was that?" Walt stopped and turned to give me his full attention.

I stood in front of him, raising my face to his. "I realized that I'm more afraid of living than I am of dying." I laughed softly. "Living is really tough. It takes so much more energy and..."

"Courage?"

I smiled. "Yeah." I looked down at my feet for a moment, not sure of how to say what I wanted him to know.

"What is it?"

"You once told me you would be whatever I needed... I'm not afraid, Walt. I don't need a protector anymore." I hesitated. "What I want is..."

"Something more?" How did he do that? It was as if he had read my thoughts. "I don't think you ever needed protection."

"Really?"

He shook his head, smiling. "No. I have a confession to make."

"You? Confession? I didn't think Anglicans did that."

"Very funny. No. I've done something really unprofessional." His eyes sparkled with a new intensity. I wanted that look to last forever and I wanted it to be for me.

"I fell in love with one of my students, Kate, and I've been afraid to tell her."

My hand trembled as I reached out to touch his face, a face that had carried me through one of the most difficult times of my life. His were the arms that had held me when Caroline died, the eyes that had guarded my sleep the night of my abduction. He had been my mentor, father figure, and friend. Now, he offered me a love I had never known before, a love that I had feared I could never have.

"You ought to tell her," I whispered, searching his eyes for a response. In their green depths I found the assurance I sought.

"It's you, Kate. I don't know when it actually happened but, it seems that I've loved you for a long time." Yet, still, he held back.

"I think I knew. I think that I was afraid to love you because I might lose you like…like my mother lost Dad."

He cupped his hands over mine. He seemed to enjoy the feel of my hands on his face. Then he closed his eyes, almost as if to shut out pain. "But I'm so much older. You could have a younger guy."

"Only if he were you," I answered. I don't know if I pulled him closer or he pulled me. Or maybe we moved together. Our lips brushed lightly. I looked into his eyes again, and then gave myself to his lips in a long kiss that carried all the love, warmth, and passion we had both longed to express. Now, here, under the stars, we could finally admit to the love that had blossomed from the seeds of our deep friendship.

When he dropped me off at my house I asked him to come in for a moment. "I need to give you something." My face was warm in the flush of our new relationship.

"Hope I like it," he answered with a chuckle.

"I don't know about that, but I hope you do!"

"You love being mysterious, Kate."

I smiled. "I thought all women were that way."

He nodded. "Of course."

Once in the house I ran upstairs and threw open my closet door. There it was, exactly as I had left it three months ago. I grabbed the box containing my manuscript, suddenly noticing how dusty it had become. When I blew the gray coating off the top, I sneezed. It had been a while since I touched it.

"Bless you," came Walt's polite response from the bottom of the stairs. I laughed as I wiped the box with a shirt that hung from the doorknob. Now I had a reason to wash that one, I thought. I felt giddy. My mind whirled with a thousand images of me and Walt doing everything that a couple does together. In those few moments we walked in the park hand-in-hand, shared kisses in the rain, read poetry to each other, and even went to a few movies—all in fond visions that hurried through my suddenly love-sick head.

I chuckled at my own foolishness. We still had to take things one day at a time, I reminded myself. It was probably a good thing that I had a practical side to hold my heart in check. I took a deep breath. "That's right, Kate," I murmured to myself, "one day at a time!"

Hurrying downstairs with my burden I presented it to my mentor with a flourish. "Here it is, finally."

He looked both surprised and pleased as he reverently took the box from my hands. "So this is it—your famous novel of the Celts."

"Yeah. Guess it's about time you saw it. Of course, 'Old Red' will probably get a lot of exercise on this one." "Old Red" was my pet name for Walt's correction pen. I had learned a great deal from its bright markings across my pages.

"He's rarin' to go!" Walt grinned, giving me a sly wink.

"Well, knock yourself out and let me know what you think of it... Oh, by the way, I've gotten an idea I'd like to work on before we leave."

He raised a hand in a reassuring gesture. "I know how that is. Just come over for our language practice—you ought to have a smattering of Chinese phrases, too—and don't worry about the research. I've got plenty of other work to do." Not only could he read my mind, he also knew when to give me the time I needed. I almost regretted asking him because part of me wanted to spend every minute with him. But I felt compelled to start this new project right away.

"Thanks," I replied gratefully.

"Don't mention it." He set the box down on the step and took me in his arms again. "Do whatever you need to do," he whispered in my ear. "I'll always be there for you."

Over the weekend I spent a lot of time racking my brain for every memory I had of my father. I kept my notebook at my side, even at meals, so I could jot down anything that came to mind. I pulled out my journals and pored over them, gleaning every detail about my dad and how his death had affected Mom and me.

I had also written about Caroline in those journals. Now I used them to jog my memory about my time with her. I took notes and fleshed out the story of our friendship. There were so many things I had not written down about her. I was glad it was fresh enough in my mind to fill all the blanks I had left in my sketchy accounts.

Though I felt almost obsessed with my new project, I often found myself staring out into space thinking about Walt. I looked forward to our trip together. My hopes for our developing relationship soared to new heights. At one point I imagined that we were picking out an engagement ring. This one had to be an emerald, I told myself. No typical diamond ring for me, I thought, gazing at my bare finger. "Oh, no!" I giggled. "I'm acting just like Holly does about Bob!" Now we could both drive Andy nuts with alternating refrains of "Bob this" and "Walt that"! I shook my head and turned the page in my notebook to continue writing.

One afternoon, after taking notes all morning, I drove over to the mall to pick up a couple of last minute items for the trip. I gasped in surprise when I saw a homeless woman at Caroline's old spot at the intersection.

Looking closely at her as she made her way down the line of cars, I noticed she was younger than my friend, middle-aged, with short, brown hair sprinkled generously with gray. Her eyes were gray, too, dulled by hunger and suffering. She smiled vacantly when someone reached out of their window to hand her some bills.

I reached quickly into my purse. This time I had five dollars. As the woman neared my car I rolled the window down all the way and smiled at her. She brightened. Life seemed to enter her eyes at my greeting. "Hello, ma'am," I called, extending my hand with the money folded discretely.

"Thank you, dear," she answered, taking my hand in hers for a moment, reminding me of another time when someone did that and called me "dear." "I hate to beg for money, but I have nothing. I've got to get to Arlington and I need bus fare."

Trying not to notice the powerful smell that surrounded her, I asked politely, "You have family there?"

"No, but a friend told me about a place where I can stay and get help. I know I've got problems," and she gestured to her head. "My friend said they're real Samaritans up there. I've got to get there." Her voice trailed off. The life seeped out of her face, leaving it dull again, almost hopeless.

"You mean Samaritan House?" I asked, excited to discover that their reputation may have spread to Fredericksburg.

"Why, yes! How did you know? Yes, I'm going there as soon as I have the money."

"They'll help you, ma'am," I assured her. The light changed and the cars in front of me began to move. I squeezed her hand again. "Good luck."

She struggled to smile, but tears filled her eyes. "I've got to get there," she repeated. Someone behind me leaned on their horn. I had to move. She wiped the tears away with her sleeve and the light returned to her face. "Don't worry. I've almost got enough. You better go." With that she turned and walked back toward the light to wait for the next line of cars to stop.

I hesitated to leave, but the drivers behind me honked impatiently. Finally, I pressed the gas pedal and drove past the woman and through the intersection. In the mall I worried about her, wondering if she would be able to find her way to Arlington. Maybe I should help her get to the bus station. Could she make it from there? But when I left the mall the woman was gone and, though I looked for her all the way down Route 3, I didn't see her again.

She had called me "dear" just like Caroline. I wondered if they had ever met. Was Caroline the friend that had told her about Samaritan House? I would probably never know. Even so, Caroline had helped start the organization that would help more and more homeless in the future. Soon there would be one in Florida. Others could follow.

I had wondered how Caroline could live as she did. Now I understood that she had given her life meaning by helping others. She had combated terrible difficulties but still managed to offer comfort to those in need. In her efforts to protect Therese she had shown incredible courage, choosing suffering over risking her daughter's life by making herself known to her.

Now I could honor her memory as well as that of her family and my own father. I would write about them all. I would write about the men who had destroyed their lives and forever changed the lives of those they left behind. Walt did say that there is often more truth in fiction than in fact. I finally understood what he meant.

With a full heart, I sat at my computer and began my second novel. The words poured themselves out onto the screen, as if of their own will. For two weeks I worked like one obsessed, hardly stopping except to eat and sleep. I told the story of losing my father. I poured out my grief at growing up without him. I wrote of meeting Caroline Rose, of our friendship and her tragic death. Was it despite these sorrows or because of them that I finally met myself—the woman and the writer?

EPILOGUE

Flying over the ocean on our way to Tibet, I mused how Caroline's ashes had been carried from that beautiful river all the way to the sea. Perhaps they might have drifted out into this very spot. Rain may have picked up some substance from them and dropped it on every continent. I imagined her essence eventually touching every place on the planet. Who knows? Certainly her memory would follow me and everyone else whose lives she had touched with her gentle ways.

Like the water, I would carry her essence wherever I went. I only hoped that I could live my own life with the same integrity and courage with which Caroline had lived hers.

"It's so beautiful," I murmured, almost to myself.

Walt leaned forward to look out the window. "It sure is." His tones soothed me, enfolding me in a feeling of warmth I had not known for a long time. The hollow pain of loss—the pain I had carried since I was a child—faded, as this new feeling flooded my heart. Instead of pushing it away as I had in the past, I embraced it without fear.

I squeezed Walt's hand and looked into his shining eyes, seeing the soft glow of love there. Yes, it was for me. He smiled and returned the pressure. Together we turned our gaze to the sea, to the destination that awaited us on the other side of the world.